Other books by this author

Seeing and Being: Ben Okri's The Famished Road.

Ceci n'est pas une fiction. Les romans vrais de B.S. John

The Fiction of Julian Barnes.

Julian Barnes. L'art du mélange.

Flaubert's Parrot *de Julian Barnes.*

NEW BRITISH FICTION

Series editors:
Philip Tew
Rod Mengham

Published
Sonya Andermahr: **Jeanette Winterson**
Mariadele Boccardi: **A. S. Byatt**
Bradley Buchanan: **Hanif Kureishi**
Vanessa Guignery: **Jonathan Coe**
Frederick M. Holmes: **Julian Barnes**
Kaye Mitchell: **A. L. Kennedy**
Robert Morace: **Irvine Welsh**
Stephen Morton: **Salman Rushdie**
Mark Rawlinson: **Pat Barker**
Philip Tew: **Zadie Smith**
Lynn Wells: **Ian McEwan**

New British Fiction

Series Standing Order ISBN 978–1–4039–4274–6 hardback
Series Standing Order ISBN 978–1–4039–4275–3 paperback
(outside North America only)

You can receive future titles in this series as they are published by placing a standing order. Please contact your bookseller or, in the case of difficulty, write to us at the address below with your name and address, the title of the series and the ISBN quoted above.

Customer Services Department, Macmillan Distribution Ltd,
Houndmills, Basingstoke, Hampshire, RG216XS, UK

NEW BRITISH FICTION

Jonathan Coe

Vanessa Guignery

First published 2016 by
PALGRAVE

Palgrave in the UK is an imprint of Macmillan Publishers Limited, registered in England, company number 785998, of 4 Crinan Street, London, N1 9XW.

Palgrave Macmillan in the US is a division of St Martin's Press LLC, 175 Fifth Avenue, New York, NY 10010.

Palgrave is a global imprint of the above companies and is represented throughout the world.

Palgrave® and Macmillan® are registered trademarks in the United States, the United Kingdom, Europe and other countries.

ISBN 978–1–137–40583–8 hardback

ISBN 978–1–137–40582–1 paperback

This book is printed on paper suitable for recycling and made from fully managed and sustained forest sources. Logging, pulping and manufacturing processes are expected to conform to the environmental regulations of the country of origin.

A catalogue record for this book is available from the British Library.

A catalog record for this book is available from the Library of Congress.

Printed in China

In memory of

Roger Coe

(1928–2013)

and

Gérard Guignery

(1940–2013)

CONTENTS

GENERAL EDITORS' PREFACE

This series highlights with its very title two crucial elements in the nature of contemporary British fiction, especially as a field for academic research and study. The first term indicates the originality and freshness of such writing expressed in a huge formal diversity. The second evokes the cultural identity of the authors included, who nevertheless represent through their diversity a challenge to any hegemonic or narrow view of Britishness. As regards the fiction, many of the writers featured in this series continue to draw from and adapt long traditions of cultural and aesthetic practice. Such aesthetic continuities contrast starkly with the conditions of knowledge at the end of the twentieth century and the beginning of the twenty-first, a period that has been characterized by an apprehension of radical presentness, a sense of unprecedented forms of experience and an obsession with new modes of self-awareness. This stage of the survival of the novel may perhaps be best remembered as a millennial and postmillennial moment, a time of fluctuating reading practices and of historical events whose impact is largely still unresolved. The new fiction of these times reflects a rapidly changing cultural and ideological reality, as well as a renewal of the commitment of both writers and readers to both the relevance and utility of narrative forms of knowledge.

Each volume in this series will serve as an introductory guide to an individual author chosen from a list of those whose work has proved to be of general interest to reviewers, academics, students and the general reading public. Each volume will offer information concerning the life, work and literary and cultural contexts appropriate to the chosen subject of each book; individual volumes will share the same overall structure with a largely common organization of materials. The result is intended to be suitable for both academic and general readers: putting accessibility at a premium, without compromising an ambitious series of readings of today's most vitally interesting British novelists, interpreting their work, assessing their influences and exploring their relationship to the times in which they live.

Philip Tew and Rod Mengham

ACKNOWLEDGEMENTS

My warmest thanks go to Jonathan Coe for his friendship and support over the years and for his generosity in giving me access to unpublished material and work in progress for this book. I am very grateful to Alexis Tadié and Emma Cypher-Dournes, as well as to the series editors Philip Tew and Rod Mengham, for their perceptive suggestions and comments on the manuscript. I would like to express my gratitude to the Harry Ransom Humanities Center and its director, Stephen Enniss, for giving me the opportunity to conduct my research in the best possible conditions at the University of Texas in Austin. Special thanks are due to Julian Barnes for having kindly introduced me to Jonathan Coe many years ago.

PART I
Introduction

TIMELINE

1960	Harold Macmillan 'Winds of Change' speech, Cape Town, South Africa John F. Kennedy elected as US President
1961	Adolf Eichmann on trial in Israel for role in Holocaust Bay of Pigs: attempted invasion of Cuba Berlin Wall constructed Yuri Gagarin first person in Space Silicon chip patented *Private Eye* magazine begins publication Muriel Spark, *The Prime of Miss Jean Brodie* Jonathan Coe born on 19 August in a suburb of Birmingham
1962	Cuban Missile Crisis Marilyn Monroe dies Independence for Uganda; followed this decade by Kenya (1963), Northern Rhodesia (1964), Southern Rhodesia (1965), Barbados (1966)

1963 John F. Kennedy assassinated in Dallas
Martin Luther King Jr delivers 'I Have a Dream' speech
Profumo Affair

1964 Nelson Mandela sentenced to life imprisonment
Commercial pirate radio challenges BBC monopoly

1965 State funeral of Winston Churchill
US sends troops to Vietnam

1966 Ian Brady and Myra Hindley sentenced to life imprisonment for Moors Murders
England beats West Germany 4–2 at Wembley to win FIFA World Cup
Star Trek series debut on NBC television
Jean Rhys, *Wide Sargasso Sea*

1967 Six-Day War in the Middle East
World's first heart transplant
Abortion Act legalizes termination of pregnancy in UK
Sergeant Pepper's Lonely Hearts Club Band album released by The Beatles
Flann O'Brien, *The Third Policeman*

1968 Anti-Vietnam War protestors attempt to storm American Embassy in Grosvenor Square
Martin Luther King Jr assassinated
Robert F. Kennedy assassinated
Student protests and riots in France
Lord Chamberlain's role as censor of plays in the UK is abolished
Lindsay Anderson, *If...*

1969 Civil rights march in Northern Ireland attacked by Protestants
Apollo 11 lands on the Moon with Neil Armstrong's famous first steps
Rock concert at Woodstock
Yasser Arafat becomes leader of PLO
Booker Prize first awarded; winner P. H. Newby, *Something to Answer for*

Open University founded in the UK
John Fowles, *The French Lieutenant's Woman*

1970 Popular Front for the Liberation of Palestine (PFLP) hijacks five planes
Students activists and bystanders shot in anti-Vietnam War protest at Kent State University, Ohio, four killed, nine wounded
UK voting age reduced from 21 years to 18

1971 Decimal currency introduced in the UK
Internment without trial of terrorist suspects in Northern Ireland begins
India and Pakistan in conflict, after Bangladesh declares independence

1972 Miners' strike
Bloody Sunday in Londonderry, 14 protestors killed outright or fatally wounded by British troops
Aldershot barracks bomb initiates IRA campaign with seven dead
Britain enters Common Market
Massacre of Israeli athletes at Munich Olympics
Watergate scandal
Anthony Burgess, *A Clockwork Orange*
Samuel Beckett, *Not I*

1973 US troops leave Vietnam
Arab–Israeli 15-day Yom Kippur War
PM Edward Heath introduces three-day working week
Martin Amis, *The Rachel Papers*

1974 Miners' strike
IRA bombings in Guildford (five dead) and Birmingham (21 dead)

1975 Microsoft founded
Sex Discrimination Act
Malcolm Bradbury, *The History Man*
Ian McEwan, *First Love, Last Rites*

1976 Weak economy forces UK government loan from the International Monetary Fund (IMF)

1977 *Star Wars* released
UK unemployment tops 1,600,000
Nintendo begins to sell computer games
Sex Pistols 'Anarchy in the UK' tour

1978 Soviet troops occupy Afghanistan
First test-tube baby born in Oldham, England

1979 Iranian Revolution establishes Islamic theocracy
Margaret Thatcher becomes PM after Conservative election victory
USSR invades Afghanistan
Lord Mountbatten assassinated by the IRA

1980 Iran–Iraq War starts
Iranian Embassy siege in London
CND rally at Greenham Common airbase, England
IRA hunger strike at Belfast Maze Prison over political status for prisoners
Julian Barnes, *Metroland*

1981 Prince Charles and Lady Diana marry in St Paul's Cathedral with 750 million worldwide television audience
Widespread urban riots in UK including in Brixton, Holloway, Toxteth, Handsworth, Moss Side
AIDS identified
First IBM personal computer
Alasdair Gray, *Lanark*
Salman Rushdie, *Midnight's Children*, which wins Booker Prize for Fiction

1982 Mark Thatcher, PM's son, disappears for three days in Sahara during the Paris-Dakar rally
Falklands War with Argentina, costing the UK over £1.6 billion
Body of Roberto Calvi, chairman of Vatican-connected Banco Ambrosiano, found hanging beneath Blackfriars Bridge, London

1983 Klaus Barbie, Nazi war criminal, arrested in Bolivia
Beirut: US Embassy and barracks bombing, killing hundreds of members of multinational peacekeeping force, mostly US marines
US troops invade Grenada
Microsoft Word first released
Salman Rushdie, *Shame*, which wins Prix du Meilleur Livre Étranger (France)

1984 Miners' strike
HIV identified as cause of AIDS
IRA bomb at Conservative Party Conference in Brighton kills four
British Telecom privatization shares sale
James Kelman, *Busconductor Hines*
Graham Swift, *Waterland*

1985 Famine in Ethiopia and Live Aid concert
Damage to ozone layer discovered
Mikhail Gorbachev becomes Soviet Premier and introduces glasnost (openness with the West) and perestroika (economic restructuring)
Thirty-eight deaths during clashes at Liverpool v. Juventus football match at Heysel Stadium, Brussels
PC Blakelock murdered during riots on Broadwater Farm estate in Tottenham, London
Jeanette Winterson, *Oranges Are Not the Only Fruit*

1986 Abolition of Greater London Council and other metropolitan county councils in England
Violence between police and protestors at Wapping, East London after Rupert Murdoch sacks 5000 print workers
Challenger shuttle explodes
Chernobyl nuclear accident
US bombs Libya
Peter Ackroyd, *Hawksmoor*

1987 Capsizing of RORO ferry, Herald of Free Enterprise, off Zeebrugge kills 193 people
London Stock Exchange and market collapse on 'Black Monday'

Remembrance Sunday: eleven killed by Provisional IRA bomb in Enniskillen
Jonathan Coe, *The Accidental Woman*

1988 US shoots down Iranian passenger flight
Pan Am flight 103 bombed over Lockerbie, 270 people killed
Soviet troop withdrawals from Afghanistan begin
Salman Rushdie, *The Satanic Verses*

1989 Fatwa issued against Rushdie by Iranian leadership (Khomeini)
Fall of Berlin Wall
Exxon Valdez oil disaster
Student protestors massacred in Tiananmen Square, Beijing
Hillsborough Stadium disaster in which 96 football fans die
Kazuo Ishiguro, *The Remains of the Day*, which wins Booker Prize for Fiction
Jonathan Coe, *A Touch of Love*

1990 London poll tax riots
Fall of Thatcher; John Major becomes Conservative PM
Nelson Mandela freed from jail
A. S. Byatt, *Possession*
Hanif Kureishi, *The Buddha of Suburbia*, which wins Whitbread First Novel Prize
Jonathan Coe, *The Dwarves of Death*

1991 Soviet Union collapses
First Iraq War with 12-day Operation Desert Storm
Apartheid ended in South Africa
PM Major negotiates opt-out for Britain from European
Monetary Union and rejects Social Chapter of Maastricht Treaty
Hypertext Markup Language (HTML) helps create the World Wide Web
Pat Barker, *Regeneration*
Jonathan Coe, *Humphrey Bogart: Take it and Like it*

1992 'Black Wednesday' stock market crisis when UK forced to exit European Exchange Rate Mechanism
Adam Thorpe, *Ulverton*

1993 Black teenager Stephen Lawrence murdered in Well Hall Road, London
With Downing Street Declaration, PM John Major and Taoiseach Albert Reynolds commit Britain and Ireland to joint Northern Ireland resolution
Irvine Welsh, *Trainspotting*

1994 Channel Tunnel opens
Nelson Mandela elected President of South Africa
Provisional IRA and loyalist paramilitary cease-fire
Homosexual age of consent for men in the UK lowered to 18
Mike Newell (dir.), *Four Weddings and a Funeral*
James Kelman, *How Late It Was, How Late*, which wins Booker Prize for Fiction
Jonathan Coe, *What a Carve Up!*, which wins John Llewellyn Rhys Prize and Prix Médicis Étranger (France)
Jonathan Coe, *James Stewart: Leading Man*, published as *Jimmy Stewart – A Wonderful Life* in the US

1995 Oklahoma City bombing
Srebrenica massacre during Bosnian War
Nicholas Hytner (dir.), *The Madness of King George*
Jonathan Coe, *What a Carve Up!* published as *The Winshaw Legacy* in the US

1996 Cases of Bovine Spongiform Encephalitis (Mad Cow Disease) in the UK
Divorce of Charles and Diana
Breaching cease-fire, Provisional IRA bombs London's Canary Wharf and Central Manchester
Graham Swift, *Last Orders*, which wins Booker Prize

1997 Tony Blair becomes Labour PM after landslide victory
Princess Diana dies in Paris car crash
Hong Kong returned to China by UK
Jim Crace, *Quarantine*

Iain Sinclair and Marc Atkins, *Lights Out for the Territory*
Jonathan Coe, *The House of Sleep*, which wins Prix Médicis Étranger (France)

1998 Good Friday Agreement on Northern Ireland
Northern Ireland Assembly established
Twenty-eight people killed by splinter group Real IRA bombing in Omagh
Sonny Bono Act extends copyright to lifetime plus 70 years

1999 Euro currency adopted
Macpherson Inquiry into Stephen Lawrence murder accuses London's Metropolitan Police of institutional racism
NATO bombs Serbia over Kosovo crisis
Welsh Assembly and Scottish Parliament both open
Thirty-one passengers killed in Ladbroke Grove train disaster

2000 Anti-globalization protest and riots in London
Hauliers and farmers blockade oil refineries in fuel price protest in the UK
Zadie Smith, *White Teeth*

2001 9/11 Al-Qaeda attacks on World Trade Centre and Pentagon
Bombing and invasion of Afghanistan
Riots in Oldham, Leeds, Bradford, and Burnley, Northern England
Labour Party under Blair re-elected to government
Ian McEwan, *Atonement*
Jonathan Coe, *The Rotters' Club*, which wins Bollinger Everyman Wodehouse Prize

2002 Queen Mother dies aged 101
Rowan Williams named next Archbishop of Canterbury
Bali terrorist bomb kills 202 people and injures a further 209
Inquiry concludes English general practitioner Dr Harold Shipman killed around 215 patients

2003 Invasion of Iraq and fall of Saddam Hussein
Death of UK government scientist Dr David Kelly, and Hutton Inquiry
Worldwide threat of Severe Acute Respiratory Syndrome (SARS)

2004 Bombings in Madrid kill 190 people and injure over 1700
Expansion of NATO to include seven ex-Warsaw Pact countries
European Union expands to 25 countries as eight ex-communist states join
Alan Hollinghurst, *The Line of Beauty*, which wins Booker Prize for Fiction
Andrea Levy, *Small Island*, which wins Orange Prize for Fiction
Jonathan Coe, *The Closed Circle* and *Like a Fiery Elephant: The Story of B.S. Johnson*, which wins Samuel Johnson Prize
Jonathan Coe named Chevalier of the Order of Arts and Letters in France

2005 UK ban on foxhunting with dogs comes into force
7/7 London suicide bombings on transport system kill 52 and injure over 700 commuters
Hurricane Katrina kills at least 1836 people and floods devastate New Orleans
After four failed bombings are detected, Brazilian Jean Charles de Menezes is shot and killed by Metropolitan Police officers at Stockwell Underground Station
Jonathan Coe, *9th & 13th*

2006 Jeanette Winterson awarded the OBE
Airline terror plot thwarted, causes major UK airline delays
Israel–Hezbollah war in Lebanon
Five prostitutes killed in Ipswich in a six-week period; Steve Wright convicted
Saddam Hussein executed by hanging in controversial circumstances

2007 March-April British sailors seized and held by Iran before negotiated release
Smoking ban in public places in England and Wales
Worst floods in the UK for 60 years; south-west England hit hardest
Salman Rushdie knighted, an honour condemned by Iranian and Pakistani ministers
Tony Blair steps down; Gordon Brown becomes Prime Minister in unopposed contest
Jonathan Coe, *The Rain Before it Falls*

2008 Benazir Bhutto assassinated after return to campaign in Pakistan elections
UK banking crisis, beginning with Northern Rock
Credit crisis and worldwide economic recession
Boris Johnson defeats Ken Livingstone in dramatic London mayoral election
Barak Obama elected as 44th US President

2009 Hamas-Israeli War in Gaza
First fears of a Eurozone sovereign debt crisis

2010 Greece bailed out by a combination of EU members and the IMF; a bailout for Ireland follows
UK general elections deliver a hung Parliament; Conservative and Liberal Democrats form a coalition government
Jonathan Coe, *The Terrible Privacy of Maxwell Sim*

2011 Osama bin Laden killed in Pakistan by American Special Forces
Portugal receives a bailout on the model of the Greek and Irish ones
Royal Wedding of Prince William and Kate Middleton
Widespread English riots
Anders Breivik terrorist attacks in Norway
Civil wars in Syria and Libya; death of Muammar Al-Khaddafi
Japanese earthquake, tsunami and nuclear plant explosion

Kim Jong-il dies
Russell Hoban dies

2012 London Olympics
Queen Elizabeth's Diamond Jubilee
EU wins Nobel Peace Prize
The Artist wins five Academy Awards, first silent film to do so since 1927
Encyclopaedia Britannica ends publication of printed versions
Maeve Binchy dies
Eva Figes dies
Jonathan Coe, *Lo Specchio dei Desideri (The Broken Mirror)*

2013 Cyprus bailout
Terrorist attack on Boston Marathon
Edward Snowden leaks NSA files
Sir Alex Ferguson retired as Manchester United manager at the end of the 2012-2013 football season
Benedict XVI resigns as Pope
Nelson Mandela dies
Hugo Chavez dies
Margaret Thatcher dies
Doris Lessing dies
Seamus Heaney dies
Jonathan Coe, *Expo 58, The Story of Gulliver* (children's book), *Marginal Notes, Doubtful Statements* (essays) and *Well Done God! Selected Prose and Drama of B.S. Johnson*, co-edited with Philip Tew and Julia Jordan

2014 Scottish referendum; Scotland votes to remain in the UK
ISIS declares an Islamic Caliphate
Russia annexes Crimea; conflict in Eastern Ukraine
Boko Haram militants kill approximately 300 people in attack on Gamboru Ngala
Ebola outbreak in West Africa, which leads to a vaccine
Sue Townsend dies
P.D. James dies

Jonathan Coe, *Loggerheads and Other Stories*
Jonathan Coe promoted to Officer of the Order of Arts and Letters in France

2015 Charlie Hebdo massacre, Paris
UK election, Conservative majority
Boko Haram militants massacre over 1,000 people, Baga, Nigeria
Mass shooting at Garissa University College, Kenya by terrorist group Al-Shabaab; 147 dead
Same-sex marriage legalised in US and Ireland
Greek debt crisis
Tunis Museum and beach resort shootings by Islamic terrorists, 22 and 38 killed
Iranian nuclear deal
Cuba Removed from US State-Sponsored Terrorism List
Günter Grass, Nobel prize-winner, dies
Jonathan Coe, *Number 11, or Tales that Witness Madness*

1

INTRODUCTION

In 2004, Jonathan Coe analysed the contemporary British novel thus:

> In the [last] three decades the British novel has reinvigorated itself … by recognizing the multi-ethnicity of modern Britain and opening itself to influences from other cultures; by tapping into the energies of popular film, music and television; by turning its back on modernist elitism and rediscovering the pleasures of humour, storytelling, demotic, and so on.
>
> (2004b, 6)

Taking this quotation as the starting point, this book invites the reader to examine Coe's fictional production since 1987 and assess the extent to which it shares the features described above. A 'novelist who loves (traditional) novels' (2004b, 7), Coe proudly belongs to that category of writers who, like Salman Rushdie, Jeanette Winterson or Graham Swift, still believe in the powerful drive of story-telling. Just as stories continue to be 'the bedrock of the novel', for Coe, 'narrative curiosity … remains the centrifugal force which draws readers back to the novel' (2004b, 6). Rather surprisingly, although Coe considers England as 'a nation of narrators' and stories as 'the Englishman's preferred method of making sense of the world' (2003), his novels are better received in France and Italy than in England. And yet Coe feels few affinities for such representatives of the French *Nouveau Roman* as Alain Robbe-Grillet, Nathalie Sarraute or Claude Simon, or for radical modernist or postmodernist writers (with the notable exception of B.S. Johnson), and asserts his attachment to such supposedly outmoded devices as plot, characterization and suspension of disbelief. When he was at university, he felt bewildered and confused by some of the experimental writers he was reading and saw 'the high modernism of Joyce and Beckett as a straightjacket the novel had to break out of' (2004b, 6): 'Someone had instilled at the back of my mind a quaint notion that novels should have an emotional as well as a cerebral impact, that they should contain characters with whom the reader was made to sympathise, that they should carry the reader, buoyed by curiosity, on a propulsive narrative journey' (2013d).

In 1994, ten years before writing about the reinvigoration of the British novel, Coe had published a fairly pessimistic essay on the state of the novel in Britain, which he would later judge too radical:

> My own impression is that the majority of literary novels being published here at the moment, while full of intelligent ideas and in general very accomplished stylistically, are none the less weak on plot, weak on character and shy of formal innovation: somehow, it would seem, we have evolved a brand of novel that contrives at once to be both middlebrow and deeply, irredeemably unpopular.
>
> (1994d, 10)

Although Coe would no longer adhere to such a statement today, it helps to delineate the types of novels he prefers and aims to produce, ones that oscillate between experimentation and tradition. In 2014, Coe remarked that he admires music composer Sean O'Hagan of The High Llamas because he 'combines experimentalism with accessibility', as Coe tries to do in his own books (in Okereke). Although he has been described a conventional inheritor 'of the liberal-realist mode of political fiction' (Head, 2006, 243), Coe's career from his debut novel, *The Accidental Woman* (1987), to his most recent book, *Number 11, or Tales that Witness Madness* (2015), is marked by several changes of direction, which should deter anyone from hastily applying constricting labels to his work. Coe is not only an heir to the tradition of the English comic and satirical novel or to the social realism of the 1950s, and not only the postmodernist writer that some critics saw in *What a Carve Up!* (1994). His experimentations with narrative, genre, perspective and voice, and his concerns with issues relating to history, class, truth, memory, loss and nostalgia, demonstrate the extent of his creative spectrum and sensibility. The aim of this introduction will be to identify and chart the main directions taken by Coe's fiction over the years, first by highlighting his interest in the depiction of contemporary Britain and his relation to political engagement, then by focusing on his fondness for humour, comedy and satire, alongside his veer towards melancholy, and finally by drawing attention to the narrative and generic polyphony of his work.

One may distinguish two trends in contemporary British fiction: one towards retro-Victorian fiction and pastiche, and another resolutely anchored in the present, dealing with topical issues, Coe belonging to the latter (Noiville, 297). In the early 1990s, the success of such novels as Rose Tremain's *Restoration* (1989) and A.S. Byatt's *Possession* (1990) 'led to a feeling that what the British novelist excelled at was a kind of historical pastiche', so that 'a generation of younger critics and reviewers', including Coe, 'grumbled that "contemporary" British life was being under-represented in our fiction' (Coe, 2013d). This fixation on the past was, for example, epitomized by the 2001 Booker Prize longlist on which only three out of 22 books were set in contemporary Britain. As a consequence of his dissatisfaction with this situation, Coe decided to write a book on the Thatcher decade: 'a large-scale, panoramic representation of what Britain looked like (to [him]) at that particular historical moment' (2013d). The result was *What a Carve Up!*, a novel which revealed Coe's ability to anchor 'his universal truths in the immediacy of contemporary society', to articulate 'the great and the small, the destiny of nations and the heartbeat of beings' (Noiville, 298–9).

In *What a Carve Up!*, two characters, Grahame Packard and Michael Owen, hold a discussion about the situation of the novel at the beginning of the 1980s. Graham, who is on a film-making course, does not understand 'why people write novels any more' (276), borrowing some of his arguments from B.S. Johnson's *Aren't You Rather Young to be Writing Your Memoirs* (11–13). This student directed a ten-minute 'efficient if unsubtle' film about the Falklands conflict called 'Mrs Thatcher's War' (280) and hyperbolically laments the fact that 'there is no tradition of political engagement' in the British novel: 'it's all just a lot of pissing about within the limits set down by bourgeois morality' (276). As for Michael Owen, he expresses a wish in one of his literary reviews: 'We stand badly in need of novels ... which show an understanding of the ideological hijack which has taken place so recently in this country, which can see its consequences in human terms and show that the appropriate response lies not merely in sorrow and anger but in mad, incredulous laughter' (277).

Quoting this passage 15 years after its publication, Coe cringes with embarrassment at that 'brazen' and 'lofty pronouncement' and wonders whether this 'little manifesto' reflected his 'personal views, or whether it was a slippery parody of them', but he admits it was 'a clear statement of the author's personal ambitions' (2013d) in a novel that combines political awareness with a comic satire of the worst excesses of Thatcherism and the ruling elite. As such, it can be related to other novels about Britain under Thatcher such as Ian McEwan's *The Child in Time* (1987), David Lodge's *Nice Work* (1988), Tim Lott's *Rumours of a Hurricane* (2002), Alan Hollinghurst's *The Line of Beauty* (2004), David Peace's *GB84* (2004) or Philip Hensher's *The Northern Clemency* (2008). While many considered Martin Amis's *Money* (1984) as 'the 1980s political novel *par excellence*', Coe argues that Alasdair Gray's *1982, Janine* (1984) 'skewered the early years of Thatcherism' with a greater 'prescience and accuracy' (2013d). Coe himself is not only interested in Thatcherism but also in the periods that precede and follow the Thatcher era: *The Rotters' Club* (2001) is a realist depiction of the effects of deregulation and the free market on the trade unions and the car industry, as well as a portrait of the growth of nationalism and xenophobia in the 1970s, while *The Closed Circle* (2004) mocks the political opportunism of New Labour, as well as the unhealthy power of spin-doctors and of the media in general. In *The Terrible Privacy of Maxwell Sim* (2010), set in 2009, the narrator regularly refers to the financial difficulties experienced by companies, relating it in particular to the 'credit crunch' (89) and to the concept of 'leverage' in investment banking (23, 121, 258), and one of the younger characters launches an impassioned attack against the previous generation: 'We may be Mrs Thatcher's children, as far as you're concerned, but *you* were the ones who voted for her, again and again, and then carried on voting for all the people who came after her, and followed exactly in her footsteps. You're the ones who brought us up to be these consumerist zombies' (37–8).

In the same novel, an elderly lady rails against England, a country 'happily allowing itself to be killed off by the power of the big corporations' (197), while a spiritual eccentric abhors 'the material world … where people spend their lives making things and then buying and selling and using and consuming them' (264). *The Terrible Privacy of Maxwell Sim* thus chimes with the emerging genre of 'Crunch Lit' which responds to the 2007–08 credit crunch and the effects of the financial crisis on British society, and is exemplified by such novels as Sebastian Faulks's *A Week in December* (2009), Justin Cartwright's *Other People's Money* (2011), John Lanchester's *Capital* (2012) or Mark Lawson's *The Deaths* (2013).

According to Richard Bradford, Coe's work raises 'the question of how the novelist is expected to deal with contemporaneity' (43). Looking back over the last 25 years of the twentieth century, Tim Adams notes that 'only a handful of significant English novels have responded directly to the monumental changes in the society of our times' – among them, Amis's *Money* and ten years later, Coe's *What a Carve Up!*. While the literary production of the 1990s in Britain was mainly interested in the past and disconnected from the here and now, Coe's novels are all set in contemporary Britain and one of his talents consists in successfully evoking a specific period and place. To give a brief survey of the time range of his novels, *The Rain Before it Falls* (2007) relates events in the life of the main character from the 1940s – a time when 'creamy, brownish white' colours were popular, 'as if people were afraid to let any real light and brightness into their lives' (92) – to 2007. *Expo 58* (2013) is set in London and Brussels in 1958 during the postwar consensus of the welfare state, but also the last days of buttoned-up Britain. *The Rotters' Club* focuses on the 'inert 1970s' (Coe, 2013d) when everything was brown-coloured: 'These were brown times', the narrator mockingly remarks (15). Coe's first three novels are set in the 1980s while *What a Carve Up!* and *The House of Sleep* (1997) deal with the 1980s and 1990s. *The Closed Circle* and *The Terrible Privacy of Maxwell Sim* are situated at the beginning of the third millennium, and Coe's new novel, *Number 11* (to be published in November 2015), covers the period from 1999 to 2015.

Coe's fictional work thus provides the reader with illuminating snapshots of the present and the recent past 'without succumbing to a kind of easy nostalgia' (2013d). In *The Rotters' Club*, from the vantage point of 2003 in Berlin, the middle-aged narrator takes her interlocutor and the reader back in time to the Britain of 1973, to a 'past that is a foreign country', 'a country that neither of us would recognize, probably' (3). In 1999, Doug Anderton also takes a retrospective glance but warns his audience against any longing for the 1970s (176), and in *The Closed Circle,* Claire, also in 1999, is reluctant to attend 'an evening of slightly morbid nostalgia' with her former school friends (26), while Paul Trotter is opportunistically pretending to have fond memories of 'the far-off, touchingly innocent days of the late 1970s' (60). In various articles, Coe points out that Britain at the time was 'a dismal and stagnant place' where the trade unions were 'perpetually involved in bitter and increasingly violent confrontations with the representatives of capital, a shabby country with a failing economy, obsessed with memories of its former Imperial glory, taking refuge in tradition and outdated ritual in an attempt to forget its contemporary problems' (2013d).

The 1980s did not see any receding of the social and political disquiet and in *What a Carve Up!,* Michael Owen remarks: 'The 1980s weren't a good time for me on the whole. I suppose they weren't for a lot of people' (102). That Tory era was indeed marked by 'a new meanness, an aggressive triumphalism' (Coe, 2013d), with such major events as the Falklands War (1982), the miners' strikes (1984–85) and the American bombing raid on Libya (1986). In *The Accidental Woman,* a character contrasts the Age of Enlightenment with the early 1980s, described as 'the age of consent' (115), while Robert Wyatt (a musician Coe admires) describes them as 'the Age of Self' in one of his songs (in Coe, 2013d). In *The Terrible Privacy of Maxwell Sim,* the protagonist's father sees the 1980s as 'vaulting, sleek and glittery', like the new tower blocks in the city of London in 1987 (246), while in an interview, Coe described the decade as 'vibrant, energetic, ruthless, dynamic', an energy he tried to infuse in his novel even if he disapproved of the main ethos (in Taylor, Charles).

Coe not only sets his novels in modern Britain, but also firmly engages with the political, social and economic failings of the contemporary world, identifying similar aesthetic perspectives in fellow British writers such as Rose Tremain, Amanda Craig, Will Self, Marina Lewycka, Nicola Barker, Martin Amis and John Lanchester (Coe, 2013d). In 'Outside the Whale' (1984), Salman Rushdie insists on the political dimension of any work of art – 'works of art, even works of entertainment, do not come into being in a social and political vacuum; ... the way they operate in a society cannot be separated from politics' (92) – and he points to 'a genuine need for political fiction': 'it becomes necessary and even exhilarating, to grapple with the special problems created by the incorporation of political material' (100). While Rushdie's words made perfect sense in the context of development of the international (or postcolonial) novel, they also fit a more national and English framework in which poetics and politics are bound to meet. Coe's own conception of the political has a particularly wide range as he argues that 'all storytelling is political, being an attempt to control and influence the imaginative life of another person for a period of time' (2013d). In his PhD thesis on Henry Fielding, he referred to *Tom Jones* (1749) as a 'political novel' because Fielding 'seizes on the form's potential for enacting change in narrative terms and for provoking it in the reader' (1986, 235). Coe himself is interested in analysing 'one of the smallest political units' – the family – and the political dynamic between parents and children (Coe, 2013d), and his writing is both politically engaged with the society it dissects and concerned with the individual's relationship to society. In Coe's words, 'the theme is always the relationship between individuals and larger social movements' (in Murphy) and the thrust of what he calls his political novels is 'to show people trying to get on with small, blameless lives without being flattened by the juggernaut of historical events over which they have no control' (in May, 2007, 69).

However, following the death of Margaret Thatcher in April 2013, Jason Cowley pointed to the lack of a figure 'with the significance and commitment of George Orwell or H.G. Wells' in the literary-political landscape, a figure one could 'turn [to] and learn from at moments of national consequence or crisis'. According to Cowley, who borrows Matthew Arnold's phrase from *Culture and Anarchy*, Orwell and Wells helped us 'to see things as they really are'. He provides a definition of the committed political novelist as 'one who simultaneously asks questions of the society in which they live and tells important truths about it'. Among the contemporary writers who can measure up to Orwell and Wells, Cowley quotes Christopher Hitchens (now deceased), Martin Amis and Ian McEwan. He adds that *What a Carve Up!* is a good political novel – although it was dismissed by some critics as a 'political tract' (Gilroy, 2011, 200) – but that Coe is not a political writer in the way Orwell and Wells were, perhaps because Coe wants his novels to entertain readers rather than be overtly didactic. For Jacques Rancière and Adorno, as Laurent Mellet points out, a work of art is political precisely when it resists the temptation of political commitment (190–91). The balance Coe is aiming for may be symbolized by the film about the arms market that a character of *What a Carve Up!* dreams of making, 'a subject which called for the politics of a Ken Loach or a Frederick Wiseman, combined with the outrageous plot and seductive glamour of a James Bond movie' (371).

Nevertheless, in our 'resolutely post-ideological age', Cowley notes a waning of the political and the ideological, and a lack of attention to issues of class in contemporary literature. He is echoed by such scholars as Dominic Head (2002), Philip Tew (2004) and Laurence Driscoll (2009) who contend that writers of the British literary establishment such as Coe, as well as Zadie Smith, Ian McEwan, Kazuo Ishiguro, Graham Swift, Will Self and Martin Amis, have constituted a middle-class canon which tends to erase the working-class subject and reassert bourgeois ideology. While Coe ironically admits to being a 'bourgeois writer', referring to the standard description of the novel as 'a bourgeois form' (2013d), the working class is not totally absent from his fiction. In *The Dwarves of Death* (1990), although William has 'had a nicely cosseted middle-class upbringing on the outskirts of Sheffield' (56), he goes on to work in a record shop and lives on a depressing council estate in South-East London, populated by pregnant women with several children, jobless men with tattoos and Alsatians, and kids with skinhead haircuts shouting obscenities, a place that makes you feel 'suicidally depressed' and where 'there are no fucking buses' on a Sunday (79). Despite this, William feels fortunate to have a roof over his head while 'a couple of miles away, men and women were sleeping in cardboard boxes under Waterloo bridge' (154). When he lived in a council flat in Bermondsey, Coe remembers noticing: 'The homeless are everywhere' (2013d).

However, such cases of interest in the underclass and the downtrodden are relatively rare in Coe's work, possibly because he recognizes the dangers inherent in successful middle-class writers attempting to ventriloquize those below them in an apparent economic-social order. Coe admits he does not 'know enough about the lives of working class men and women to write about them with real confidence' (2013d). In an article on contemporary London novels, he aptly points out that 'many of the most successful

British writers live in London, command large advances for their novels, inhabit some of the capital's most gracious districts, and own substantial homes' (although this is not so in Coe's case), and he very pertinently asks: 'is this really the best vantage point from which to chronicle the lives of the underprivileged and the urban poor?' (1996a, 320). In *The House of Sleep*, a film producer derides the angry young men and middle-class lefties of the late 1950s: 'every other movie was made by some public school-educated romantic giving us his view of working-class life' (202). In *The Closed Circle*, Benjamin shares his doubts about his legitimacy as a writer in the new millennium: 'I'm a middle-aged, middle-class, white, public school-, Oxbridge-educated male. Isn't the world sick of hearing from people like me now? Haven't we had our say? Isn't it about time we shut up and moved over and made way for somebody else?' (259). One cannot help but feel that such rhetorical questions may well mirror Coe's own sincere and honest misgivings about his status.

Apart from an interest in current social and political issues, a central dimension of Coe's work is his attachment to humour, comedy and satire. Coe remarks that 'the need for laughter is universal and absolute' and he remembers his childhood when laughter was 'something that drew people together ... something shared. It forged bonds of sympathy between people, among friends and among families'. He recalls that his first ambition was to 'become a television comedian' and then 'a writer whose words would make people laugh', and he calls the Monty Python, Spike Milligan, Flann O'Brien and Laurence Sterne 'entertainers', adding: 'it's one of the highest compliments in the English language'. As he became aware of the different 'kinds of laughter: melancholy laughter, mad laughter, despairing laughter, angry laughter', Coe realized that 'laughter itself could be a weapon in the battle against injustice' (2013d).

As a writer of comic fiction who has been praised for his self-deprecatory humour, Coe has often been placed within a tradition of serio-comic British writing incorporating Evelyn Waugh, Tom Sharpe and David Lodge, but also P.G. Wodehouse whom Coe called 'the elephant in my comic room' (2013d) and whom Thomas Foley (in *Expo 58*) reads 'for a bit of light relief' (37). While Coe's grandfather – a man who 'had a deep vein of warm, ironic humour' – enjoyed the creator of Jeeves, Coe admits he had been for a long time 'stupidly snobbish about Wodehouse and reluctant even to read him' because of the lack of satire and moral seriousness in his novels. When he finally decided to read Wodehouse, he immediately admired his 'pure, unpolluted humour' and declared: 'all humour should really aspire to the condition of Wodehouse' (2013d). In *The Closed Circle*, a character is working on 'a history of English humour, starting with Chaucer and coming up to P.G. Wodehouse' (375), and in the short story 'V.O.', the local French translator Henri, wearing 'a three-piece, double-breasted tweed suit' and smoking 'a shockingly pungent meerschaum pipe', is 'busily engaged upon an as yet unpublished French edition of the complete works of P. G. Wodehouse'. His 'plummy English drawl' and vocabulary recall those of Wodehouse's characters, with expressions such as 'old bean', 'old fellow', 'Blighty', 'a jolly poor show' or 'Toodle-pip' (2014a), which also pepper *Expo 58*.

For Coe, it is 'in the field of comedy … that we find some of Britain's most impressive post-war cultural achievements' (1994d, 10) and he himself is drawn to the kind of humour found in the *Carry On* films and such figures of British post-war comedy as Tony Hancock, Eddie Braben and the Two Ronnies (Barker and Corbett). Coe remembers Kenneth Williams and Frankie Howerd in *Carry On Doctor*, both gay and in the closet, both 'fully tapped into that vein of sexual subterfuge and masquerade which has always been central to the British sense of humour' (2013d), and in the short story 'Ivy and her Nonsense', during a game of charades, the protagonist impersonates British comedians Tommy Cooper and Harry Worth. Coe is also a great fan of such situation comedies as *Porridge* (first shown on the BBC from 1974 to 1977 and repeated ever since) or light entertainment programmes such as *The Morecambe and Wise Show*, which the Trotters watch on Christmas night in *The Rotters' Club* (272), like so many other Britons. It is while watching the show and imagining millions of families 'convulsed with joy' that Benjamin surmises that 'perhaps his ambitions were all wrong – his desire to be a writer, his wish to be a composer – and that to be a bringer of laughter was in fact the holiest, most sacred of callings' (274). In an article on British comedy and the *Carry On* series, Coe alludes to the 'great divide between elitism and populism' in Britain, to 'our chronic inability to reconcile the competing claims of high and low culture' (2013d). He remarks elsewhere: 'There is a bit of snobbery, about what is high art and low art' (in Lakin) and praises Umberto Eco for his genuine and uncondescending love of popular fiction (1989b).

Like Salman Rushdie, Coe has always strived to reconcile these claims in his work, combining cinema, television and literature. He explains that the satirical British sitcom *Yes Minister* (BBC Television, 1980–84) was a 'source of inspiration' (2010b) for *What a Carve Up!*, together with the satirical puppet show *Spitting Image* (ITV, 1984–96) and the early 1960s comedy stage revue *Beyond the Fringe*, considered as seminal to the rise of satirical comedy in Britain. In *The Closed Circle*, Coe pays indirect homage to one of its performers, Peter Cook, by quoting his line: 'I've learned from my mistakes, and I'm sure I could repeat them perfectly', and identifying its author merely as 'some crusty old pillar of the British establishment' (5).

As a child, Coe would watch *The Fall and Rise of Reginald Perrin*, broadcast on the BBC between 1976 and 1979, and based on a 1974 novel by David Nobbs, which Coe first read when he was 15 and to which he wrote a preface for an Italian edition in 2011. Built on 'the collision of two seemingly incompatible modes: high seriousness, and low comedy', Nobbs's novel deals with a middle-aged sales executive driven to despair by the monotony and triviality of his job. In so doing, it depicts the stagnant and drab British society of the 1970s, yet 'manages to find joy in the trivial and creates farce out of monotony' (Coe, 2013d). As a 15-year-old teenager, Coe found in Nobbs's book 'the perfect crystallisation of [his] own hazy literary vision' as, at that time, he wanted 'to write something that offered a portrait of society as a whole, but filtered through the individual consciousness', and that intertwined humour and melancholy (2013d). Coe told Philip Tew that the book's 'combination of melancholy, satire, farce, seriousness and a distinctive melange of tones' may have found their way into *What a Carve Up!* (in Tew, 2008, 37). A comic quote from Nobbs's novel is used as one of the epigraphs to *The Terrible Privacy of Maxwell Sim*, thus announcing the tone of the book, while the character who tells the story of Donald Crowhurst (who faked a voyage around the world by boat) has a friend called Martin Wellbourne, the name assumed by Reginald Perrin after he faked his suicide (45). Coe's fascination for Nobbs's use of the absurd – 'a vein of absurdism which recalled Flann O'Brien, and the early novels of Samuel Beckett' – has thus partly influenced his own creation:

'Nobbs's critique of consumerism, industrialisation and globalisation … is truly radical: to imply that capitalism is absurd, after all, is far more scathing than simply to point out its failings and corruptions' (2013d).

The absurdist perspective is not one that is usually applied to Coe's novels, and yet, from his early novels, Coe has clearly been drawn to that approach, praising for instance N.F. Simpson as 'Britain's greatest postwar absurdist playwright' for the way he 'combined the rarefied absurdism of Ionesco with the downtrodden melancholy of the suburban sitcom' (2013d). On the other hand, Coe says he has been intent on trying to avoid irony, 'that baneful, ubiquitous, superior mindset which has gripped so many people (especially in the media) in the post-Thatcher years' (2013d). In *The Rotters' Club*, in particular, he tried to portray the mid-1970s without looking down on the characters when considering them from the perspective of 'our notably glossier, spin-doctored, Starbucks-infested era' (2013d).

Coe has often been called a satirist, following the tradition of Jonathan Swift, Alexander Pope and Henry Fielding. Coe himself wrote about *Gulliver's Travels* in an essay in 2007 and adapted the novel as a children's book in 2011 under the title *The Story of Gulliver* for an Italian series called *Save the Story*, which invited authors from around the world to retell one of their favourite stories. In *The Closed Circle*, Doug Anderton refers to Swift but the allusion is comically lost on the editor of the newspaper he is working for (124). Among other things, Coe admires *Gulliver's Travels* for its 'concentrated and calculated intensification of satiric outrage', a book Swift wrote 'to vex the world, rather than divert it' (Coe, 2013d). Satire differs from humour in that the former is usually endowed with a moral purpose, advocating a better world. The specificity of Coe's satire might be that it is more ethical than moralising because it appeals to the reader's empathy. According to Northrop Frye, in *Anatomy of Criticism*, 'two things are essential to satire; one is wit or humour founded on fantasy or a sense of the grotesque or absurd, the other is an object of attack' (224). In Coe's novels, but more particularly in *What a Carve Up!* – which, according to Coe, is 'the only genuinely satirical book' he has ever written (in Armitstead) – all kinds of domains of contemporary life are subjected to the irreverent gaze of satire, be it the world of advertisement, new technology, educational reforms, the academic microcosm, the press, television, private enterprise, Thatcherism, New Labour, investment banking, the National Health Service or food production. Coe's satire is militant as it is obvious where his allegiances lie.

However, reflecting on *What a Carve Up!* some 17 years after its publication, Coe finds the book 'preachy' (2011), maybe because it lacks what, in his PhD thesis on Fielding's *Tom Jones*, he described as 'a quality which we nowadays tend to expect of satire if it is not to fall into preachiness, namely a sense of complicity with the objects satirised' (1986, 295). In addition, Coe remarks that the problem with most satire is that 'it preaches to the converted', sharing rather than challenging their assumptions (2011). For satire (but also irony) to be efficient, the reader must indeed share the same standards as the implied author, and thus, to quote Wayne Booth in *The Rhetoric of Fiction*, feel 'a sense of collusion with the silent author' against the butt of the satirical or ironical attacks (304). Coe goes so far as to argue that there is too much political satire in modern Britain and too little opposition to it as a majority of people share the same acceptable rhetoric, including part of the political establishment (at least in public): 'What was, back in the 1960s, a genuinely galvanising movement, sweeping aside centuries of conservatism and deference, has now become a sort of toothless default setting' (2010b). To quote Paul Gilroy, Coe's 'refined sense of the absurdity of contemporary political culture is attuned to the possibility that in Britain greed and selfishness have been normalized to such an extent that satire becomes effectively impossible' (198). Satire will not tear down the established order and people will not take to the streets. Instead, satire:

> creates a welcoming space in which like-minded people can gather together and share in comfortable hilarity. The anger, the feelings of injustice they might have been suffering beforehand are gathered together, compressed and transformed into bursts of laughter, and after discharging them they feel content and satisfied. An impulse that might have translated into action is, therefore, rendered neutral and harmless.
>
> (Gilroy, 2011, 198)

The political and economic establishment can feel safe as the balance will not be upset. In his thesis dissertation, Coe had already referred to this conservative type of satire which resolves 'into a comfortable feeling (laughter)' (1986, 105). In 2013, Coe identified 'a growing disillusionment with the role played by laughter in the national political discourse' and argued that 'Britain's much-vaunted tradition of political satire was itself an obstruction to real social change, since it diverted everyone's contrarian impulses into harmless laughter' (2013d). Referring to such revues as *The Last Laugh* and *Beyond the Fringe* (in the late 1950s), *That Was the Week That Was* (in the 1960s) and *Have I Got News for You* (in the 1990s and 2000s), Coe affirms that anti-establishment humour has become innocuous and can no longer be subversive: 'laughter is not just ineffectual as a form of protest, but … it actually *replaces* protest' and becomes 'a substitute for thought rather than its conduit' (2013d). As everything becomes subversive and everyone becomes cynical, Britain is 'sinking giggling into the sea', to quote Peter Cook in the 1960s (in Coe, 2013d), and the politicians, economists or bankers who should be made accountable for what happens in the country are gently let off the hook. Instead of disrupting the established order, laughter, 'a unifying, not a dividing force', 'brings us comfort, and draws us into a circle of closeness with our fellow human beings'. Rather than force us into action, into trying to change the world, satire is 'one of the most powerful weapons we have for preserving the *status quo*' (Coe, 2013d). This is what Coe depicts in *The Closed Circle*, when the New Labour MP Paul Trotter is invited to 'a satirical TV show: a weekly panel game on which young comedians would sit around making scathing jokes about the news, sometimes joined by a high-profile politician' (68). Although the invited MPs often have to face a 'barrage of mockery' (68), they know their careers will not be fundamentally disrupted by it. Satire thus 'actually suppresses political anger rather than stoking it up. Political energies which might otherwise be translated into action are instead channelled into comedy and released – dissipated – in the form of laughter' (Coe, 2011). This dissatisfaction might explain why, after *What a Carve Up!*, Coe turned towards a gentler form of humour and comedy, tinged with melancholy.

Already as a teenager and as an apprentice writer, Coe recalls that his 'sensibility was being pulled in two different directions – towards humour and towards melancholy – and [he] wanted to find a way of writing that would reconcile these two opposite approaches' (2013d). He refers to Robert Burton's *The Anatomy of Melancholy* (one of B.S. Johnson's favourite books) as 'a masterpiece of humour' (2013d) and takes his cue from Italo Calvino in his lectures on the value of literature, *Six Memos for the Next Millennium*, when he writes about the 'lightness of thoughtfulness' and 'thoughtful lightness', and points to the 'special connection between melancholy and humour': 'As melancholy is sadness that has taken on lightness, so humour is comedy that has lost its bodily weight' (in Coe, 2013d). If B.S. Johnson invites the reader 'to share in a private sadness', Coe himself has 'been writing about loneliness and depression for most of [his] working life now, from one book to another' (Coe, 2013d), and the vein of melancholy which runs through all his novels is buried under the comedy, satire and social commentary.

Will Self has described his friend as 'quiet and melancholy' and Coe himself considers the novel as 'an introvert's form' (in Laity). The author's wry humour and thoughtful melancholy are often directed against his male characters, who are portrayed as self-effacing, isolated, unassuming. If two of Coe's novels offer portraits of female characters – the emotionally crippled Maria in *The Accidental Woman* and the reminiscing and nostalgic Rosamond in *The Rain Before it Falls* – his other books dwell on figures of weak masculinity or, as Coe puts it, 'passive, slightly depressed men – often failed writers or composers or both – who show a rather uncommitted sexuality and tend to fixate on past romantic disappointments' (2011). Among those are Robin Grant in *A Touch of Love*, Michael Owen in *What a Carve Up!*, Robert in *The House of Sleep*, Benjamin Trotter in *The Rotters' Club* and *The Closed Circle*, the anti-hero of *The Terrible Privacy of Maxwell Sim*, and Thomas Foley in *Expo 58*.

In *The Rotters' Club*, Benjamin describes himself as just 'an ordinary teenager in an ordinary family' (275), with 'no natural authority … None at all' (292). He believes he has been assigned 'little more than a walk-on part' in his own life: 'Sometimes I feel that I am destined always to be offstage whenever the main action occurs. … I feel that my role is simply to be a spectator to other people's stories, and always wander away at the most important moment, drifting into the kitchen to make a cup of tea just as the denouement unfolds' (107, 389). Doug, whose destiny it is 'always to be at the centre of things' (389), warns him: 'You won't take life by the throat and give it a good old shaking. You'll never do that, will you, Benjamin? You'll never take your chances.' (147) – prophecies which will be confirmed in *The Closed Circle* when Malvina describes Benjamin as 'the king of understatement' (103). In *The House of Sleep*, Robert defines himself as 'weak and indecisive' (239), and Coe conceived Maxwell Sim as an Everyman, wanting 'to make him as ordinary as possible: an ordinary man, doing an ordinary job in an ordinary town' (Website, *Sim*). Thomas Foley's 'distinguishing feature' in *Expo 58* is his quietness (2). Many scenes involve these anti-heroes in comic and ludicrous situations reminiscent of some of the best productions by Tom Sharpe or David Lodge.

These indecisive rudderless characters – who Coe says are all a part of himself and who recall the middle-aged lonely male protagonists of Nobbs's *The Fall and Rise of Reginald Perrin* and Gray's *1982, Janine* – often fail to fulfil their dreams, whether this means the completion of a book, the achievement of a satisfactory relationship or a successful professional career. As vulnerable heroes longing for an ideal and selfless love (Michael for Shirley Eaton in *What a Carve Up!*, Benjamin for Cicely in *The Rotters' Club*), they look like paler versions of the archetype of the knight in medieval romances, on a quest for an unreachable goal. In their inability to seize the propitious moment, they resemble Britain, teasingly described by Coe as 'world leader in the field of anti-climax, of missed opportunities' (2013d). In *The Rotters' Club*, Benjamin, who has only been able to 'snatch a moment's eye contact' with Claire Newman, finds himself gripped 'by an overwhelming sense of lost opportunity' (95).

While Coe's male heterosexual characters are often presented as inadequate and helpless in their love lives, homosexual and lesbian relationships are usually portrayed in a more positive light. According to José Ramón Prado Pérez, 'the crisis of masculinity addressed by male writers indicates both the historical appearance and acceptance of various sexualities in society, and the direct reaction against the conservative ideology, mostly masculine in its principle of fiery competition and individualism' (971). Female homosexuality is a familiar feature in Coe's novels and the recurrence of certain names is striking, suggesting hidden links between the books: in *The Accidental Woman*, Maria has a comforting relationship with Sarah; in *The House of Sleep*, Veronica first goes out with Sarah and then lives with Rebecca for nearly 11 years; in

The Rain Before it Falls, Rosamond has long-term relationships with Rebecca and then Ruth; in *The Closed Circle,* Cicely and Helen are believed to have been lovers (199). Contrary to the series of disastrous heterosexual pairings, some of these relationships are presented as serene and satisfactory, offering a welcome alternative. Rosamond and Rebecca are fortunate to have found 'someone with whom you can share absolutely everything' (141), and later in life, Rosamond and Ruth, who have been 'lifelong companions' (254), have eased into a comfortable silence. Male homosexuality is less smooth and often not entirely assumed: in *A Touch of Love,* Aparna accuses Robin of 'flirting with homosexuality' (176) without making a clear decision; in *Expo 58,* Thomas's face is 'pinkening with indignation' when he understands he is being asked if he is a homosexual (38). At the end of *The Terrible Privacy of Maxwell Sim,* Max finally recognizes his father's homosexuality as well as his own, but the promise of a harmonious homosexual relationship is curtailed by the author who suddenly appears in the novel and kills off his character with a click of his fingers. Male characters thus often remain in an in-between position, indecisive as to their sexuality and desires.

Coe's novels cover a wide narrative spectrum that ranges from relatively daring experiments in his first three novels, exploiting such devices as self-reflexivity and embedded narratives, to more conventional and linear narratives in his most recent novels, including his latest, *Expo 58. What a Carve Up!,* and to a lesser extent *The Rotters' Club* and *The Closed Circle,* include a multiplicity of genres and narrative modes, meant to reflect the plural and fragmented dimension of contemporary society. Both *What a Carve Up!* and *The House of Sleep* exploit the device of overlapping and intertwined narratives, and in these two novels, the frontiers between fiction and reality, dreams and the real world, are often blurred so that both characters and readers wonder about the ontological status of events, a question that is familiar to readers of eighteenth-century as well as postmodernist fiction.

In *The Closed Circle,* Benjamin describes the type of novel he is writing: 'what I'm trying to achieve … is a new way of combining text – printed text – with the spoken word. It's a novel with music, … there's going to be a CD-Rom. And some passages you have to read on the screen … The text scrolls down at intervals that I've programmed myself … and certain passages of the text trigger bits of music' (257). Richard Bradford sums it up as a groundbreaking epic 'combining prose narrative with CD, visual images and music to create a genre of its own, capable of capturing those dense layerings of immediate and objective experience which resist the linearity of standard prose fiction' (45). Benjamin never gets to write that novel but it may hint at the type of creation Coe would have achieved if he had chosen to be more of an experimental writer. He said he could 'envisage a kind of multimedia novel' which would bring music, images and text even further to the centre of what he is doing (in Guignery, 2013, 37). In 2001, Coe recorded an album of music and readings entitled *9th & 13th* (in collaboration with French singer Louis Philippe and Danny Manners), a 'peculiar collection of melodies and recitatifs' which he says 'represents a small but significant step towards one of [his] long-held goals as a writer: finding a new way of integrating music and the spoken word' (2001b). Coe's novels include numerous references to music and films, especially pop and rock songs and bands from the 1970s (in *The Dwarves of Death* and *The Rotters' Club*) and the 1980s, deploying such popular cultural coordinates in a way that is reminiscent of Hanif Kureishi's *The Buddha of Suburbia* (1990) and *The Black Album* (1989), Nick Hornby's *High Fidelity* (1995) or Salman Rushdie's *The Ground Beneath Her Feet* (1999). Arguably, the intermediality of Coe's work also echoes the modernist call for hybridity and for the crossing of frontiers between arts in order to explore the limits of the literary.

The combination of references to literature, popular films and television shows in Coe's novels testifies to a deconstruction of the hierarchy between genres and a preference for syncretism that is emblematic of the postmodernist episteme. Although Coe's production is sometimes described as realist and conventional, it really oscillates between postmodernist inventivity and more traditional narratives, emotion and comedy, nostalgia for the past and political commitment to the here and now. Through the devices of pastiche and parody, and the intermingling of various literary traditions, Coe interrogates the notion of Englishness with irony, emphasizing the corruptness of the contemporary world. He also raises more intimate questions about individual identity, moving beyond the supposed playfulness of postmodernism to encompass broader issues and combine epistemological and ontological concerns.

2

A BIOGRAPHICAL READING

In his biography of B.S. Johnson, Coe argues that the novel should be a self-contained statement: 'a work of literature should speak for itself, without the need for glossing, interpreting and contextualizing by reference to its writer's life' (2004b, 7). However, Coe willingly admits to the autobiographical dimension of some of his work, though none is as autobiographical as his unpublished novels, *The Sunset Bell*, a book about a university graduate who has been disappointed in love (it was completed in the early 1980s but never published), and *Paul's Dance* (the title of a 1981 tune by the Penguin Cafe Orchestra), a conventional *Bildungsroman* mainly set in Birmingham during a long summer vacation, dealing with the friendship between two Cambridge undergraduates who had been schoolfriends, a book which was abandoned after some 300 pages (Website, *Touch*; Message Board 14 February 2013). Coe defines *What a Carve Up!* as a 'political novel alongside this personal story about my childhood' (in Lappin, 11), and admits that in *The Rotters' Club*, he 'satirised [himself] as much as [he] could in the character of Benjamin Trotter' (in Laity) so that the book feels like '"semi-autobiographical" fiction: a thorough and sometimes uneasy blend of memory and invention'. Coe drew inspiration from the diary he kept when he was in sixth form, but subsequently learned more about the political climate of the period (of which he was unaware at the time). He remarks: 'The background detail is authentic – or at least, as accurately researched and remembered as I could manage – but all the main narrative threads are entirely fictional' (2013d). The aim of this chapter is not to suggest, as Sainte-Beuve did, that awareness of an artist's biography is crucial to understanding his work, but a brief presentation of Coe's family life, social background and education may be useful as a first point of entry into the geographical, literary and social landscapes of his novels.

Here we go, then. Jonathan Coe was born on 19 August 1961 and brought up in Lickey, a middle-class suburb of south-west Birmingham, in the West Midlands, close to a small town called Bromsgrove, 'a solid Tory constituency', 'overwhelmingly white' (Coe, 2013d). Both Birmingham and the regional area regularly feature as locations in his work, as Coe feels 'part of an English provincial tradition rather than being a metropolitan writer', like David Lodge, who was also born in Birmingham, but unlike such contemporaries as Will Self, Iain Sinclair or Zadie Smith whose works are firmly set in London (Coe, 2013d). *The Accidental Woman* starts and ends with a vision of a park overlooking Birmingham (10, 163), and in *A Touch of Love*, a narrator describes Birmingham as 'a gentle and leafy city', which 'can look beautiful' in autumn, before facetiously adding between brackets 'I write this for the benefit of those who have never been there' (153). In *What a Carve Up!*, Michael Owen comes from the fringes of Birmingham, 'the point where Birmingham's outermost suburbs began to shade into countryside, in a placid, respectable backwater, slightly grander and more gentrified than my father could really afford' (159). Coe's home city plays a major role in *The Rotters' Club* and *The Closed Circle*, both as the place where the characters live and as a city where historical events took place. In the former, Benjamin goes through an epiphanic moment when he fuses Birmingham with the woman he loves, Cicely, and emphatically exclaims: 'I LOVE THIS CITY! I LOVE THIS CITY!' (109) – maybe an echo of the beginning of B.S. Johnson's *The Unfortunates* (1969) in which the sentence 'But I know this city!' is repeated three times on the first page (1). In *The Closed Circle*, after being away for five years, Claire comes back to Birmingham 'homesick, absurdly, for a place she didn't even like that much' (92), while Benjamin, from his desk, relishes the 'grey panorama of the city he still loved, despite all his cravings to break free from it' (167). In *The Rain Before it Falls*, Rosamond's family lives in Hall Green, a few miles south of the centre of Birmingham, a place of small, unyielding, redbricked semi-detached houses (35–6). In *Expo 58*, Thomas and his family leave monotonous Tooting to settle 'on the Lickey Hills on the outskirts of Birmingham' (251). *The Terrible Privacy of Maxwell Sim* also reads like a melancholy nod towards places of the author's and character's childhoods as Max nostalgically remembers the pools his mother and he 'used to walk past whenever she took [him] for a walk on the Lickey Hills, all those years ago, at the back of The Rose and Crown pub, on the edge of the municipal golf course' (7). On his way to Birmingham, he takes the scenic route and drives through the landscape of his childhood – 'I wanted to drive straight over the crest of the Lickey Hills' (151) – and wonders how his GPS will react to this 'nostalgic impulse' (151).

However Birmingham is not only the gentle city eulogized by Coe's characters: it is also the place where IRA bombs exploded in two pubs in November 1974 and where strikes were led by Derek Robinson and the unions in the 1970s to protest against the shutting down of plants such as the Longbridge branch of British Leyland. In *The Rotters' Club* in 1977, a character remarks: 'everyone who lives in Birmingham is affected by Longbridge. … The life of a factory this size has an impact on every part of the local community' (238). This was the case of Coe's own family as his father 'helped to design the batteries which were fitted in the British Leyland cars' (Coe, 2015b). In 2009 however, when Maxwell Sim drives past the old factory, he only sees 'a gaping hole in the landscape': 'an entire complex of factory buildings which used to dominate the whole neighbourhood, stretching over many square miles, throbbing with the noise of working machinery, alive with the figures of thousands of working men and women entering and leaving the buildings – all gone. Flattened, obliterated' (155). Coe himself remembers taking that drive and seeing the former British Leyland car plant transformed into 'a massive, windswept post-industrial vacuum awaiting redevelopment' (2013d). As recorded in *The Terrible Privacy of Maxwell Sim*, factories were knocked down to leave room for 'exclusive residential units' and 'retail outlets' (155), and Max can no longer get his bearings in Birmingham where so 'many new buildings had gone up – shopping malls, most of them' (164). In Coe's unpublished 'spoken musical theatre piece' *Say Hi to the Rivers and the Mountains* (2008), a 1960s housing estate is being demolished and replaced by retail businesses, leading a character to reflect on the intimate link between space, memory and history: 'Sometimes I think that these spaces we inhabit aren't physical places at all. Just layer upon layer of memories. They are built out of experience, human experience, not steel or pre-cast concrete'. His ultimate question is heart-rending: 'When this place is gone, what will be left of the people who lived here?'.

Other important provincial places of Coe's childhood appear in his fiction, such as 'the Llŷn peninsula in North Wales' where Benjamin and his family go on holiday every summer in *The Rotters' Club* (107–8), and which has become for Benjamin 'a repository of some of his own most treasured childhood memories' (315). It is also the place where his brother Paul and his daughter Malvina find refuge at the end of *The Closed Circle* (407). Every year Coe spent his summer holidays with his parents in a caravan in Porth Ceiriad bay, a beach on the Llŷn peninsula in Gwynedd, North Wales, where B.S. Johnson's film *Fat Man on a Beach* was shot in 1973. Coe also spent vacation time and Christmases with his grandparents in Shropshire, outside Newport, a place which inspired the short story 'Ivy and Her Nonsense' as well as *The Rain Before it Falls*. Both texts refer to two Shropshire houses belonging to siblings and closely based on Coe's grandparents' country house 'The Rise' in Cherrington (an hour's drive from the outer suburbs of Birmingham) and his great uncle's farm. In *The Rain Before it Falls*, Rosamond explains that after her father retired, her parents 'moved to Shropshire, to a large very lovely cottage which lay only a mile or two from Warden Farm and indeed formed part of Uncle Owen's estate' (198). In 'Ivy and Her Nonsense', the narrator – Rosamond's nephew – nostalgically remembers 'the weekly visits [they] used to pay to Shropshire as children; the summer holidays, with their morning fishing trips and long afternoons sitting alone in the dining room, reading books and listening to the slow tick of the grandfather clock' (2005a, 6). In real life, Coe sees Shropshire as 'an entire emotional topography, … a landscape of the heart' because of the glimpses of the past it offers (2013d), while in *The Terrible Privacy of Maxwell Sim*, the protagonist views Staffordshire where his grandparents used to live as 'the lost landscape of [his] childhood' (185).

On his website, Coe remarks: 'My grandfather, James Kay, was a great influence on me when I was growing up. He was a warm, funny man, slightly to the left politically' (Website, *Rain*). On the other hand, Coe's father, who passed away in January 2013, only a few months before Margaret Thatcher, voted Tory: 'He was a great admirer of Thatcher, my dad. An instinctive and lifelong

Conservative, he was full of praise (as much as such a quiet man can be) for the Iron Lady and all those who surrounded her' (2013d). Coe's own political stance evolved during his secondary education at the selective direct-grant school King Edward's in Birmingham (1972–79): 'it was a high-pressure environment, and because I was anyway quite shy and introverted, I withdrew. I don't thrive on competition' (in Laity). When he read English at Trinity College, Cambridge – 'a big, intimidating college full of Harrovians, Etonians and Westminster school people who would not give me the time of day' (in Kellaway) – just after Thatcher's electoral landslide, he came 'to fear and despise' every credo of the Conservative Party (2013d). In an essay on the 1980s, Coe recalls how some of his friends from Cambridge went to work in the City, making a lot of money, while he drifted into academia. In a 'state of hopeless political and literary naivety', breathing 'the rarefied air of political puritanism' and feeling 'despair at the state of Michael Foot's Labour Party', Coe was on a 'constant search for a political home elsewhere' (2013d).

Coe declares that he comes 'from a fairly ordinary middle-class family, and had a routine suburban upbringing in which books never loomed very large' (2004b, 451). His childhood was 'very happy and very uneventful', 'almost unnaturally untraumatic'; he lived 'a sheltered life' (Coe in Laity). His father Roger worked in the motor industry as a research physicist; his mother Janet was a music and PE teacher; his older brother was to become a regional sales manager in Worcestershire, maybe an inspiration for Maxwell Sim's professional background. As Coe recalls, 'in my youth there were no book-lined rooms, no bookish family. My Dad used to read Harold Robbins and Arthur Haley, my Mum Agatha Christie' (in Tew, 2008, 36). As a child, Coe read comics, Sherlock Holmes stories and James Bond books, and wrote his first stories at the age of eight, in particular a detective thriller called *The Castle of Mystery* which amounted to 180 typed pages, 'a long mock-Victorian detective story … full of cliff-hanger chapter endings and bizarre historical detail' (Coe, 2013d), which Coe described as a 'stylish marriage of Doyle and Wodehouse' (in Vincent). The beginning of the story is reproduced in *What a Carve Up!* (284–7), attributed to Michael Owen, and the Victorian detective and his assistant are described as 'Holmes and Watson revisited, with a healthy dash of surrealism' (284). Like Coe, Michael is said to have been 'brought up on a diet of Hercule Poirot and Sherlock Holmes' (232), and is assisted in his investigation on the Winshaws by a gay sleuth whose Islington apartment is furnished exactly like that of Thaddeus Sholto in Conan Doyle's *The Sign of Four* (221). In addition, when the young artist Phoebe arrives at Winshaw Towers, she is greeted by Hilary who welcomes her to 'Baskerville Hall' (193). In 'Diary of an Obsession' (2005), Coe explains that his passion for Sherlock Holmes's stories dates back to discussions with his maternal grandfather (45) and has even taken the form of an obsession when it comes to Billy Wilder's adaptation of *The Private Life of Sherlock Holmes* (1970) which he has watched dozens of times and refers to in *The House of Sleep* (127). In *Expo 58*, the Russian spy Andrey Chersky 'has an encyclopaedic knowledge of the Sherlock Holmes stories' (114).

While in Lickey County Primary and Middle School, Coe's teacher read Tolkien's *The Hobbit* (1937) to the class every day and Coe remembers that part of what appealed to him about Tolkien was 'his qualities as a local, provincial writer – a writer of the Midlands' (Coe, 2013d). In *The Rotters' Club*, Benjamin pins on his bedroom wall 'a picture of Bilbo Baggins's house at Bag End, drawn by J.R.R. Tolkien himself, and another Tolkien illustration, a detailed map of Middle Earth' (57–8), while his friend Philip, whose 'favourite reading matter' is *The Lord of the Rings* (179), suggests that their music band bear the name 'Minas Tirith' (58), all places that appear in *The Hobbit* and *The Lord of the Rings*. Benjamin nurses 'a residual fondness for Tolkien' because in the landscape of *The Hobbit*, he 'found sentimental echoes of the area where he himself had grown up', more particularly 'a place just a mile or two south of Longbridge: the Lickey Hills, where his grandparents lived' (134–5). While in *The Terrible Privacy of Maxwell Sim*, Max confesses he has never read *The Lord of the Rings* (101), in *The Rain Before it Falls*, when Rosamond thinks of Beatrix's bloodshot, rounded eyes staring at her and her daughter, the image reminds her 'of the character of Gollum from *The Lord of the Rings*', a comparison which she slyly hopes 'doesn't seem too grotesque or inappropriate' (190).

Coe also remembers reading George Orwell's *Animal Farm* (1945) at the age of 11 or 12, which had a profound influence on him as he admired the way 'a political allegory was smuggled into what appeared to be a children's fable' (2013d) – a combination he would emulate many years later in his children's book *The*

Broken Mirror (2014). In *The Terrible Privacy of Maxwell Sim*, Miss Erith admits she has been 'an old lefty' ever since she 'started reading George Orwell and E.P. Thompson' (195), while in *The Rotters' Club*, Malcolm's friend advises him to buy some Orwell for Benjamin so he can 'wake up to what's happening in this country' (99). The notion of the novelist as critic of society is certainly one which was bound to appeal to Coe.

As a teenager, Coe watched television shows like *Rising Damp* (1974–78) and remembers being in thrall to Monty Python, 'that bunch of Oxbridge-educated surrealists', and skipping school to go to the cinema and watch *Monty Python and the Holy Grail* three times in one week in 1975: 'I got my first exhilaration at the idea that a TV show, or a film, or a novel, could parody itself, deconstruct its own conventions' (2013d). *Monty Python* instilled in him 'an early love of parody, surrealism and subversion': 'I was interested in comedy and especially interested in the ways in which comedy could subvert our perceptions' (2013d). In *The Terrible Privacy of Maxwell Sim*, when the PR officer asks Max to think of an archetypal story of a quest, a journey, a 'voyage of discovery', such as that of 'King Arthur and the Holy Grail', he confesses to himself he can only think of Monty Python (101). Coe was also drawn to Spike Milligan, comedian and co-writer of the radio comedy programme *The Goon Show*, as well as author of the comic novel *Puckoon* (1963), which Coe particularly enjoyed because it 'plays Shandean games with narrative convention and includes several dialogues between the narrator and his central character' (2013d). At 15, Coe wrote a full-length satirical novel entitled *All The Way* (which he sent to a publisher, unsuccessfully, and then burnt), which he describes as 'would-be Kingsley Amis, or actually would-be Spike Milligan' (in Laity): 'I was trying to write like Evelyn Waugh and I wound up writing like Kingsley Amis' (in Taylor, Charles). When he was 16, Coe read Fielding's *Joseph Andrews* (1742), 'a revelatory reading moment' for him: 'Fielding just opened up for what could be done with the novel in terms of architecture, you could have multiple plotting and complicated interrelationships on a large scale. That really set me thinking about the novel in a completely new way' (in Taylor, Charles).

At the age of 17, Coe read the novels of Joseph Heller and Flann O'Brien's *At Swim-Two Birds* (1939) – which he liked for 'its formal playfulness, its mixture of Irish melancholy and pessimism, and its subversive humour' (in Tew, 2008, 37) – as well as Laurence Sterne's *Tristram Shandy* (1759–67). He enjoyed what the Monty Python, Milligan, O'Brien and Sterne had in common, namely 'an amused, radical scepticism about the form in which they were working': 'What I was really looking for were writers *within whose work itself* were inscribed doubts about the validity of what they were doing; or, if not that, a recognition of its potential absurdity; or if not that, at the very least, a note of self-examination and self-criticism' (2013d). At that time, Coe started writing another novel, *Half Asleep; Half Awake* (the title of a track on the 1974 album *Unrest* by British avant-rock group Henry Cow). He describes the book as 'a highly melodramatic exploration of [his] own teenage angst', which was 'experimental in form, with nods towards the novels of Laurence Sterne and Flann O'Brien' (Coe, 2015b), but he wrote no more than 40 pages of the book. In *The Rotters' Club*, Benjamin becomes enthralled with Flann O'Brien (317) and refers to his surreal comic novel *The Third Policeman* (1967).

Coe developed a passion for music at an early age. As a child, he played the piano and like Joseph in the short story 'Rotary Park', who gets a guitar for Christmas, Coe was given his first guitar for his ninth birthday. His heroes were such improvisers as Miles Davis, Keith Jarrett and Pat Metheny (Coe, 2014b). Like Benjamin (45) and Philip (179) in *The Rotters' Club*, Coe dreamed of writing a rock opera but did not learn to read music and therefore lacked the solid foundation of musical theory. Influenced by progressive rock music and jazz, he started 'writing tunes and recording them' on a cassette recorder, creations that he considers a diary of his emotions at that time. Coe recalls how in 1978, at the age of 17, he was 'in thrall to many different kinds of music: the density and elaborate structures of the classical repertoire, the wild but disciplined freedoms of jazz, the energy and directness of pop music' (2013d). The first classical music he enjoyed and understood was not that of great composers like Beethoven, Schubert or Verdi (whom he hardly ever listens to), but the three piano pieces by French composer Erik Satie, the *Gymnopédies* (1888), which he considers at the origin of modern music for their use of repetition and of slightly dissonant accords (2014b).

Coe arrived at Trinity College, Cambridge, in 1980 and remembers being 'slightly full of [him]self … and yet at the same time inexperienced, diffident and narrowly educated'. He was still 'locked into an adolescent mindset' and did his best to make himself invisible. As a consequence, his memories of Trinity are 'positive', but also 'complicated, and sometimes unsettling' (2013d). Coe's early novels are situated in an academic background: in *The Accidental Woman*, Maria studies in Oxford, while in *A Touch of Love*, a bittersweet campus novel, Robin, after graduating from Cambridge, becomes a postgraduate student in Coventry. His friend Ted nostalgically conjures up their college days, embellishing what probably took place and comparing what he experienced to 'a scene out of *Brideshead Revisited*' (64) – Evelyn Waugh's famous 1945 campus novel – and to 'a scene out of *The Glittering Prizes*' (66), a British television drama about a group of Cambridge students, which follows them from 1952 to their middle age in the 1970s. Referring to *A Touch of Love*, Coe admits: 'The main character, Robin, is identifiably a version of myself, and several of the other characters are also based on friends and acquaintances from my time at Warwick University' (Website, *Touch*). In later books, characters at university (the group of students in *The House of Sleep*, Graham who is on a film-making course in *What a Carve Up!*) are more loosely based on autobiographical material.

After graduating in 1983, having completed a BA dissertation on Byron's *Don Juan*, Coe moved to Warwick University in Coventry where he 'began to read feminism, structuralism, the nouveau roman, Beckett' (Laity). He wrote an MA dissertation entitled 'Samuel Beckett and the Double Act: Comic Duality in Fiction and Drama' (1984) and completed in 1986 a doctoral thesis entitled 'Satire and Sympathy: Some Consequences of Intrusive Narration in *Tom Jones* and Other Comic Novels'. The 343-page dissertation draws analogies between Fielding and such well-known satirists as Jonathan Swift and Laurence Sterne, but also points to affinities with more unexpected writers such as Flaubert, Dickens, George Eliot, Brecht and Beckett. Coe sees *Tom Jones* as 'a playground in which Fielding was able to let his contradictory impulses engage with each other in friendly combat' (1986, 2) – be they literary, moral or political – and he analyses several devices that point to the ambiguities of form, such as the figure of the intrusive narrator, the narrator-reader relationship, and various dialogical aspects of narrative.

Many years after writing this erudite thesis, Coe still considers *Tom Jones* 'the first great English novel and the first great English essay on the art of novel-writing' (2013d), as well as his 'great inspiration, the English novel that towers over everything else' (in Kellaway). What Coe likes about it is that it is 'at once a social panorama' of England in the mid-1740s, and an 'experimental novel' full of self-reflexive remarks on the writer's own procedures (Coe, 2013d); at the same time, Coe remarks, 'it excels at all the thrillingly vulgar devices without which a novel is dead on its feet: it's full of jokes, suspense, cliffhangers, narrative reversals and pathos' (2007b, 55) – from which Coe drew inspiration. Coe remarks that Fielding 'turned [his] writing around completely, set it on the path it [has] followed ever since' (in Taylor, Charles), and he notes he still hasn't 'found anyone who was doing for the novel of the late twentieth century what Fielding had done for his era, or Sterne for his' (2013d). In *The Rotters' Club*, during a summer holiday in Denmark, Benjamin reads Fielding's novels in preparation for his English A-level classes, while the picaresque dimension of *The Terrible Privacy of Maxwell Sim* may have found its origins in Fielding's works.

While 'eighteenth-century literature has influenced [Coe's] writing most' (in Kellaway), the nineteenth-century production has not left the same mark, although he admires Dickens – 'an almost mythical figure to [him]' (in Taylor, Charles) – 'for his social commitment and his high spirits' (in Tew, 2008, 38), and devoted some 20 pages of his PhD thesis to an analysis of the shifts in narrative perspective in Dickens's novels and in particular *The Old Curiosity Shop* (1986, 19–38). Referring to the Victorian novel, Coe explains why its model is inadequate to the modern times, echoing B.S. Johnson's own misgivings (Johnson, 1973b, 14): 'If there is a problem with the nineteenth-century model, it's not so much that it is invalid or irrelevant but that, paradoxically, it is too formally satisfying to suit our current state of mind. It induces the stolid consolations of closure and catharsis and I'm beginning to think that these are not what our present difficulties require' (2013d). Some of Coe's work has nevertheless been considered as a 'parody of prim Dickens', borrowing from 'the Dickensian grotesque' (Vianu, 157), and Coe himself has been called a 'second-rate Dickens', although it was supposedly offered as a 'compliment' (Beck, 33). *What a Carve Up!* has been compared to *Bleak House* (Thurschwell, 31) and *The House of Sleep* includes quotes from and a witty pastiche of Chapter 59 of *Great Expectations* (83, 306, 308), when Pip and Estella meet again. While Dickens's Pip can assert 'I saw no shadow of another parting from her' (493), melancholy Robert/Cleo, in the *House of Sleep*, feels he/she has lost Sarah forever: 'Cleo saw no shadow of another meeting with her' (311). In *Expo 58*, Thomas confesses to being 'rather parochial in [his] tastes' and slyly mentions that he likes Dickens (37).

As a student, Coe did not share in the general enthusiasm for the work of his immediate contemporaries of the *Granta* generation – the 'Young Turks' Martin Amis, Graham Swift, Julian Barnes or Ian McEwan, who had appeared on the 1983 *Granta* selection of 'Best of Young British Novelists' – whom he found 'too suave, too urbane' examples of 'metropolitan cool'. Coe's gravitation towards experimental fiction also had limits: 'I had dipped my toe into Robbe-Grillet, and Pinget, and possibly even Christine Brooke-Rose, but had withdrawn it again quickly and with a sharp intake of breath, finding the waters chilly and unwelcoming' (2013d). On the other hand, he enjoyed the works of such innovative writers as Samuel Beckett and Alasdair Gray to whose *1982, Janine* he devoted an essay, praising its playfulness and 'raw vulnerability' (2013d); a quote from the novel appears as an epigraph to *The Terrible Privacy of Maxwell Sim*. At the same time, Coe came across the works of B.S. Johnson – whom he thinks 'most deserves to be thought of as Laurence Sterne's heir' (2013d) – and of the female writers of the Virago Modern Classics (Rosamond Lehmann, Dorothy Richardson, May Sinclair, Antonia White), an imprint founded in 1973 by Carmen Callil, which primarily published works by women writers and re-issued books by neglected authors, most of them from the upper middle class. Coe explains in an essay that, in the 1970s, readers enjoyed these novels for their 'good old-fashioned escapism' at a time when people were watching television or film adaptations of Evelyn Waugh's *Brideshead Revisited* and E.M. Forster's *A Room with a View*: 'As the last flurries of Britain's experiment with socialism descended into chaos, and the dampening realities of the Thatcher revolution started to sink in, the nation was beginning to take refuge in nostalgic fantasies of elegance and privilege' (2013d).

These literary love affairs led Coe to write *The Accidental Woman*, whose metafictional devices and narratorial interventions are very much indebted to Sterne's *Tristram Shandy* and Johnson's *Christie Malry's Own Double-Entry* (1973). Coe's first published novel and his second, *A Touch of Love*, would be echoed in the titles of the two novels by Michael Owen in *What a Carve Up!*: *Accidents Will Happen* and *The Loving Touch* (284). Such hints might be a way to suggest parallels between the hapless hero of Coe's fourth novel and the writer himself.

In 1986, Coe moved down to London, to a council flat in Bermondsey, and became a proofreader for a City law firm: 'For four hours every day I huddle over British Telecom privatisation documents, checking the indentations and making sure the commas are in the right place' (2013d). This was the place where he met his future wife, an Australian aptly named Janine. They were married on 28 January 1989 – having lunch to the sounds of 'protestors marching against Salman Rushdie, and burning copies of *The Satanic Verses*' (2013d) – and as an homage both to his wife and to Gray's *1982, Janine*, *What a Carve Up!* was dedicated to '1994, Janine'. Although Coe has lived in London for nearly 30 years, 'he still feels like an outsider writing about the capital and doesn't believe he could write with the confidence of Londoners such as Peter Ackroyd or Zadie Smith' (in Lakin). His third novel, *The Dwarves of Death*, is set in London and its narrator, William, who comes from Sheffield, lives on a council estate in Bermondsey (40) and positively hates the capital for its unfriendliness and impersonality. In *What a Carve Up!*, as Colin Hutchinson remarks, Michael Owen contrasts his life in London, 'given over to the aggressive pursuit of self-interest', with what 'he encounters in Sheffield, where Joan and her lodgers are perceived to be enjoying a more intimate and socially cohesive life' (94).

While working at the law firm, Coe was still writing his novels as well as composing music for jazz and cabaret and playing the keyboards in a band called the Peer Group (formed in 1985 when Coe was still studying at Warwick University). He was also composing for a radical feminist cabaret group named Wanda and the Willy Warmers: 'It was quite raucous, in-yer-face, let's-make-fun-of-the-men-in-the-audience. I would be given these scabrous lyrics, and I would write my typical melodic, melancholy, wistful tunes to them' (in Laity). Coe remembers writing lengthy, jazzy instrumentals 'in the vein associated with Canterbury-school bands like Caravan and Hatfield and the North' (Website, *Dwarves*), and that the Peer Group sounded like 'the bastard child of Prefab Sprout, Everything But The Girl and The Average White Band' (2013d). Coe's experience as a musician inspired him to write *The Dwarves of Death* which focuses on several aspirant musicians in 1988 in London, and in which each chapter starts with an epigraph from a song by Morrissey, the lead singer of The Smiths, of whom Coe is a huge fan. *The Rotters' Club* and *The Closed Circle* are also replete with references to pop, rock and funk bands of the 1970s through to the 2000s, and Benjamin's 'short-lived part-time musical career in the 1980s' (2004a, 45) might be an echo of Coe's. In the 1970s, as Coe explains, young people 'defined themselves by what kind of music they listened to', so that music 'said everything about you, about your intellectual pretensions, about your political views'. As a consequence, the musical references in Coe's books are 'very much part of the characterization' (in Guignery, 2013, 37).

In several essays on music and in interviews, Coe explains that he distrusts words and gets irritated by them – 'I get very frustrated by words, of what they will not do for you' (in Guignery, 2013, 37) – thus echoing the narrator of *The Accidental Woman* who remarks: 'words are tricky little bastards, and very rarely say what you want them to say' (37). In *The House of Sleep*, Coe offers a satirical parody of a psychoanalytical paper, in which its author reflects upon the treachery of language, comically accumulating improbable metaphors:

> Language is a traitor, a double agent who slips across borders without warning in the dead of night. It is a heavy snowfall in a foreign country, which hides the shapes and contours of reality beneath a cloak of nebulous whiteness. It is a crippled dog, never quite able to perform the tricks we ask of it. It is a ginger biscuit, dunked for too long in the tea of our expectations, crumbling and dissolving into nothingness. It is a lost continent.
>
> (282–3)

> … language is a cruel and faithless mistress; it is a sly cardsharp, who deals us a pack full of jokers; it is a distant flute on a misty night, teasing us with half-forgotten melodies; it is the light on the inside of the fridge, which never goes off when we are looking; it is a fork in the road; it is a knife in the water.
>
> (293)

The indiscriminate mixture of images makes the list ludicrous and comic, satirising the stereotyped discourse on the unreliability and inadequacy of language. While this passage is deliberately parodic, it nevertheless contains some degree of truth. Coe actually ascribes more power to notes, chords, melodies and harmonies, and argues that music always appears to him as a more truthful expression of the emotions he is trying to convey. He remarks: 'Music, for me, will always be my doorway into imagined worlds, and also to remembered ones' (2013d). For Benjamin in *The Rotters' Club*, 'music always made sense. ... He would never understand the world, but he would always love this music. He listened to this music, ... and knew that he had found a home' (100). In an article on Hitchcock, Coe notes that the director 'reminds us that cinema is at its most emotionally powerful when it speaks in sounds, music and images, not words. In life, as in movies, people talk to each other because chatter fills the void' (2013d).

Coe himself interviewed several musicians for *The Wire* (Bill Frisell, Annette Peacock, Steve Reich, Brian Eno) between 1989 and 1991, and at the same period wrote book reviews for the *Guardian* (1988–92), the *Sunday Times* and the *Mail on Sunday* (1992–94). In 1988–89, he wrote film reviews in two magazines (*The Metropolitan Magazine* and *LAW London Australian Weekly*), before working as a film critic for the *New Statesman* in 1996–97. He was also commissioned to write the biographies of two American actors: *Humphrey Bogart: Take it and Like it* (1991) and *James Stewart: Leading Man* (1994), and is regularly invited to film festivals in Britain and other European countries. Coe's fondness for the cinema explains why the inspirations for his books are more often visual and cinematographic than literary.

Back in 1994, when he was 33 years old and had just published *What a Carve Up!*, Coe wrote a piece about 'parent's block', focusing on his lack of 'impulse towards fatherhood': remembering the 'humiliations at school, stomach-churning fear of visits to the doctor or afternoons on the rugby field', he argued he did not want to have to deal with 'emotions of such intensity' all over again as, according to him, children 'present us with the entire spectrum of our joys and sorrows grotesquely enlarged and vivified' (1994c). And yet, in 1997 and 2000, Coe's daughters, Matilda and Madeline, were born and Coe explains that having children has transformed his work, adding a 'tenderness to everything [he's] written' since he has had them (in Kellaway). He has also 'become interested in children as fictional characters because they offer an extreme instance of powerlessness' (Coe, 2013d). *The Rain Before it Falls* is the first novel Coe conceived completely since having children: 'A lot of it has grown out of my own relationship with my daughters and seeing how they relate to their mother' (in Page, Benedicte 20). The caring relation between Gill and her grown-up daughters in the novel, which comes as a welcoming counterpoint to the defective relationships among other characters, may thus be read as a fictional projection of Coe's own family in the future. His children's book *The Broken Mirror* is dedicated to Matilda and Madeline.

In 2013, having published ten novels, Coe remarked that 'they're starting to feel less like a series of disconnected books and more like a kind of continuum. As if each book is a chapter in a longer story' (in Snoekx). In the author's note to his 2014 collection of short stories, *Loggerheads and Other Stories*, Coe refers to his literary project of 15 books called *Unrest* – which is also the title of the novel-in-progress of his fictional alter ego Benjamin in *The Closed Circle* (102, 257), inspired by the title of a 1974 album by Henry Cow (414). *The Rain Before it Falls* and *Expo 58* (which includes a chapter entitled 'Unrest') are part of this project, as well as three short stories, 'Ivy and Her Nonsense' (written in 1990), 'Pentatonic' and 'Rotary Park' (both written in 2012). Coe aims to trace the history of a fictional middle-class Midlands family from the 1940s to the present and look at Britain's relationship to Europe. He recalls how, in his mid-20s, he had become fascinated 'by the idea of narrative as a repository of lost time: the notion that a long sequence of novels could, by exhaustively tracing the life story of one character, make readers feel that they had actually lived that character's life, in rich, imaginatively continuous detail' (2013b). Coe's ambition for such a sequence confirms his areas of interest as being the provinces rather than London, the contemporary world (or recent past) rather than the distant past, the middle class rather than other strata of society. The next chapters will show how these interests come together in Coe's novels.

Part II
Major Works

3

'FUNNY, BRUTALIST AND SHORT': *THE ACCIDENTAL WOMAN, A TOUCH OF LOVE* AND *THE DWARVES OF DEATH*

Jonathan Coe's first three novels, *The Accidental Woman* (1987), *A Touch of Love* (1989) and *The Dwarves of Death* (1990), seem to echo B.S. Johnson's dictum that the novel should 'try simply to be Funny, Brutalist, and Short' (1973a, 165). In interviews, Coe can be unjustly harsh about his early production and regularly points out that his first novel was rejected many times by agents and publishers. He gives the number of copies sold for each book (around 300 for each in hardback), considering *The Dwarves of Death* to be his weakest novel and remarking that: 'My first three novels had been very pinched and constrained' (2011). Philip Tew argues for his part that Coe's early fiction 'combines a reflexive, self-aware experimentation with a blend of caricature and satirical, ironic distance' (2008, 47). This aptly captures the specific mode, tone and mood of these novels, all set in the bleak and dreary atmosphere of Britain in the 1970s and 1980s, but frequently illuminated by bouts of fierce humour and farcical comedy. Among the common features of these three novels are the characterization of most protagonists as placid and hapless, the dark humour, the use of self-reflexivity and deconstruction of narrative conventions, as well as the reflexions on memory and the relativity of truth.

It was under the influence of the female writers of the Virago Modern Classics that in his mid-twenties (in 1984–85), Coe 'abandoned straightforward autobiographical writing and chose a female protagonist for [his] first published novel, *The Accidental Woman*' (2013d), a book whose title is not meant as a response to Iris Murdoch's *An Accidental Man* (1971), which Coe says he has never read (Website, *Accidental*). Before that, Coe says his work was 'full of received ideas and forms' and his unpublished novel *The Sunset Bell*, although written in 1981, 'reads as though it were written in the 1950s' (in Laity). Apart from the Virago writers and B.S. Johnson, the main influence behind *The Accidental Woman* is Beckett whom Coe admires for his 'morbid, obsessive humour' and the way he 'looks the worst of the human condition head on' (2013d). 'Bordering on pastiche Beckett', *The Accidental Woman* is 'greatly influenced by *Watt* and *Murphy*' to the point that the name Maria for the main character was chosen as 'a deliberate homage to Beckett's "M" characters – Murphy, Molloy, Malone' (in Magarian, 13).

Alliteratively nicknamed 'Miserable Maria' and 'Moody Mary' at school and at work (2, 107), the protagonist is described as quiet, placid, imperturbable, indifferent, of 'a silent and studious disposition' (2), and belonging to 'the withdrawing type' (51). Her emotional blockage is anaphorically summed up by her friend Sarah: 'nothing excites you. Nothing amuses you. Nothing moves you' (38), and foreshadows that of Coe's later male characters. In the early work however, it is women who are presented as dispassionate and indecisive. In *The Dwarves of Death*, Madeline's typical infuriating (but also comic) cue is 'I don't mind' (25): when her boyfriend William slides his arm beneath hers, she offers 'neither resistance nor encouragement' (93), and when he suggests seeing her again five days later, she is fine with it but 'would have said the same if I had suggested meeting tomorrow or in six months' time' (46). William's childhood friend Stacey fares no better as she is described as 'down to earth', 'uncomplaining' and 'unflappable' (142). These drab portraits of unemotional young women in Coe's early fiction point to a deep void in their lives, but also to a broader sense of incommunicability between people. For instance, William's lack of attention and sensitivity make him fail to understand that his roommate is repeatedly being beaten up by her boyfriend. The difficulty of connecting and ethically reaching out towards the other is also evidenced by the recurrent allusion to the absence of any genuine contact with next-door neighbours (1989a, 42; 1990, 42), or with people on public transport: 'I could stand with my body pressed up against another man's on a crowded tube, and our eyes would never meet' (1990, 42).

In *The Accidental Woman*, Maria's life is a series of failures, accidental events and dead-ends that belie any notion of the novel as a *Bildungsroman*. The anti-heroine – '(for it is she, as chance would have it)' (1), the narrator writes in the third sentence of the book, thereby introducing the figure of the 'accidental woman' – does not mature or develop, and her life seems merely driven by chance: 'All her life she had, it was starting to seem, been at the mercy of forces beyond her control' (105). The novel, which D. J. Taylor judges 'a convincing study of the random impetuses by which human lives tend to be governed' (40), therefore follows no teleological direction, but goes in a circle back to the family unit at the end of the book – 15 years after Maria left – and to the park where the young woman has memories of a childhood episode when, 'by chance' (10), she had been separated from her parents. But no epiphany takes place there and the scene is anticlimactic, marked by a 'curious lack of emotion': 'the recollection was pale, ... the park appeared to have nothing to do with her memory' (164). As Maria and a lark stare at each other, the narrator decides to lend his sympathy to the lark, whose perspective from above is offered until Maria becomes a mere insignificant 'speck in the unseen ... indifferent even in the face of death which who knows may be the next thing chance has in store for her' (165). At the end of *A Touch of Love*, Aparna also returns to the city of her college days, Coventry, before going back home to her parents in India, 'with a mixture of longing and fear' (232). In *The Dwarves of Death*, William returns to his childhood home in Sheffield, prompted by the lyrics of a Gaelic song by John McLennan, which also forms the epigraph to the book: 'I'd set my course to the land I love, / The land my people dwell in' (133, 135). For William, coming home, a place that seemed 'warm and gentle and clean' compared to London, 'had been the easiest thing in the world' (211), while Aparna, in *A Touch of Love*, 'had not forgotten that home can be the strangest place of all' (231). Unlike Maria however, both William and Aparna have 'grown up' (1990, 213), learning from their painful experiences, and years later, in the short story 'V.O.', the former aspirant musician William will reappear as a fairly famous film composer acting as jury member at a film festival (2014a).

Despite such faint hopes for a better future, the idea of a life driven by accident and out of one's control is what prevails in Coe's early fiction. In *A Touch of Love*, postgraduate student Robin fails to write his dissertation and is depressed by current world affairs; he asks his former college friend: 'Do you ever feel ... that you've never really *made* any decisions?' (19). Later on, just before he makes an innocent move that will lead to his being accused of an improper act, he muses: 'Forces would seem to be conspiring against me' (71, 131). In *The Dwarves of Death*, the narrator seems more confident when he declares in the incipit: 'I thought I'd made some good decisions' (2), but he backtracks only three pages later: 'I realized that I had not made a proper decision today at all' (5). When remembering his teenage years with his friend Stacey, he realizes: 'Decisions were taken, often quite major decisions, without either of us realizing it' (142), and at the end of the book, he wonders why he should let 'senseless, random circumstances' defeat him (163). However, he has to admit that he has no control over the drift of his life: 'circumstances were sweeping me away, carrying me beyond the realm where decisions could be made and free will exercised' (178). Only a gun aimed at him appears as 'an aid to decision-making' (201). According to D. J. Taylor, Coe's protagonists resemble the heroes of Evelyn Waugh's early novels, 'to whom things happen' (40): they are passive and seemingly unable to influence their own destiny.

This fatalist philosophy which denies free will is summed up in the second embedded story written by Robin in *A Touch of Love*, 'The Lucky Man' – perhaps an oblique homage to Lindsay

Anderson's film *O Lucky Man!* (1973) that Coe particularly admires – in which Lawrence argues that his 'life has been a chain of accidents' (97), and adds: 'everything we do is merely determined by chance ... Our so-called choices, these supposedly responsible decisions – ultimately they have to be made in the context of factors over which we have not the slightest control' (99). Thus, when Amanda unexpectedly takes him in her arms at the end of the story, he wonders if 'all that it meant was that another decision ... had just been made on his behalf' (112). In an almost perfect symmetry, the protagonist is echoed by another Lawrence in the fourth embedded story, 'The Unlucky Man', when he tells his friend Harry (who has had his whole life planned out since he was 25): 'You can't assume that people will always behave in the way you want them to. Life is chaotic. It's random' (207). Lawrence argues for his part that the only way to 'prove that *you* have control over what becomes of you' is to commit suicide (208, 222), which is the course chosen by Robin and several other characters in Coe's novels, and by B.S. Johnson in real life.

This discussion about chance, randomness and the lack of control or free will in Coe's first two books will recur in later novels and is reminiscent of B.S. Johnson's reflections. In *Aren't You Rather Young to be Writing Your Memoirs?* Johnson writes: 'Life is chaotic, fluid, random' (14), anticipating fictional Lawrence's words, and he notes that he tried to reproduce this chaos and randomness in his work, for instance by refusing any teleology, causality and linearity. In his film *Fat Man on a Beach*, Johnson faces the camera and asks: 'Why can't a film be a celebration of accidents?' (168). He concludes: 'let's celebrate the chaos. Let's celebrate the accidental' (169), possibly providing inspiration for the title of Coe's first novel. In Johnson's *The Unfortunates*, the unexpected development of cancer in his friend Tony's body is also seen as a sign of the randomness that rules the world: 'it is all chaos, I accept that as the state of the world, of things, of the human condition, yes, meaningless it is, pointless ... it was just random, arbitrary, gratuitous' ('Just as it seemed', 3). In *The Dwarves of Death*, in which a band is called 'The Unfortunates', a character named Tony reflects upon his father's death and eerily echoes Johnson when he says: 'It doesn't make much sense, does it? The randomness of it' (41). Several characters of Coe's early novels thus share Johnson's fatalist belief in the randomness and chaos of life, driven by forces beyond one's control. They will find an echo a few decades later in Rosamond's hypothesis in *The Rain Before it Falls*: 'Perhaps chaos and randomness are the natural order of things' (224), but also in Benjamin's bitter comments in *The Closed Circle* when he loses his faith in God: 'there are no such things as miracles. Just random sets of circumstances, intersecting in ways that make no sense. … Chaos and coincidence. That's all it is.' (178) He will only be contradicted later on by Claire who refuses to shrug her shoulders and say: 'Life is random' (369). She believes on the contrary that one can cut one's way 'through all the chaos and randomness and coincidence' and find causes and patterns (370).

Claire's positivist belief in causality is however rarely shared and most characters in Coe's novels are fatalistic and often presented as passive, emotionless and inevitably defeated. Coe recalls that when he was writing *The Accidental Woman*, the motto he had pinned over his desk was 'Hitchcock's formula for engaging an audience: torture the heroine' (in Magarian, 13), and he indeed does not spare his protagonist. Beyond the character of Maria, *The Accidental Woman* would appear cynically and ironically to highlight the unhappiness and solitude of an entire generation, perhaps parodying the bleakness of Beckett's own writing: 'more and more she began to see the sexual cravings of the human race, including her own, as the symptom of a far greater craving, a terrible loneliness, an urge for self-forgetfulness' (12). When Maria goes to parties, 'on none of the tired and wasted faces which thronged around her did she see the marks of real happiness, only the marks of a hateful delusion' (48). The novel thus communicates 'a sense of universal emptiness, an exacerbated general loneliness' (Vianu, 154), which seems related to a nihilistic perspective, and so does *A Touch of Love*, in which Coe stages a hapless young man suffering from a sense of alienation and despair: 'I look inside myself and I see this emptiness at the centre … It scares me almost to death' (143). Robin's suicide is foreshadowed by this morbid fear but also by allusions in his own short stories: in the first story, a 'small, noisy family' dies in 'a concerted suicide' (42); in the second, Lawrence is pressed to 'perform a premature and involuntary suicide' (111); in the third, Nick was 'on the point of killing himself' a few months before (160); in the fourth, suicide is presented as a way to prove that '*you* have control over what becomes of you' (208) and Robin has scribbled a quote by philosopher Simone Weil on the last page of his notebook: '*Two ways of killing ourselves: suicide or detachment*' (223). Here again, a short piece by B.S. Johnson springs to mind, 'Everyone Knows Somebody Who's Dead' (1973), in which the narrator evokes the memory of his colleague Robin who committed suicide, soon after his girlfriend did away with her own life.

Despite their bleak and dismal mood, Coe's early novels are also characterized by farcical, cynical and tongue-in-cheek humour, even when dealing with such dramatic issues as suicide or domestic violence. In *The Accidental Woman*, when a housewife asks for help from a woman's magazine after her husband has assaulted her because she replaced carrots with parsnips for his Sunday lunch, the journalist responds with advice on how to remove gravy stains from a dress and recommends keeping a stock of carrots in the deep freeze (109). At times, the playful narrator resorts to Beckettian humour, for instance when describing Maria's room in the simplest terms at Cribbage House: 'There was a table, near the window, and a chair, near the door. She put the table near the door and the chair near the window' (52), perhaps echoing the stage directions at the beginning of Beckett's *Endgame* (1957). In *The Dwarves of Death*, the narrator proposes a hilarious and absurdist description of his endless wait for a bus on a council estate on a Sunday, and confesses he hates the old woman going past and 'pulling a little trolley full of dirty washing' because 'even though she is walking at the rate of a mile a century, you know that she will have time to go down the launderette, do three loads of washing, call in on her sister for Sunday lunch, eat the whole meal, wash up, watch the omnibus edition of *Eastenders* and walk all the way back before the next bus comes' (80–1). At a linguistic level and thus in a more oblique way, *The Accidental Woman* debunks clichés and set phrases such as Charlotte's 'there is a certain sort of silence between people, where no words are necessary, and which signals not the end but the start of understanding' (18, 136), and the narrator ironically mocks stereotypical attitudes towards the past: 'she thinks, just this once, to try not to forget the past, but to recreate it, and thereby, perhaps, to come to terms with it. Worth a try, at any rate' (150). In *A Touch of Love*, comedy emerges from satirical portraits of academics who have written such supposedly 'radical and provocative' books (56, 57, 58) as *The Failure of Contemporary Literature* (26, 56) or *Culture in Crisis* (57). When an obsequious and expectant student asks a professor if this means 'the end of literature', the latter exclaims: '"Ah! No, no … indeed not. Far from it. In fact I think –" here there was an almighty pause, far surpassing any that had gone before "– I think …" … "I think I'd like another macaroon."' (58) Coe is very fond of such anticlimactic and mocking comic effects.

Such a tongue-in-cheek debunking of academic discussions goes hand in hand with a recurrent self-reflexivity about conventional narrative techniques in Coe's first two novels. *The Accidental Woman* starts with a chapter entitled 'Beforewards' and ends with one called 'Afterhand', thus already defamiliarising linguistics and rules of temporality. Lidia Vianu argues that '"Beforewards" is one way of saying "towards before", of announcing that the direction of the novel … is not towards an end but actually to a place and time before the novel was born' (154). Such an interpretation may be related to the first words of the novel – 'Take a birth. Any birth.' (1) – which happen to be misleading as they do not lead to the discussion of an actual birth, but to the announcement that the main character has won a place at Oxford. This birth should therefore be interpreted metaphorically and metafictionally as the creation of a character, the birth of a novel and the simultaneous advent of a novelist. Right from the start, Coe deconstructs the conventions of the traditional *Bildungsroman* by exposing the mechanisms of creation and playfully thwarting the reader's expectations. A major point of interest in Coe's early novels is indeed his use of metafictional devices and of an intrusive narrator, which could be compared to Beckett's and B.S. Johnson's own self-reflexive techniques and direct addresses to the reader, but which also involves fictional strategies traceable to Fielding and Sterne. In his introduction to *Tom Jones,* Coe points to 'the novel's most ingenious formal trick', which is that 'it tells a complex, engrossing story while at the same time commenting upon itself reflexively, either in the introductory chapters which preface each of the 18 books, or in the hundreds of shrewd, jocular asides with which Fielding peppers his narrative' (2013d). Coe's early narrators also pepper their narratives with such commentaries addressed to the reader, thus exposing the artefact and countering any suspension of disbelief.

Coe describes *The Accidental Woman* as 'a novel about authorial intentions', in which 'the central character is the intrusive narrator' (in Magarian, 13), while 'the heroine is pushed aside' (Vianu,

152). The facetious narrator thus frequently refuses to describe some scenes in ways that are reminiscent of Fielding's narrator in *Tom Jones* or Johnson's in *Christie Malry's Own Double-Entry*. For instance, Coe's narrator is deliberately and archly frustrating the reader's expectations when he writes: 'Here you are to imagine a short scene of family jubilation, I'm buggered if I can describe one' (14), or when he refuses to discuss the love affair between Maria and Nigel: 'How long it lasted, how much pleasure it gave them, these are details which we needn't bother with' (44), or declines to ponder over another character's reaction: 'what his response would have been is nobody's business. I have enough difficulty predicting Maria's behaviour, without bothering about his' (75). Subsequently, he refers to Maria's state of mind as one of misery, 'a misery such that I cannot describe and you probably can't imagine, so we'd better just leave it' (86), and when the family is reunited at the end of the novel, he remarks: 'I see no need to describe the ensuing scenes, in fact it would be difficult to do so with accuracy. No, we shall move on' (157).

Such jocular reticence on the part of the narrator comes not only from a supposed sense of inadequacy and incompetence as a storyteller, as suggested by the quotes above, but also from an impatience with the conventions of realism and verisimilitude, and from a dread of boredom: 'This is going to make for rather boring reading, I'm afraid' (103), he remarks, and later on: 'Let's be honest, I begin to weary of Maria, and her story, just as Maria begins to weary of Maria, and her story. ... Let us move on, for I have only one more episode to relate of Maria's life, and then we shall be done, and we can say goodbye' (148). As in Sterne's *Tristram Shandy*, the narrator thus regularly addresses the reader in a playful tone, turning him/her into a confidant and an accomplice in the very act of creation, and systematically reminding him/her of the status of the book as an artefact. In *A Touch of Love*, the narrator of the main narrative also resorts to self-reflexive devices, for instance when he remarks that Ted's wife, Katharine, 'is not, in case you were wondering, going to be allowed a voice in this story, because it is the story of Robin and Ted, who have both, in their different ways, resolved to keep her out of it. Which is a pity, in a way, because I think you would have preferred Katharine to either of them, had you been allowed to meet her' (64–5). The suggestion that a fictitious character might have met the extradiegetic reader amounts to a transgression of the ontological boundary that separates incompatible worlds, and as such draws attention to the construction of fiction, preventing the reader from suspending his/her disbelief as in conventional realist fiction.

In *The Accidental Woman*, the narrator also shares with the reader his thoughts about narrative conventions. At some point, he casually asks a rhetorical question: 'Do you mind if we revert to the past tense? I find the other so exhausting' (150). Contrary to what some modernist writers' and B.S. Johnson's narrators would have done, Coe's narrator decides against telling an episode in fragments, even though it was the way his character remembered it: 'There was one time which kept coming back to her … it came back to her in fragments, … but this is not how I shall narrate it' (72). The narrator also seems concerned with the need to maintain a straightforward narrative (even though his constant interruptions actually provide many digressions): 'But there, you start chatting with the reader and before you know where you are you find that you have forgotten all about narrative' (148). Lidia Vianu argues that Coe's texts are therefore 'explanatory' ones, as the narrator 'explains to us each of his moves' (151), thus seemingly taking good care of the reader and making him/her share in the various steps of his creation, but also probably causing some frustration with his constant interruptions.

Coe's third novel, *The Dwarves of Death*, a first-person narrative, is more conventional in form – Coe wanted to write 'something simpler' after 'the tricksy, multilayered narrative of *A Touch of Love*' (Website, *Dwarves*) – but the narrator nevertheless shares with the reader his reticence at telling his traumatic story: 'I find it hard to describe what happened' (1); 'It's hard to know where to start' (20). Laurent Mellet reads in such confessions gnawing doubts as to what literary description can achieve (2015, 258), and quotes E.M. Forster: 'By describing what has happened one gets away from what happened' (Forster 48). Coe's narrator decides to get 'the difficult part [of the story] out of the way' (20), resisting the temptation to go straight on and say how it all ended. Instead, he moves backwards and carefully explains the background to what happened, and when he comes to the night of the murder, makes a promise: 'I'll try not to exaggerate, and I'll try to say exactly what I mean: and for your part, you must take these words and really think about them' (161). Thereby, the narrator is reaching out to the reader and asking for his/her participation and leniency, if not for his/her sympathy.

The narrator of *The Accidental Woman* is also keen on treating the reader fairly and honestly, for example when he implicitly recalls Johnson's motto of truth-telling in *Albert Angelo* (1964) – 'the novel must be a vehicle for conveying truth' (175) – and confesses various cases of embellishment in his narrative (as Johnson's does at the end of his novel). When Maria remembers her time in Oxford as always bathed in sunlight, the narrator remarks: 'We can safely assume, I think, that this was in reality not the case, but then who said our concern was with reality' (17), thereby also forcefully distancing himself from the realist tradition. Later on, he again truthfully refers to weather conditions: 'Three years later, and it is still raining. I tell a lie, of course, there have been intervening periods of sunshine, but they do not concern us' (140). The narrator thus regularly echoes Johnson's plea to tell the truth, 'never a bad thing to do occasionally in a novel' (73), but while trying to be honest and truthful, he is simultaneously undermining the foundations of realism, maybe anticipating Ruth's unapologetic 'dislike of pure realism' in *The Rain before it Falls* (243).

In *A Touch of Love*, the influence of Johnson's self-reflexive techniques is again palpable, for instance in Robin's first embedded story, 'The Meeting of Minds', when the narrator interrupts his stream-of-consciousness technique to state: 'I dislike this mode of writing. You pretend to be transcribing your characters' thoughts (by what special gift of insight?) when in fact they are merely your own, thinly disguised. The device is feeble, transparent, and leads to all sorts of grammatical clumsiness. So I shall try to confine myself, in future, to honest (honest!) narrative' (34). Such a passage advocating honesty could easily have come out of Johnson's *Albert Angelo* or the last page of *House Mother Normal* (1971) when the eponymous character reveals that she is 'the puppet or concoction of a writer', and that her previous interior monologue was actually his: 'this is from his skull. It is a diagram of certain aspects of the inside of his skull!' (204). In *Christie Malry's Own Double-Entry*, the narrator also offers a 'transcursion into Christie's mind' but immediately qualifies it as 'an illusion of transcursion, that is, of course, since you know only too well in whose mind it all really takes place' (23). In all the examples quoted above, the narrators expose the devices they are using in the name of honesty, thus forbidding the reader any suspension of disbelief or adherence to an outdated form of realism. According to D. J. Taylor, Coe thereby borrows from such experimental writers of the 1960s as B.S. Johnson, Ann Quinn and specifically Eva Figes whose motto was 'not to comfort', but 'to subvert', and who used 'the novel as *device* rather than credible illusion' (40). In a talk about the Flemish writer Louis Paul Boon, Coe remarks that, even after the advent of modernism, Boon understood that 'readers still expect, still demand those old, confident Augustan certainties from their writers. They come to fiction expecting to be comforted, to be reassured, to see order recreated from chaos. But they will no longer find it: they *cannot* find it'. If Boon's narrator in *Chapel Road* (1953) denies the reader these comforts, he nevertheless offers 'the consolations of his presence, and his voice', sharing with us 'his own anxieties, his neuroses, his doubts' (2013d). That might be what the narrators of Coe's early novels also offer the reader through their self-reflexive comments. Nigella Lawson, in her review of *The Accidental Woman,* argues that 'the Maria-figure remains a device rather than a character' in that she has no 'inner reality', and the novel is marked by 'an authorial voice that is both knowing and irresponsible' (515).

If *The Accidental Woman* is regularly interrupted by metafictional remarks, it nevertheless follows a linear progression as in a traditional coming-of-age novel. *The Dwarves of Death,* on the other hand, opens with a murder that takes place on a Saturday in December 1988, and then moves backwards in a series of analepses to explain the circumstances of what happened that night, until it rejoins the storyline. The narrative structure of *A Touch of Love* is more complex and uses the device of interlocked or embedded stories, which Coe would later develop in *What a Carve Up!* and *The Terrible Privacy of Maxwell Sim. A Touch of Love* is divided into four parts, each containing a main narrative focalized through a specific character (first Ted, then Emma, then Robin and finally Hugh – the postscript being written in the first person by Aparna); each also includes an embedded story written by Robin (in the original Duckworth edition, the stories appear in a smaller font, while in the Penguin edition, the text of the stories is aligned to the left, which sets it apart from the main narrative whose text is justified). Parts one and three echo and complement each other as the first story 'The Meeting of Minds' focuses on the beginning of a love relationship between Richard and Karen, while the third story, 'The Lovers' Quarrel', narrates the end of a friendly relation between Robert and Kathleen. These fictional couples resemble very much Robin (the author of the embedded stories) and Katharine (Ted's wife) in the main narrative, two college friends who were attracted to each other but never confessed their love to each other. Robin's friend Aparna, who also has a platonic relationship with Robin, notices the coincidence in names – 'These sets of lovers you always write about. Always R and K' (178) – and she understands the stories are an oblique but fairly obvious way for Robin to write about his own life and feelings. Parts two and four also work symmetrically, as the second embedded story, 'The Lucky Man', focuses on Lawrence, a homosexual who ends up in the arms of Amanda at the conclusion of the story, while in the fourth story, 'The Unlucky Man', Harry tells another Lawrence that his wife Angela is being unfaithful to him, unaware that Lawrence is her lover.

As Robin tells Ted early in the main narrative, the stories form a sequence and are 'all interrelated. They're about sex and friendship and choices and things like that' (16), which could also be a faithful description of the novel as a whole. The four embedded stories are all concerned with the fragility of love relationships and friendships, and the novel's title is inspired by a quote from Simone Weil's *Gravity and Grace* (1947) which Robin has been reading and taking notes from, and which Coe says (in the foreword) has influenced his novel. Weil writes about the 'I' which can be dead or half dead, and Robin has copied out the following quote: '*as soon as the 'I' is half dead, it wants to be finished off and allows itself to sink into unconsciousness. If it is then awakened by a touch of love, there is sharp pain which results in anger and sometimes hatred for whoever has provoked the pain*' (223–4). This quotation might explain the attitude of some of the lovers in the main narrative and the stories, who fail to reach out to each other. Weil's book will reappear in *The House of Sleep*, in which two characters read it, pondering over its epigrams about loss and absence (160, 302).

Coe explained that he originally wrote the four self-contained stories of *A Touch of Love* with the intention of publishing them separately in small literary magazines in case he did not find a publisher for his novel (Website, *Touch*). This device, which allows for a multiplicity of perspectives and characters, is obliquely echoed in the fourth story when detective Vernon Humpage is said to look like Mervyn Jones (203) in *Dead of Night* (1945), a horror film made up of five separate stories within one larger framework, thus mirroring the intricate construction of *A Touch of Love*. In addition to the multiple viewpoints offered by such a structure, the novel is characterized by a diversity of narrative techniques and literary genres: it starts with a phone conversation of which the reader hears only one side, contains several letters in italics, a first-person interior monologue (in part three), as well as an imagined interview between Robin and a television presenter, thereby making for a variety of voices, tones and viewpoints. In the early novel, Coe was thus already trying his hand at a small-scale mixture of genres and intertwining of stories, which he would bring to a more challenging complexity in *What a Carve Up!*. *The Dwarves of Death*, though more conventional in form, is still remarkable for its generic plurality as it oscillates between the psychological thriller, romantic comedy and black farce, and follows the pattern of a musical piece: each chapter bears the title of a musical movement and the narrative includes song lyrics and music scores.

In *A Touch of Love*, the diversity of perspectives and voices points to the elusiveness of truth, as contradictory versions of the same event sometimes coexist. The lawyers Alun and Emma have to decide which version of events in Coventry's Memorial Park on 18 April 1986 they should trust: Robin tells an imaginary interviewer he needs to relieve himself in 'a discreet clump of rhododendrons' because he has had 12 cups of tea that day (144), while a man – 'a reliable and trustworthy witness' (87) according to Alun – says Robin followed his son in the bushes when the latter went there to retrieve his ball, and the boy – whose testimony is 'not very coherent, … not very conclusive' (85–6) – says Robin 'exposed himself and he was very frightened' (86). As Alun points out, the facts 'are open to quite different interpretations' (85) and the question is 'Whom do we trust, … which of these people is the most trustworthy?' (86). These differing versions raise the question of the reliability of the people involved and point to the relativity and possible manipulation of truth.

Coe further emphasizes the notion of subjectivity and the elusiveness of truth when Ted and Robin, who have grown apart, compare their memories of their college days as they walk in the aptly named Memorial Park. While Ted embellishes the past about which he reminisces with fond nostalgia, Robin provides blunter and bleaker versions of the same events. Ted's self-delusional reason for plumbing 'the well of shared memory' is to remind Robin 'of a time when their friendship was fresh and sustaining; to show him that the past, if it lives on in their minds, cannot be irretrievable' (64). But the four scenes conjured up by Ted are remembered by Robin in a completely different light, leaving Ted 'daunted by the number of disparities between their different accounts of the same, supposedly shared, experiences' (68). Memory appears as an unreliable medium and the two characters can neither retrieve the past nor find comfort in common memories and thereby reconnect. Through this unsparing comparison, Coe bars the way to any cheap sentimentalism, replacing it with a sardonic tone.

In *The Accidental Woman*, Maria also embellishes her memory of listening to her friend Stephen play the organ in a chapel, a scene described through a series of clichés and smooth sound echoes: 'the pale glowing tetragon of sunlight on the slabs, the shaft of sunlight connecting this figure to her nearest window, the dust-clouds dancing before her, the shade around' (73). But the narrator undercuts the drift towards mawkishness and debunks the scene by announcing 'Now: irony coming up', and revealing that Stephen's teacher was actually playing the organ. However, he also adds: 'her inaccurate memory meant much more to her than our knowledge of the facts can ever mean to us, so we needn't feel superior' (73). Truth is therefore not only elusive but also secondary to the facts, and memory is meant to prevail over accuracy, as suggested by another quote: 'It started, as far as Maria's memory and therefore as far as we are concerned, in the afternoon' (67). For Maria, the memory of an experience, though erroneous, is 'more important than the experience' (72), for it can be treasured and conjured up at any time. To quote a poem from Coe's *Say Hi to the Rivers and the Mountains, 'Nothing on this planet is more fragile than a memory'*. Several of Coe's subsequent novels would dwell on the vagaries of memory, which can lead to distortions, reconstructions and fabulations of the past.

Although Coe's early fiction sometimes points to the doubtful nature of memory, it is nevertheless firmly set in a contemporary time period which can be precisely dated. *A Touch of Love* in particular gives specific dates as it goes back and forth in time, moving from 17 April 1986 – the day Robin and Ted meet again and two days after the United States bombed Libya – to 4 July

1986 – when Emma is reflecting on the case she has to defend, in which Robin is accused of being a child molester – back to 18 April 1986 – just before the event that led to the accusation against Robin – and then forward to 15 July 1986 – the date of Robin's suicide – 19 December 1986 – when Emma meets Hugh in order to read Robin's fourth story – and 28 October 1987, when Aparna returns to Coventry before going back to India. In addition, in part three, Robin, aged 26, imagines a discussion with a journalist that would take place in 2006 when he is 46 and has become a successful writer who looks back on his life and on the historical events of April 1986. This non-linear progression with a shift of inner focalization for each new period, together with the insertion of embedded stories, each introducing a set of new characters, forces the reader to constantly adapt to a new storyline, a different viewpoint and tone, but the precise temporal indications also help the reader situate the plot with great accuracy, both at the microlevel of the narrative and at the macrolevel of world history.

A Touch of Love is indeed concerned with the American bombing raid on Libya on 15 April 1986 carried out in response to the bombing of the TWA flight 840 on 2 April and of *La Belle* discotheque in West Berlin, frequented by American soldiers, on 5 April. The scandal at the time was that the US planes took off from British air bases, thus testifying to the political collaboration between Ronald Reagan and Margaret Thatcher, and the congruity of their foreign policies. Coe said that this American imperial episode was for him 'a defining, apocalyptic historical moment' and he wanted 'to capture that feeling in fiction' (2013d), just as he would write about the 1991 American invasion of Iraq in *What a Carve Up!*, and that of 2003 in *The Closed Circle*. In *A Touch of Love*, the first reference to the 1986 attack appears in Robin's direct speech but remains oblique as no specific names are given: 'She let him use our air bases. They used our air bases to bomb Libya' (12). Later on, in the interview imagined by Robin, the journalist explicitly asks the latter about '*Reagan's bomb attack on Libya, carried out with the complicity and co-operation of the British government*' (137), which leads to a four-page didactic presentation of what happened, with the insertion of authentic quotes by Reagan, Abu Nidal and Gorbachev. As Coe himself admitted, the disquisition on the subject is quite disconnected from the narrative, but it clearly reveals the writer's keen interest in the contemporary. In addition to the Libya affair,

A Touch of Love alludes to the conflict in Northern Ireland, both in the first story when Richard and Miles begin 'to go over the pros and cons of the British military presence' (35) and in the second story where 'IRA sympathizers in Sheffield' (95) invite a terrorist to 'give an informal lecture on the subject of the Troubles' (96). Through such references, Coe shows his wish to engage with contemporary political issues, a dimension he will further develop in later novels.

Among these pressing issues is racism, first approached in *A Touch of Love* through the character of Aparna Indrani, Robin's friend and an Indian PhD student who gets 'tired of being thought of as foreign' (18), of simply bringing people their 'bit of local colour' (19, 171) and of not being taken seriously, including by her supervisor who dismisses her work but asks her out for dinner when his wife is away. When Ted sees her in the street, he is 'dismayed to find that she was Indian', for now 'he would probably have difficulty making himself understood' (8). Aparna resents such 'clever, middle-class, well-educated, heterosexual Englishmen' (168) who push people like her into a mould and want them to be 'strange and exotic' (171). The young woman is eventually defeated by the system as she never gets her degree and has to return to India, but it is her voice, in the first person, and her poetic tones, which are heard in the postscript. While the issue of racism is only touched upon in Coe's early fiction, it will be addressed on a larger scale in *The Rotters' Club* and *The Closed Circle* through references to the rise of the National Front in the 1970s in Britain and to numerous instances of everyday racial insults, aggressions and crimes.

Published in the 1980s, Coe's early novels show the first steps of a promising writer experimenting with the various possibilities of the novel in terms of self-reflexivity, generic multiplicity and narrative modes. The books strike a balance between the sense of alienation and despair of the young protagonists and a prevailing black humour, comedy and farce. However, Coe felt the need to extend his scope and ambition: 'I dashed off *The Dwarves of Death* in just five months and, afterwards, wasn't very happy with it. That dissatisfaction led me to *What a Carve Up!* and the impulse to write a book that I really wanted to write, over a much longer period of time' (in Magarian, 13). Four years later, in 1994, Coe was indeed to publish the novel that would prove to be his breakthrough on the British literary scene.

4

WHAT A CARVE UP!: A STATE-OF-THE-NATION NOVEL

Referring to *What a Carve Up!* (1994), Coe remembers that his decision to open himself up to 'the idea of writing a socially panoramic story was incredibly liberating' (2011). A social and political satire, the novel focuses on the Thatcher era of the 1980s, marked by the triumph of materialism and free enterprise, and the disavowal of community and social welfare. In an article devoted to the 'fondness and predilection of Britain for state of the nation writing', Coe pointed out that *What a Carve Up!* had been 'written as a response to the seismic changes in British political culture during the 1980s' (2013d). He was 'flushed with political and literary certainties' at the time and the most fixed of these certainties was his anti-Thatcherism (2013d). Coe explains that he used the upper-class Winshaw family as a 'metaphor for the British ruling elite, whether they were involved in politics, finance, food production, culture or any other area of national life' (Blog, *What a Carve Up!*). His undertaking echoes the work of film director Lindsay Anderson who, in *If* … (1968), depicted a rebellion in a boarding school to offer an anarchic vision of Britain in the late 1960s and in *Britannia Hospital* (1982) used the institution of a hospital as 'a metaphor for the whole of British society as it stood on the threshold of the Thatcher revolution in the early 1980s' (Coe, 2013d). Coe's commitment to grapple with the contemporary world in his novels and 'create hybrid spaces for social contestation'

(Prado Pérez, 972) seems to confirm Linda Hutcheon's hypothesis that postmodernist art is 'engaged in contesting the modernist (humanist) premises of art's apolitical autonomy' (1988, 230). Coe thus recalls the tradition of the writer's political commitment that Jean-Paul Sartre defended in *What is Literature?* in 1947. As noted by Andrzej Gasiorek and David James who reflect on the question of 'postmillennial commitments', Sartre vindicated 'a literature of praxis' and 'saw commitment as a form of open-ended engagement with contemporary history' (613). In the third millennium however, reflecting on state-of-the-nation novels, Coe has doubts about their effectiveness: 'If we find ourselves living through an era where everything – economically, socially, culturally – seems to be going wrong, why do we think that reading a novel about it is going to help?' (2013d). One wonders indeed whether the portrayal of one's dissatisfaction with society in a fictional work could make readers wish to change that society or if a work of art is necessarily detached from political action.

Among the pioneering Condition-of-England novels of the nineteenth century are Disraeli's *Sybil or the Two Nations* (1845) and Anthony Trollope's *The Way We Live Now* (1875), a satire of London society in the 1870s. According to Tim Adams, 'each of these novels was of its moment, and in the broadest sense political; each had a particular vision of the society of its day, the ways in which people connected and power corrupted' (Adams). Contemporary avatars of the genre may be Julian Barnes's *England England* (1998), James Hawes's *Speak for England* (2005), Amanda Craig's *Hearts and Minds* (2009) or Martin Amis's *Lionel Asbo*, subtitled *State of England* (2012). From these few books, one gauges how many different forms the state-of-the-nation novel may take, from the most traditional and cathartic to the most avant-garde, interspersed with self-referential comments and denying readers the 'comfort of closure'. For Coe, 'one of the most impressive state-of-the nation novels of the last forty years' is the challenging *Lanark* (1981) by Alasdair Gray, a novel which combines two narratives: a realist *Bildungsroman* set in pre-War Glasgow and a dystopian depiction of Unthank, a Glasgow-like city on the verge of disintegration (Coe, 2013d).

Coe's own engagement in political satire is epitomized by *What a Carve Up!* which depicts the crimes perpetuated in the 1980s by the members of the Winshaw family, hyperbolically described as 'the *meanest, greediest, cruellest bunch* of backstabbing penny-pinching bastards who ever crawled across the face of the earth' (209). The family's chronicler provides a hyperbolic and satirical list of the criminal activities of the family who have 'carved up the whole bloody country between them' (107): 'swindling, forgery, larceny, robbery, thievery, trickery, jiggery-pokery, hanky-panky, plundering, looting, sacking, misappropriation, spoliation and embezzlement' (88). The vertiginous sound echoes and inner rhymes create a playful and jaunty rhythm which trivializes the listed crimes, but also highlights the comic dimension of the book. Coe explains that *What a Carve Up!* was written 'in response to a slew of pamphleteering and rather morose novels about Thatcherism that had started to come out in the early' 90s' and which he found 'dampening'; he wanted instead to entertain the reader (Coe in Taylor, Charles). His ambition was 'to write something intensely political which didn't make readers feel that they were being harangued. To combine anger with warmth and humanity' (Coe, 2014c, 9).

In a mixture of comedy and tragedy, humour and anger, the even-numbered chapters of the sprawling book, named after the Winshaws and adopting generic and narrative modes that reflect their occupations (newspaper articles, diaries, political debates, lists …), throw light on the obnoxious power and manipulation of the press (Hilary), the drastic cuts in health budgets which lead to the severe deterioration of the National Health Service (Henry), the submission of culture to speculation and the law of the market (Roddy), the mass production of food high in saturated fats that clog arteries and cause heart diseases (Dorothy), the rip-off of pension funds by bankers, depriving elderly people of their life savings (Thomas), and the manufacture of arms sold to rival countries which will end up killing soldiers and civilians in Iraq (Mark). In all areas, 'the logic of late capitalism', to use Fredric Jameson's famous phrase, and the money economy prevail. As one character states, 'the only kind of … values anybody seems to care about are the ones that can be added up on a balance sheet' (102).

In the odd-numbered chapters of the book, dated from August 1990 to January 1991, Michael informs the reader of the progress of his research into the Winshaws, while at the same time giving information about his personal life and childhood through a series of analepses in first-person narration. Michael provides the link between odd and even chapters, between the public and the private, the political and the personal. For instance, it suddenly dawns on him that the heart attack from which his father (or the man he believes is his father) died was probably caused by Dorothy's junk food; the narrative reflects: '*Does this mean that Dorothy killed my father?*' (256), a question later echoed by the assertion 'Dorothy was the one who killed off my father' (413). Equally Thomas has taken over the company for which his father had worked all his life, emptying the employees' pension fund, leaving them to survive on a meagre state pension. The question '*Does this mean that Thomas was an accessory to my father's murder?*' (324) finds a clear answer later on: 'Thomas added a twist of the knife' (413). Moreover, the death of Fiona, Michael's girlfriend, has certainly been precipitated by a series of errors in the understaffed hospital where she was admitted.

Beyond the fate of his own family and friends, Michael's investigation into the careers of the cynical Winshaws unveils a series of direct or indirect crimes committed against a large portion of the population in the name of greed. Like Alan Hollinghurst's *The Line of Beauty*, the novel depicts 'the gap between Thatcher's meritocratic political rhetoric and the actual protection of a small metropolitan elite' (Marsh, 80) and points to the 'destruction of the British community' (Simons, 54). The unequal distribution of wealth in British society is what the (almost untranslatable) title suggests. For Michael, the Winshaws have 'pretty well carved up the whole bloody country between them' (107): while the merchant banker Thomas takes sadistic pleasure in 'snatching these huge state-owned companies from the taxpayers' hands and carving them up among a minority of profit-hungry shareholders' (321), the arms dealer Mark and his colleagues share production among munitions companies and take their million-dollar commissions. 'What a carve up, eh …?', one of them gleefully exclaims (396). While the Winshaws and the ones they stand for 'sit at home getting fat on the proceeds', the country is being crushed as Michael emphatically points out in another example of a euphonic and hyperbolic list: 'Our businesses failing, our jobs disappearing, our countryside choking, our hospitals crumbling, our homes being repossessed, our bodies being poisoned, our minds shutting down' (413). Coe admits he wanted to write 'a big political novel' (Lappin, 11), and it is certainly what he achieved in a book that is toying with what B.S. Johnson called 'the enormity of life' (1964, 170) and which Coe glosses as 'chaotic, multifaceted, complex, infinite' (2003).

In terms of form and narrative structure, *What a Carve Up!* can be regarded as a postmodernist novel for its polygenericity, its fragmentation, its self-reflexivity, its use of parody and of popular forms and its shifts from one narrative mode to another. One of the characteristic features of postmodernist writing consists in overtly acknowledging, and borrowing from, the literary past, acknowledging that legacy both consciously and ironically through the use of pastiche and parody. Coe explains that he conceived the Winshaws as '19th century Dickensian villains' (in Taylor, Charles); the book starts with a Victorian address to the reader – 'my friendly readers' (3) – and the revelation of the identity of Michael's father is quite Dickensian, with echoes of *Great Expectations* in particular. As such, the novel seems both to conform partly to the postmodernist agenda and to revert to more conventional realistic fiction, maybe recalling Coe's admiration for Umberto Eco's *Foucault's Pendulum* (1988) as a book which 'has absorbed the tenets of post-modernism only to move beyond them', so that 'at its centre lies a core of profoundly old-fashioned humanism' (Coe, 1989b). According to Eagleton, 'Coe's novel is so flagrantly Post-Modern, so shrewdly conscious of its own busily parodic technique, that it has the curious effect of parodying Post-Modernism too, raising it to the second power, and so, to a certain degree, allowing it to cancel itself out. What it then cancels into is realism' (12). The two forms (realism and postmodernism) thus end up being both incorporated and interrogated.

This process of use and abuse of conventions is remarkable in the way the novel first seems to comply with the codes and conventions of classic detective fiction – the novel starts with two mysterious deaths – before veering off into parody, satire and farce, and resisting narrative closure. The second part of the novel, set at the gothic Winshaw Towers and told in the third person, grotesquely parodies the 1961 comedy horror film also entitled *What a Carve Up!*, 'about this wealthy family who turn up at a big country house for the reading of a will, and get bumped off one by one' (152), a film Michael saw as a child (36) and which becomes an obsession as he believes he is 'inhabiting it' (152) and later re-enacting it (466). According to José Ramón Prado Pérez, Coe deconstructs the authoritative discourse of history by 'equating it with a comic and farcical film' (968), while for Ryan Trimm, the linking of Thatcherism to a film fusing comedy and horror 'positions Coe's novel as an angry satire framing the Thatcher era as a gross inversion of social values, a distorted mirrorworld simultaneously comic and tragic' (159). This recurrent mixture of tragedy and farce in the novel could also be related to Coe's analysis of the scene from Hitchcock's *Sabotage* when a cute little boy is shockingly killed by a bomb that explodes in a bus, immediately followed by the shot of a domestic scene with a character laughing. For Coe, Hitchcock is here 'insisting on the fact that the carnage and laughter aren't as far apart from each other as the audience would like to think, that they belong in the same world' (1997b).

In terms of genre, *What a Carve Up!* contains all the conventional ingredients of an enjoyable whodunnit with clues (the smell of jasmine, a coded message ...), red herrings, manuscripts, the theft of photographs and private documents, and a mysterious man tailing Owen and skulking in the shadows. The main enigma is probably the reason why Michael was chosen by Tabitha Winshaw as the author of the chronicle. Detective Onyx, who refuses to believe it was just 'by chance' (87), tells Michael: 'the real mystery is you' (234). By bringing together all the various clues and threads as the French surrealists assembled words, the reader may come up with unexpected 'exquisite corpses', unless s/he prefers to view the novel as a macabre version of Happy Families or of the Cluedo board game, which Michael and his friends are playing in June 1982 amidst timely cracks of thunder and flashes of lightning, until Michael realizes he is himself the culprit (303). In the book as well, he who had assumed the role of uninvolved observer (as in classic detective fiction), realizes little by little that his life is intricately linked with that of the Winshaws as he probes into his own past and the Oedipal trauma he has been repressing. Terry Eagleton actually compares Michael to Oedipus, 'the detective in pursuit of the criminal who is himself' (12).

The book's playfulness is also embedded in the postmodernist narrative games played by an author who starts his novel with a prologue and ends it with a preface, alternates chapters in first- and third-person narration, and does away with chronology by gleefully sprinkling his text with analepses and prolepses. On the one hand, the book seems to achieve a reassuring moral closure typical of Victorian novels and of detective fiction through the series of murders committed at the family mansion, which put an end to the Winshaw dynasty and bring individual and poetic justice (as the Winshaws are killed in a way that is related to their own crimes). On the other hand, instability is re-introduced through the detective-writer-narrator's untimely death at the end of the novel, before he has completed his chronicle, and the insertion of a 'preface' which, in a circular mode, ends with the repetition of the first sentence of the book, whose narrative voice is uncertain. Coe's brio has also led him to interweave a multiplicity of literary genres (including tabloid newspaper articles, the minutes of a board meeting, interview transcripts, a diary, autobiography, letters, parodies of horror stories and gothic tales) and, in the process, erode the distinction between high and popular culture – a typically postmodernist trait according to Jameson – but also privilege fragments over the presentation of a unified whole. Coe explained the reason for this multiplicity of genres and narrative modes: 'the fragmented, fast-changing nature of the reality I was trying to capture dictated that no single narrative approach would be adequate' (Coe, 2011). The negation of any narrative and formal coherence mimics the thorough collapse of moral and ethical principles in Thatcherian Britain, while offering 'formal refutation of the homogeneity stressed by Thatcher' (Trimm, 160).

In addition, Coe deliberately confuses ontological levels and blurs the frontiers between fiction and reality, a common feature of postmodernist writing as well: Michael, for whom film images (or simulacra) have taken over the real world, walks through the screen and becomes the main actor in the film he is watching (40–2) or rather '*living*' (462); his dreams become reality and fictional characters meet real-life figures. The detective strands which had been introduced at the beginning seem forgotten when the narrator tells us about his personal story or when he probes into the careers of the abominable Winshaw children, so that the genre to which the book belongs (autobiography? chronicle? detective fiction? gothic melodrama? political novel?) becomes uncertain. Michael's editor, keen on sensationalism, finds some passages of his chronicle 'so laudably academic in tone, so rigorous in their historical perspective' that they might prove a bit daunting to some readers, who, she mischievously suggests, could 'safely ignore the main body of [Michael's] narrative' (498). In a postmodernist way, the main story often ramifies into a multiplicity of adjacent stories and forking paths, thus subverting any sense of a continuum in narration as well as in history, and the novel pays homage to popular genres of English entertainment, such as the melodrama and horror story, or the lowbrow comedy films of the 1950s and 1960s. In a self-reflexive moment, Tabitha provides a description of the book she had envisaged, which might well fit *What a Carve Up!* – 'part personal memoir, part social commentary, all stirred together into one lethal and devastating brew' (476) – while Michael's review of a 'fantastic, funny, angry, satirical book' could also be considered as a self-reference, both to his chronicle and to Coe's novel (299).

As postmodernist narrator and writer, Michael is self-conscious and thus repeatedly lays bare narrative devices, addresses the reader, breaks the frame of fiction, reveals his awareness of the constructedness and instability of narrative and discourse, and confesses that he is sometimes 'fleshing out incidents …, speculating on matters of psychological motivation, even inventing conversations' (90) when solid and demonstrable facts are missing: 'Yes, inventing: I won't fight shy of the word' (90), so that parts of the book 'read like a novel and parts of it read like a history' (91). He knows he should 'decide once and for all whether to present it as a work of fact or fiction' but he eventually has to acknowledge his status as a character in the story and no longer as a detached observer: 'I thought I was supposed to be writing this story … but I'm not. At least not any more. I'm part of it' (472). The issues of authorship and authority – but also of complicity as Michael has to admit his unwitting support of Thatcherism by his 'willingness to tolerate greed, and to live alongside it' (485) – are therefore regularly questioned as the narrative voice keeps shifting from one chapter and one genre to the next, and the origin of the voice in some chapters remains uncertain.

In the end, the mystery which remains unsolved pertains to the status of the book itself. In the prologue, Michael self-reflexively refers to Tabitha Winshaw, 'the patron and sponsor of the book which you, my friendly readers, now hold in your hands' (3). The chronicle of the Winshaws commissioned by Tabitha cannot however be *What a Carve Up!*, the book the reader holds in his/her hands, as the latter includes chapters dealing with Michael's own life (which would have no place in a chronicle of the Winshaws) and the last chapter relates Michael's death, which he could not have written himself. Moreover, the section devoted to Henry Winshaw is composed of extracts from his diary, published in 1995, and a footnote directs the reader to 'Michael Owen, *The Winshaw Legacy: A Family Chronicle* (Peacock Press, 1991)' (120), which is indeed the title that appears on the facsimile of the cover of Michael's book, just before the editor's preface (495). In her cheeky preface, the editor, Hortensia Monks, reveals herself as the author of the second part of the book, 'An Organization of Deaths', a 'sensational' account of the 'horrific murders' which took place at Winshaw Towers in January 1991 (498), but also as the author of the 'Prologue 1942–1961' as she states: 'my intention in the remainder of this Preface is to summarize, in a few concise, vivid pages, the entire early history of [the Winshaws]' (498). The last sentence of her preface ('Tragedy had struck the Winshaws twice before, but never on such a terrible scale') is also the first of the Prologue, which confirms her status as the author of both. The last part of that sentence refers to the 1991 murders and so cannot have been written by Michael as he died in a plane accident without having completed his chronicle. Is the Prologue therefore written entirely in the first person by Hortensia Monks? But then, on the fourth page, the narrative voice refers to some of Tabitha's relics which 'came into the hands of the present writer' (6), i.e. Michael. Coe admitted that there is 'meant to be some ambiguity about whether Michael writes that first sentence or not. At the very end of the novel, the reader is supposed to realize that the opening scene is in fact a continuation of Hortensia's "Preface". At some point, Hortensia's words must stop and Michael's must begin – but it's never clear where that point is' (in Guignery, 2011, 433). The narratorial ambiguity and the generic polyphony of the book may well be meant to echo the confusion and chaos of the political era depicted.

In order to represent the atmosphere of the 1980s in *What a Carve Up!*, Coe decided to 'tap into the energy and unpretentiousness of British popular culture' (in Laity), a remark which equally applies to *The Rotters' Club* and *The Closed Circle*. For these three books, Coe drew from television shows, movies and songs of the 1970s to the 2000s. In *The Rotters' Club*, when Benjamin is watching TV and thinking of the millions of people watching the same programme at the same time, he feels 'an incredible sense of … oneness' (274). In *What a Carve Up!*, a TV producer idealistically suggests that television is 'one of the fibres that holds the country together. It collapses class distinctions and helps create a sense of national identity' (68), a motto Hilary Winshaw will shamelessly and cynically plagiarize a few years later (70), thus questioning the supposedly egalitarian and humanist ambition of television.

What a Carve Up! is also teeming with filmic references which self-consciously point to a postmodernist awareness and acknowledgement of the cultural popular past. Coe thus takes delight in having the fictitious Thomas Winshaw meet the real-life actors Dennis Price, Esma Cannon, Sid James, Shirley Eaton and Kenneth Connor during the shooting of the 1961 film *What a Carve Up!*, directed by Pat Jackson (316). As the first three unsuccessfully try to remember which film Thomas played in, they cite famous 1960 British comedies (*Two-Way Stretch, Dentist in the Chair, Watch Your Stern, Follow That Horse, Inn for Trouble, Life is a Circus, School for Scoundrels*), as well as actors (Ian Carmichael, Terry-Thomas, Walter Hudd, Stuart Saunders) and directors (the Boulting brothers), while Thomas later refers to the TV comedy series *Hancock's Half Hour* starring Tony Hancock and Sid James (320) – a world of comedy Coe would pay tribute to 20 years later in *Expo 58*. The film *What a Carve Up!* is described as 'a loose comic remake of an old Boris Karloff feature' (316), namely the 1933 adaptation of Frank King's comedy gothic potboiler *The Ghoul* (1928) – also alluded to in *The House of Sleep* (126) – starring Boris Karloff and Cedric Hardwicke, and set at the Blackshaw Towers. As revealed in the 'Author's Note', the first paragraph of Part Two (423) is directly copied from the first chapter of the original book *The Ghoul* (except for one word), and 'there are several smaller instances of what Alasdair Gray has called "Implags" (imbedded plagiarisms)' (500). The mesh proves even more intricate as the film *What a Carve Up!* echoes the plots of John Willard's play *The Cat and the Canary* (1922) and Agatha Christie's *Ten Little Niggers* (1939) – both referred to in the novel (444, 452) – as well as that of *Kind Hearts and Coronets* (1949), also quoted (316). Such echoes point to Coe's broad filmic culture and place him firmly in the generation of Britons born in the 1950s and 1960s, who watched these films on television. They also confirm his attachment to popular genres, even if he remains wary of pedant attitudes. In the short story 'V.O.', which takes place during a 'Festival of Horror and Fantasy Cinema', the protagonist pompously declares: 'I think that serious artistic statements ... can be made within any kind of generic restrictions. It doesn't do to be snobbish about these things'; he adds that horror films 'don't tend to be taken seriously by critics' even if some are 'the works of real *auteurs*, real visionaries' (2005a, 31). However, the parodic titles of films shown at the festival (*Mutant Autopsy 3*, *One Corpse at a Time, Please!*, *Vampire Brainsuckers Get Naked*) seem to gently mock such noble aspirations.

Coe's reliance on popular culture, his playfulness and interest in social and political satire do not however preclude ethics and emotion. In *What a Carve Up!*, although the Winshaws appear particularly ruthless and unethical in their selfish greed for power, and Michael passive and inefficient at first, as the novel progresses, his encounter with Fiona opens up a new ethical and emotional dimension which culminates on her deathbed when Michael finally discloses the identity of his father, a traumatic revelation which had led to his self-imposed isolation and loss of a sense of self for years. Thanks to Fiona, Michael relinquishes the solipsistic world of simulacra on television – 'cracks had started to appear in the screen' (411) – to risk a face-to-face encounter with the Other, to borrow Emmanuel Lévinas's terminology. The writer-turned-detective drifts away from rational explanations and the satirical and farcical vein to offer an emotional response. Michael is indeed not only searching for a specific truth and resolution of an enigma outside of himself: he is also struggling with his own sense of identity that has been shattered by his mother's revelation about his biological father. The deathbed scene is an example of melodrama and tragedy but also a subtle avoidance of pathos as Michael shifts from internal focalization to external focalization to describe the scene in the third person as if he were the spectator of a film, thus preserving decency (416–9). Considering the novel 15 years after its publication, Coe is no longer sure it can fit the label of a state-of-the-nation novel, and feels that it might rather be 'the story of a depressed young hero going through a crisis of identity, while being swept along on a current of historical forces towards a destiny over which he has no control' (2013d). It is not so much a story about 'how Britain was changing as the 1970s drew to a close' as 'a story about growing up, and how children make their first, clumsy steps into the world of adult emotions' (2013d). One might argue that the book is both a postmodernist Condition-of-England novel and a sensitive *Bildungsroman*, as well as a *Künstlerroman* (with the reader witnessing the development of a writer). A similarly stimulating mixture of genres will reappear in the diptych *The Rotters' Club* and *The Closed Circle*.

5

THE ROTTERS' CLUB AND *THE CLOSED CIRCLE*: THE CHILDREN OF LONGBRIDGE

Like *What a Carve Up!, The Rotters' Club* (2001) and *The Closed Circle* (2004) involve social and political satire and can be regarded as state-of-the-nation novels. *The Rotters' Club* portrays England in the 1970s, in particular the dismantling of post-war consensus, the shift towards capitalism, the crisis in the car industry, the stifling of trade unions – which still 'had real power in those days' (176) – as well as the growth of ultranationalist and neo-fascist organizations. *The Closed Circle* deals with the disillusionment provoked by the New Labour of Tony Blair in the 2000s, when most people 'still believe that they've voted in a left-wing party. Whereas really they've just voted for another five years of Thatcherism. Ten years. Fifteen, even' (130). Both novels show that Coe resents the economic ideology people have come to take for granted in Britain: 'Thatcherism, Majorism, Blairism, Brownism – it doesn't matter how you label it' (2013d).

In *The Rotters' Club*, which the author considered subtitling 'a novel of innocence' while *The Closed Circle* would be 'a novel of experience' (Coe, 2015b), Coe used the genre of the coming-of-age novel or *Bildungsroman* and the perspective of a teenager (Benjamin Trotter, an alter ego of Coe himself) to intertwine the personal and the national levels, drawing from well-documented historical events of the 1970s, and relating them to the everyday lives of Birmingham dwellers. David Mitchell would achieve similar effects in *Black Swan Green* (2006) through the perspective of a maturing 13-year-old boy living in England in the 1980s. The local society in which Benjamin evolves becomes a microcosm for British society at large, thus offering a panoptic point of view, where Birmingham is depicted as 'a site for contestation and desire' (Tew, 2004, 108). Coe says he feels a 'great responsibility to historical fact in [his] fiction' and it was therefore very important to him that whatever he wrote in the novel 'could have happened factually' (in Tew, 2008, 39). As a result, every event is precisely dated (including the day of the week) and historical figures are regularly referred to. A crucial moment in the book is when Benjamin's sister Lois witnesses her boyfriend Malcolm being killed in the actual 21 November 1974 IRA bombing of the 'Tavern in the Town' pub in Birmingham (104), fuelling the fierce anti-IRA feelings that had already been violently expressed in a notice pinned to the board of the Longbridge factory: 'IRA BASTARDS KILLED 12 PEOPLE ON MANCHESTER BUS YESTERDAY REFUSE TO WORK WITH IRISH BASTARD MURDERERS' (37). Malcolm's left-wing friend Reg provokes Benjamin, who defines himself as a 'Tory cunt', when he tells him: 'I bet you think the IRA are a bunch of murdering Micks, don't you? And our boys in Belfast are the salt of the fucking earth?' (99). Doug Anderton also deplores the 'anti-Irish sentiment' (235) which has developed in Birmingham, leading to several 'lynchings and unprovoked assaults on Irish citizens' (235).

Claire later reflects upon Malcolm's death, her sister Miriam's disappearance and the death of an Irish maintenance worker at Longbridge factory, all within the same few days, and is tempted to weave threads between them: 'Three curtailed narratives, then. Three stories, with no connection between them except that they had been truncated, savagely, when their opening chapters had barely been written. … What days those had been, for unfinished stories' (226). In the process, she is metatextually describing the writer's craft, turning facts and history into narrative and stories, whose incompleteness can leave room for uncertainty, suspense and further revelations. In *The Closed Circle*, Claire will again interweave the macro and the micro levels of history when pondering over the origins of 'the Irish problem' and the way ordinary lives are 'fucked up by forces outside their control' (369): 'Is Oliver Cromwell to blame for the fact that Lois had to spend so many years in hospital? Or is he to blame for the fact that Miriam was killed?' (368). By doing so, Claire is intertwining incompatible ontological realms, blaming a historical figure for the distress and demise of fictional characters.

In *The Rotters' Club*, the Irish conflict occupies a large part of the historical background of the 1970s, while the Welsh nationalist demands for separatism conveyed through the didactic speech of Uncle Glyn, Cicely's uncle, echo the growing call for Welsh and Scottish independence at the same period (350–2). Hywel Dix argues, however, that Coe trivializes the issue of Welsh nationalism by letting an 'over-zealous extremist' be its spokesperson, while racial, class and gender antagonisms are portrayed with greater seriousness and more subtlety (35). The 1970s were indeed a time when racism was thriving in Britain, creating further dividing lines in society. Conservative MP Enoch Powell had delivered his 'Rivers of Blood' speech in Birmingham on 20 April 1968, in which he warned his audience against what he saw as the consequences of unchecked immigration to Britain. In a mock letter to the editor of the school's magazine (Benjamin's school), the outrageous persona of Arthur Pusey-Hamilton (an elitist and far-right conservative puritan, modelled on Peter Cook's comic creation of Sir Arthur Streeb-Greebling) comments on a production of *Othello*: 'I found that the climax illustrated, most powerfully, Mr Powell's chilling vision of "rivers of blood", and provided an ample demonstration of the perils of unrestricted immigration' (192). In addition, the novel alludes to 'The Association of British People' – 'a far-right offshoot, more cranky and less organized even than the National Front' (37), believed to have been 'behind a recent attack in Moseley on two Asian teenagers, who had been found beaten half to death outside a chip shop' (38) – and refers to the authentic demonstration in Southall against a National Front election meeting in the town hall that led to the death of activist Blair Peach (390–2).

Beyond specific historical events, racism is portrayed as an ordinary everyday attitude, for instance when one of the workers at British Leyland pulls a face on climbing into the car of a turbaned taxi driver and is 'ready to share some blokey, insulting witticism' with his companion (20). A boy at school provocatively refers to the black man in Harper Lee's *To Kill a Mockingbird* (1960) as a 'nigger', 'Wog. Coon. Darkie' (25), and argues that the book is 'propaganda' (26). Racism also infiltrates vernacular culture as epitomized by Eric Clapton's memorable racist outburst during the 1976 Birmingham concert (131) and recalled by one of the teenagers: he said 'something about Britain becoming one of its own colonies. He mentioned Enoch Powell, anyway. I'm sure of that. Said that Powell was right and we should all be listening to him' (133). The comment seemed all the more uncalled for as Clapton had recently performed cover songs by Bob Marley, viewed by one of the characters as 'pure cultural appropriation', 'Neo-colonialism in a musical setting' (45): 'Coming out in support of Powell, after all the things he's lifted from black music himself ... It was so out of order' (159). Mr Warren, the school's games master, argues for his part that 'the only Tory he would vote for, – the only one with integrity – was Enoch Powell' (52), while in a mock version of a by-election, a teenager named Sean Harding reads from a National Front's leaflet that speaks of 'droves of dark-skinned sub-racials' and 'race-degeneration' (178). In London in 1976, Doug meets a young man who describes Birmingham as 'full of Pakis' (163). These recurrent disturbing references reveal how profoundly racial antagonisms divided Britain at the time. More than 20 years later, in December 1999, Doug feels no nostalgia for the glaringly racist 1970s:

> People forget about the 1970s. ... They forget about the Ugandan Asian refugees who arrived at Heathrow in 1972, and how it made people say that Enoch had been right in the late sixties when he warned about rivers of blood, how his rhetoric echoed down the years, right down to a drunken comment Eric Clapton made on stage at the Birmingham Odeon in 1976. They forget that in those days, the National Front sometimes looked like a force to be reckoned with.
>
> (176)

In *The Closed Circle*, racism still looms large but 'the battle-lines, which had seemed so stark and simple back in the 1970s, were now almost impossible to define with any clarity' since 'the nationalist movement in Britain had splintered' (272). Steve Richards (who used to be the only black boy in King William's school) writes to Philip in June 2001 to discuss racist crimes that actually occurred in Telford, Shropshire, and especially the racist threats against Afro-Caribbean Errol McGowan that culminated in him being found hanging from a doorknob in July 1999 (194). Steve refers to 'Combat 18' (195), a neo-Nazi organization formed in 1992, whose members are suspected to have been involved in numerous deaths of immigrants. In the Author's Note, Coe lists Nick Lowles's *White Riot: The Violent Story of Combat 18* (2001) as one of his historical sources. Alluding to the actual race riots in Bradford and Oldham, Steve argues that, although Britain in the new millennium is supposedly 'a successful multicultural society', 'these people are still out there' (195). Philip, worried at 'the number of council seats the BNP has been winning' (234), decides to write a book about the far right and the modern forms of British fascism. Novelists such as Salman Rushdie, Hanif Kureishi, Zadie Smith, Andrea Levy or Monica Ali have shown to what extent the optimistic concept of a harmonious multicultural Britain had to be qualified, and Coe's novels share such doubts, by regularly drawing attention to ordinary and organized cases of racism. As Paul Gilroy points out, obstacles 'inhibit the formation of a multicultural polity at ease with itself nationally and transnationally' (201), and racism and nationalism, by targeting alien minorities, help mystify the country's chronic economic, social and political problems.

In *The Rotters' Club*, the major social issue pertains to the bitter strikes that took place in the 1970s in Britain, in particular the 1976–78 labour dispute at Grunwick Film Processing Laboratories in Willesden, West London, which is evoked through a massive demonstration in November 1977, called by the historical Jayaben Desai, the inspirational leader of the strike, whom Bill Anderton admires (262). As Hywel Dix remarks, the violence unleashed at the rally is depicted in an 'impressionistic' (rather than strictly realist) way, through a series of 'disjointed fragments', that reflects the dissolution and 'overall unravelling of Britain's social fabric' (34). Another major historical figure inserted into *The Rotters' Club* is Derek Robinson, the notorious union convenor who caused hundreds of walkouts at government-owned British Leyland between 1978 and 1979, and who, in the novel, urges Bill to keep the faith (240). He is referred to as 'the man soon – very soon – to be demonized in the newspapers as "Red Robbo", and to be sacked by Michael Edwardes [British Leyland's new Chairman] for trying to orchestrate protests against his programme of redundancies' (303). The encounters between a fictional character (Bill) and real-life figures (Desai and Robinson) – a device frequently used by Coe – amount to an 'ontological scandal' (McHale, 85), as they blur the frontiers between incompatible ontological realms, but they also firmly situate the novel in a realistic historical context. The effect is quite different in *What a Carve Up!* when Henry refers to his first conversation with Margaret Thatcher (122) or when Mark is seen chairing a meeting with Saddam Hussein (379), as the unreliability of the Winshaws makes the reader sceptical about the (fictional) authenticity of the scenes, or else gives the historical figures a fictitious dimension.

In *The Rotters' Club*, Bill, a shop steward at Longbridge and trade unionist, insists that 'the class war was alive and well and being waged with some ferocity at British Leyland, even in Ted Heath's egalitarian 1970s' (16). The 'struggle between labour and capital' (239) is indeed fiercely underway at Longbridge which Bill considers as 'a microcosm … of society as a whole. The ruling class versus the labouring class. Management versus workers' (239). The issue of class (which Coe does not sidestep) is a moot point and Bill's boss mischievously and provocatively comments on the fact that Bill's son and the son of Colin Trotter, a junior manager at British Leyland, go to the same school: 'What does that tell about the class war? It's over. Truce. Armistice. … Equality of opportunity' (16), thus anticipating Tony Blair's pronouncement at the 1999 Labour Party Conference that 'the class war is over'. Bill's colleagues criticize him fiercely for not sending Doug to the 'local comprehensive' but to a fancy direct-grant school (modelled on Coe's own school), that 'fucking … toffs' academy in Edgbaston' (20, 79) – a rebuke which will find an echo in the short story 'Pentatonic' in which the narrator feels embarrassed at sending his daughter to a private school (2014a). Doug himself will humorously sever 'a lifelong allegiance' to the working class and yield 'his sense of self, his sense of belonging, his loyalty to the place and the family he came from' (164) when having sex with Ffion ffoulkes in London: 'That night, in short, he became enamoured of the upper classes' (165). In *The Closed Circle*, some 25 years later, Doug still considers himself Old Labour, despite being married to 'The Hon. Francesca Gifford' and having 'a house worth something in the region of two or three million pounds, spreading over five floors' (76–7). His protests of loyalty to his class may thus be considered with some irony: 'Just because I've married into a posh family … doesn't mean I've forgotten where I came from. Where my loyalties lie. I haven't given up on the class war' (88). As for the

Longbridge car plant, after being privatized in 1988 and renamed Rover, the risk of closure leads to a massive demonstration in June 2000, in which the characters of *The Closed Circle* all participate. The whole city feels concerned by the situation, so that pensioners are seen 'walking with teenagers, Bangladeshis alongside whites and Pakistanis' (105), leading Doug to exclaim, gleefully, nostalgically but also naively: 'It's just like being back in the 1970s' (107).

Along with social class, *The Rotters' Club* and *The Closed Circle* are concerned with the politics and ideology of the times, represented through brief and efficient references to the tenets of the two main political parties, usually conveyed in direct speech by various characters. The first novel charts successive British governments and prime ministers in the 1970s, from the Conservative Edward Heath (1970–74) to the Labour Harold Wilson (1974–76) and James Callaghan (1976–79), with the shadow of Margaret Thatcher looming in the last pages through the ominous poster of her, Paul Trotter has pinned to his wall (370) and through Sam Chase's ironically incorrect prediction that 'that woman will never be Prime Minister of this country' (399). Before that, when one of the teachers talks politics with Sam, they both rail 'against the incompetence of Edward Heath's government' and shake 'their heads at the scandal of a nation held to ransom by obstreperous, strike-happy miners, the shame of a once-great country reduced to measures more often associated with Eastern Europe or the Third World: power cuts, petrol rationing, three-day weeks' (51). With the general election scheduled for 28 February 1974, Colin Trotter is concerned that they 'are going to vote for Wilson', letting 'the socialists back in' (51). In 1978, his youngest son, Paul, criticizes the Callaghan government in a tone and rhythm that may remind one of the cynical rhetorics of Shakespeare's Richard III (until the final comic disambiguation): 'Was ever an administration more mired in the past, more hopelessly adrift, more feebly in thrall to the whims and demands of a selfish, militant faction? (I mean the unions, of course)' (287). In his 1999 speech, Doug Anderton recalls a Guy Fawkes' night in 1976 after the Tories had won in a by-election, when Paul had shown him his sparkler fizzling out, slyly calling it 'the death of the socialist dream' (262). Back in 1977, Doug's father could see that 'these were bad times to be a socialist. … He could feel the old certainties slipping away' (262). For Doug, it became clear that his father's 'beautiful ideas' and 'noble aspirations', were never going to happen: 'A national health service, free to everyone who needed it. Redistribution of wealth through taxation. Equality of opportunity' (182). Instead of that, 'a new breed of Tory' was waiting in the wings and their 'rhetoric was fierce: it was anti-welfare, anti-community, anti-consensus' (181). In *The Closed Circle*, the reader learns that Benjamin and Cicely's daughter, Malvina, was conceived on 2 May 1979, the day before the general election that would make Margaret Thatcher Britain's first woman Prime Minister (420). Doug could thus not have been closer to the truth when he exclaimed: 'You really are one of Thatcher's children, aren't you?' (110).

However, *The Closed Circle* sets the Thatcher years aside to focus on the New Labour under Tony Blair. As Paul triumphantly points out, the more radical members of New Labour intend to '"roll back the frontiers of the state" to a point which even the author of that phrase (Margaret Thatcher) would not have recognized' (206). Private finance has now firmly made its way into the public sector: 'Responsibility for substantial areas of health provision, state education, local government, prison services and even air traffic control were now in the hands of private companies whose duty of care lay towards the interests of shareholders rather than the general public' (206). As suggested by David Osler in *Labour Party Plc* (2002), which Coe quotes in his 'Author's Note' as a source for background material, New Labour has become a party of business, and Gordon Brown's famous declaration in the *Financial Times* of 28 *March 2002* is quoted in the novel: 'The Labour Party is more pro-business, pro-wealth creation, pro-competition than ever before' (344).

In *The Closed Circle*, which Coe considers as 'a traditional third-person social realist novel' (in Tew, 2008, 45) and 'a mild variation on social realism' that was 'probably too traditional' (2013d), Benjamin has completed a circle of sorts, moving to a comfortable suburb of Birmingham with his wife and working as an accountant despite his earlier ambition to become a writer, a trajectory that may remind the reader of Christopher's own (shamefaced?) return to suburbia in Julian Barnes's *Metroland* (1980). The age is marked by a sense of apathy, a lack of political ideals and the triumph of Guy Debord's 'Society of the Spectacle', as encapsulated by Doug's description of Britain in 2002: 'the obscene *weightlessness* of its cultural life, the grotesque triumph of sheen over substance'

(325). Coe explains that in *The Closed Circle*, he tried to 'draw a portrait of a class and a culture in a state of flux and disorientation', marked by 'a sense of drift, and a vague undercurrent of resentment' at Blair's betrayal of their hopes. The writer thus points to the confusion and contradictions of his generation of middle-class Middle Englanders who 'disapprove of Thatcherism and Blairism, for good, old-fashioned left-liberal reasons, but ... rather like the material benefits it confers upon us' (2013d). The straightforward satire of *What a Carve Up!* has thus become blunted in the two later books, mirroring the sense of fluctuation in political convictions, while the farcical outrages of the early book have given way to a more subdued form of realism.

The Rotters' Club and *The Closed Circle* are indeed quite traditional and realist in form, even if the former begins with a 30-year analepsis and does not follow a strict chronology. *The Rotters' Club* starts and ends with the same temporal and geographical landmark – 'On a clear, blueblack, starry night, in the city of Berlin, in the year 2003' (1, 401) – and with Sophie getting ready to tell Patrick the story of Benjamin's life in the 1970s, a story which might leave Philip and the reader 'frustrated' because 'It doesn't end. It just stops' (3). She joyfully announces the analepsis – 'Let's go backwards. Backwards in time ... Britain, 1973' (3) – and the next chapter starts with as much enthusiasm and precision: 'Imagine! November the 15th, 1973. A Thursday evening' (9). Her voice as self-conscious oral storyteller lingers for a few more lines – 'I'm doing my best, Patrick. Really I am. But it's not an easy one to tell, the story of my family. ... I'm not even sure this is the right place to start' (10) – but then disappears behind the voice of an omniscient narrator who regularly provides the reader with precise dates from 1973 to 1978, so that the progression is clearly charted and is mainly chronological though the narration sometimes jumps forward in time, for instance to 1981 for a glimpse into the future (305), or to 1999 to provide a retrospective glance at the 1970s (174).

Frequently, the omniscient narrator steps aside to let other characters speak (or write) in various 'speech genres', to use Mikhail Bakhtin's words, types of utterances (oral or written) which are specific to a determined sphere of language and area of human activity (60). *The Rotters' Club* and *The Closed Circle* are thus marked by a polyphony of voices and genres, with the insertion (usually in a different font to set them apart), in the latter, of several letters, emails and texts, newspaper articles (110, 136), a piece of fiction (117–20), the minutes of a meeting (204–8), a phone conversation (243–6), a log-book entry (276–9) and several poems (380–7). This combination contributes to a kaleidoscopic picture and a polyvocal symphony rather than allowing a monological truth and a single voice prevail. The plurality is even more visible in *The Rotters' Club* which includes extracts from Miriam's diary (28–9), as well as Lois's (326–34), letters by various correspondents (35–6, 221, 305–13), a handwritten notice, a propaganda tract (37, 38–9), interviews, the review of a play, letters to the editor, an article and an editorial, all published in the school's newspaper, *The Bill Board* (62–3, 184–95, 225, 227–8, 235–7, 266–7, 286–90), an 'unpublished story' by Benjamin (107–29), dictionary entries (140–2) and a commemorative speech by Douglas Anderton (174–83). The penultimate chapter, Benjamin's first-person stream-of-consciousness, consists of a 37-page sentence without any punctuation (363–99), an homage, Coe declares, not so much to Molly Bloom's interior monologue in Joyce's *Ulysses* (1922) – a book Benjamin has been struggling with (134) and which Sam Chase is reading at the pub (399) – as to *Dancing Lessons for the Advanced in Age* (1964) by Czech writer Bohumil Hrabal, a 90-page novella written in one continuous sentence (Coe, 2013d). Coe remarks that he meant to convey the idea that 'all the thoughts which pass through Benjamin's mind in that section occur to him in the space of a moment' and he wanted readers to 'feel this sense of compression and simultaneity as vividly as possible' (2013d). In addition, the device helps Benjamin draw out a rare moment of happiness with Cicely – 'how can I prolong this moment, how can I stretch it, how can I make it last for ever' (363) – an instant which is one of those 'moments in life' that are 'so replete with emotion that they become stretched, timeless' (128, 363). In *The Closed Circle*, Paul also savours a 'suspension of time' when pedalling on a tandem with his childhood friend Rolf – conceiving 'of that moment as being stretched, eternal' (161) – and when holding Malvina in his arms: 'he was being offered another of those moments that would never end' (190).

The Rotters' Club is probably characterized by a great formal variety because it witnesses the birth of Benjamin as a writer: his precocious first-person narration of his family's holiday in

Denmark in July 1976 (107–29) even contains self-reflexive comments on the art of story-telling. Benjamin is thus upfront about not knowing how 'the story' ends (just like Sophie) or at least about having only one version of it (107). When he tries to 'make sense of it', he realizes that 'slowly, irresistibly', it is 'beginning to dissolve into the hazy falsehood of memory', and adds: 'That is why I have written it down, although in doing so I know that all I have achieved is to falsify it differently, more artfully' (128). One might hear in this confession B.S. Johnson's own doubts voiced in *Albert Angelo,* when he deplores the writer's temptation 'to impose his own pattern, an arbitrary pattern which must falsify, which cannot do anything other than falsify' (170). Benjamin also wonders: 'Does narrative serve a purpose? ... I wonder if all experience can really be distilled to a few extraordinary moments' (128). The question remains unanswered but testifies to Benjamin's (and Coe's) interrogations as to what narrative might do and to what extent it can distort and simplify. In *The Closed Circle,* set in the era of spin doctors and the tyranny of the media, the generalized suspicion pertaining to narrative has contaminated language: 'Words can mean what we want them to mean. In the age of irony', Paul remarks (54).

In his teenage years, Benjamin is not only a budding writer but also a composer who believes he may have found his creative vocation: 'These pieces, he already realized, were merely stepping stones at the start of a journey towards something – some grand artefact, either musical, or literary, or filmic, or perhaps a combination of all three – towards which he knew he was advancing' (2001a, 137). *The Rotters' Club* is therefore a *Künstlerroman* as well as a novel in gestation. In *The Closed Circle,* Benjamin's book – called *Unrest* (102, 257, 414) like Coe's own project of a saga – has reached 'several thousand pages' (45) and its scope corresponds to Coe's two novels: 'it's about some of the political events from the last thirty years or so, and how they relate to ... events in my own life' (257). Benjamin views it as 'an unprecedented marriage of old forms and new technology' (103), which entails 'putting together words and music – literature and history, the personal and the political' (260), and which will 'change the relationship between music and the written word for ever' (103). However, Benjamin never completes the novel: like the protagonist of Johnson's *Christie Malry's Own Double-Entry* but also like 'T.S. Eliot [who] worked in a bank' (198), he becomes an accountant, glad to 'think of himself as the Emile Zola of the double-entry system' (58).

Since Benjamin's novel remains unfinished, one might surmise that the intradiegetic author of the two books is Sophie who has been the oral story-teller throughout and 'a walking encyclopedia of [Benjamin's] past' according to Benjamin in *The Closed Circle* (253). In that novel, Benjamin foretells that his niece might 'turn out to be the writer in the family' and remarks: 'You have … a very advanced sense of narrative' (253). In the last chapter of *The Rotters' Club*, as she has finished telling her story, Patrick deems it 'beautiful' and proposes a catchy description of it: 'It was full of nice things: friendships, jokes, good experiences, love. It wasn't all doom and gloom. … it even has a happy ending', except that to Sophie, 'it doesn't feel like the ending' (402). An author's note tells the reader that there 'will be a sequel to *The Rotters' Club*, entitled *The Closed Circle*, resuming the story in the late 1990s' (403). The sequel starts indeed with a letter by Claire, dated 7 December 1999, and ends as *The Rotters' Club* began and ended, on 'a clear, blueblack, starry night, in the city of Berlin, in the year 2003' (420), with Sophie and Patrick 'telling each other stories' and discussing an era (the 1970s of the first novel) that 'seemed to belong to the dimmest recesses of history' (419–20). The echoes between the two books are striking as several short passages from the beginning of *The Rotters' Club* (1–3) are repeated at the end of the sequel (419–20) to introduce the story Sophie is about to tell, but in *The Closed Circle*, the narrative premise is more enigmatic, as it is not explicitly suggested that Sophie is telling Patrick the story of her family in the 1990s. *The Closed Circle* is also marked by a more nostalgic mood as the middle-aged characters often recall their youth in the 1970s, fixing their gazes 'backwards, back in time' (30), 'back across the years to the schooldays which kept tugging at them: the past that wouldn't let go' (286), contemplating lost opportunities and missed chances, or indulging in 'melancholy inertia' (114). While most people live 'in the present' and 'for the future', Benjamin and his friends are 'locked in the past', 'the past that kept reaching out to them with subtle tendrils whenever they tried to break away and move forwards' (284–5).

The Rotters' Club and *The Closed Circle* were supposed to be the first and sixth volumes of a sequence involving the same characters, but Coe eventually decided to write only those two, calling the second a 'companion piece' or 'mirror image' of the first (Website, *Closed*), and he implemented a number of formal devices to suggest this mirroring dimension. For instance, 'the two novels have exactly the same number of chapters, but in *The Closed Circle* they are numbered in reverse order', so that, after Claire's letter, the novel starts with Chapter 28 and ends with Chapter 1, and 'the last words of each of the three sections of *The Rotters' Club* are also the titles of those sections, whereas in *The Closed Circle*, the same is true of the first words of each section' (Coe, Website, *Closed*). The titles of the two books also regularly recur in the novels, with their meaning and origin explained. *The Rotters' Club* is the title of the second album (1974) by Hatfield and the North, a Canterbury rock band, and Benjamin Trotter tells his sister: 'that's us, Lois, isn't it? Do you see? That's what they used to call us, at school. Bent Rotter, and Lowest Rotter. *We're* The Rotters' Club' (173), an explanation confirmed by Emily in a letter to Claire (310) as well as in *The Closed Circle* (252).

The first novel introduces 'The Closed Circle', 'a select debating society ... cloaked in impenetrable (and somewhat infantile) secrecy' (145), made up of 16 members and modelled on a similar élite society Coe had been asked to join at King Edward's (Coe, 2015b). Defined by these members as 'a "think-tank" composed of the finest minds in King William's' (228) and 'an alternative power-base for carefully chosen, like-minded individuals' (286), it is dismissed by Doug as 'a nasty, divisive bit of elitist bollocks': 'It's like a bunch of schoolkids pretending to be fucking masons' (145). In the sequel, an adult version of The Closed Circle has been founded in 2001 by Labour MP Paul Trotter and is composed of six members chosen from the 18 members of the Commission for Business and Social Initiatives. A 'circle-within-the-circle', it is 'clandestine' and meant to encourage 'private finance initiatives' into the public sector (206). The image of the circle should therefore be understood in terms of exclusion and homogenization of political opinion. As Doug tells Paul, 'the left's moved way over to the right, the right's moved a tiny bit to the left, the circle's been closed' (139). The notion of closure and circularity also applies to the narrative situation. Coe's original idea for a six-volume sequence entailed a circular narrative, with the first volume called *The Learning Curve*, and the six books forming a complete circle (Coe, 2015b). In *The Closed Circle*, when Benjamin reflects on his loss of affinity with his sister and his 'growing and deepening fondness' for his niece, he finds some comfort in the symmetry, 'the sense of a circle being closed' (253), and at the end of the book, as Sophie and Patrick are having dinner in a restaurant whose platform does a complete turn in 30 minutes, they understand it is time for them to go – and for the novel to end – when 'the circle had closed for the last time' (420). The sense of a neat closure but also the promise of a new cycle (as the young people expect 'to repeat the mistakes their parents had made' [428]) certainly fit the general realist vein of the novel which avoids the postmodernist ploys of *What a Carve Up!*.

In 2005, when Hatfield and the North issued a new CD with a selection of their songs from the 1970s (*Hatwise Choice*), they asked Coe to write an introduction to the accompanying booklet. Coe remarked:

> Perhaps I was never happier than in those far-off days as a spotty teenager, on my way home from school on the number 62 bus, with a copy of *The Rotters' Club* in my Virgin Records plastic bag, all a-quiver with anticipation at the thought of the aural delights to come. … It was in an attempt to recapture some of that youthful excitement, the sense of freedom, possibility, artistic horizons suddenly blown open, that I used *The Rotters' Club* as the name of one of my novels.
>
> (2005b)

Paul Laity remarks that this music 'fits almost too well with Coe's fiction' as it is 'known for combining the avant-garde with the popular and catchy – the silly with the serious'. The numerous musical references in *The Rotters' Club* – a novel that belongs to the 'Punk or Rock Against Racism generation' (Gilroy, 199) – participate in the representation of Britain in the 1970s, from progressive rock to the advent of punk. In the early 1970s, Doug Anderton buys *Stranded* by Roxy Music (1973) and insists 'it blew the socks off his poxy Genesis albums' (26); Malcolm introduces Benjamin to Henry Cow (46) and Hatfield and the North (94); Philip's Christmas present from his parents is *Tales from Topographic Oceans* (1973) by progressive rock band Yes (60), which inspires him to compose a 'rock symphony in five movements', which is 'even longer than "Supper's Ready" from the Genesis album *Foxtrot*', and is ambitiously 'narrating the entire history of the universe from the moment of creation up until roughly ... the resignation of Harold Wilson in 1976' (179). But Philip's 'personal bid for progressive rock superstardom' (180) fizzles out as specialists in 'fifteen-minute instrumentals' and such prog rock bands as 'Camel and Curved Air and Gentle Giant' now provoke 'howls of derision' (250) among his friends. In 1976, a new kind of music springs up (160, 162), that of The Damned with their single 'New Rose', the Sex Pistols and 'Anarchy in the UK', The Clash with 'London's Burning' and 'Janie Jones'. To quote Doug, 'it was the glorious rebirth of the two-minute single. No more guitar solos. Concept albums were out. Mellotrons were *verboten*. It was the dawn of punk or ... dole-queue rock' (180).

However, when 'the characters dream of transcendence, it is through classical music' (May, 2014, 229). Benjamin thus becomes infatuated with the symphonies and orchestral pieces of English composer Vaughan Williams – also conjured up by the art teacher to rhapsodize over Philip's mother (139) – such as the 'long, wandering tune, impossibly noble, impossibly sad' of 'Norfolk Rhapsody No.1' (256), by which Paul's taxi driver in *The Closed Circle* is also enraptured (317) and which Sean Harding solemnly listens to (377). In *The Rotters' Club*, for his girlfriend's birthday, Benjamin selfishly and comically buys '*Voices and Instruments*, one of the new releases on Brian Eno's Obscure Records label. One side consisted of e.e. cummings poems set to music by John Cage, sung by Robert Wyatt and Carla Bley. On the other, a Birmingham musician, Jan Steele, had composed some minimalist settings of texts by James Joyce' (296–7). The reference to Robert Wyatt is significant as he is one of Coe's favourite musicians and Coe wrote the introduction to his biography by Marcus O'Dair (2014c). The record that, for Coe, captures the essence of the 1980s is Wyatt's *Old Rottenhat* (1985), an album that 'crystallized the emerging ruthlessness of the Thatcherite tendency better than any other' (Coe, 2014c, 10), with songs that 'foresaw the rise of New Labour, and the disengagement of the Labour Party from its roots' (2013d). Coe enjoyed 'being welcomed into that lyrical space where political engagement had always co-existed with generosity and humour' (2014c, 10), and drew inspiration from Wyatt's 'way of combining music with a political consciousness' (in Okereke). While accurately representing the cultural and political background in Britain, the intermediality of Coe's novels functions as an exemplar of the complete work of art, which combines the auditory, the visual and the literary, echoing the rich cultural combinations of books by Salman Rushdie or Nick Hornby.

From a literary perspective, Coe's portrait of adolescence in *The Rotters' Club* may be partly indebted to Rosamond Lehmann's *Dusty Answer* (1927), a study of the 'complex period when nostalgia for childhood momentarily overlaps with the dawning of adult sensibilities', a period marked by the 'sense that friendship and romantic relationships will always be the most crucial testing-grounds for our standards of commitment and integrity' (Coe, 2013d). In Coe's novel, the young Benjamin suffers from such overwhelming emotions as 'a paralyzing nostalgia', a 'heaviness and apathy' (250), 'an almost unbearable longing' (250–1) and 'an aching, insupportable sense of loss' (252), all caused by his hopeless unrequited love for Cicely, so much so that in *The Closed Circle*, his niece both jokingly and suggestively remarks that all his friends have learned to avoid using the C-word (424). In both novels, Benjamin's intense feelings of nostalgia, apathy, longing and loss, conveyed with a mixture of mockery and sympathy, point to Coe's genuine interest in grappling with the emotional conflicts of private lives, beyond the obvious political, ideological and comic content of the novels. This attention to the intimate world of individuals is an aspect Coe more particularly developed in *The House of Sleep* and *The Rain Before it Falls* as the next chapter will outline.

6

IN SEARCH OF LOST TIME: *THE HOUSE OF SLEEP* AND *THE RAIN BEFORE IT FALLS*

Ten years separate the publication of *The House of Sleep* (1997) from that of *The Rain Before it Falls* (2007), but the two novels share an interest in the intimacy of private emotional lives and evoke 'an understanding of the workings of human nature' (Coe, 2013d). Like Sarah in *The House of Sleep*, the books combine 'ease and melancholy, lightness and weight' (1997a, 154) and explore close human relationships – between friends, lovers, family members – and the sense of connectedness and sharing they achieve or fail to conjure. To borrow Coe's comment on Rosamond Lehmann's work, a central theme is 'nothing less than the moral responsibility of human beings towards one another' (2013d). Unlike *What a Carve Up!*, *The Rotters' Club* and *The Closed Circle*, both novels essentially leave the historical and political context in the background even if it is never totally absent.

While *The Rain Before it Falls* is almost devoid of comedy, Coe describes *The House of Sleep* as a 'comedy on the effects of willed insomnia' (2013d): it was inspired by Coe's own fits of sleepwalking, which led him to inquire into various sleep disorders (insomnia, somnambulism, narcolepsy, somniloquy). The mood and tone are quite different from *What a Carve Up!* which preceded it, as the new novel is less political and more melancholy, romantic and dreamy; it still employs humour and comedy, but shuns the bluntness of satire. And yet, the character of Gregory Dudden, the fanatical sleep specialist, is, in Coe's terms, 'a leftover Winshaw' (in Taylor, Charles): he admires America's 'efficient system of private medical insurance' (179) and argues that 'Britain stood poised on the edge of greatness' when Thatcher was in charge (175), attributing her success – and that of great men like Napoleon and Edison – 'to the fact that she only needed two or three hours' sleep a night' (176). Gregory considers sleep a 'disease' and a 'plague', 'shortening your life by a third' (180), and despises it for putting 'even the strongest people at the mercy of the weakest and most feeble' (176), for being 'the great leveller', like 'fucking socialism' (177). He thereby echoes Doctor Bordeu in Denis Diderot's philosophical dialogues *D'Alembert's Dream* (1769), who says that while asleep, 'the master is thrown on the mercy of his servants' (158). In a neoliberalist vein, Gregory looks for ways of reducing sleeping hours so as to decrease vulnerability and increase profitability and, for that purpose, he deprives several animals and human beings of sleep to observe how long they might survive. The balance of power is clearly drawn between those who need long hours of sleep and those who remain awake and alert: as an adult and film critic in 1996, Terry develops insomnia, a quality much coveted by Gregory who exercises power by looking down on 'people as they lay helpless, unconscious, while he, the watching subject, retained full control over his waking mind' (18). A Winshaw-like sinister character, Gregory clearly subscribes to a hierarchical conception of society dominated by the strong and wealthy.

Terry himself believes in the hegemony of capitalism in the mid-1990s: 'Left and right have become meaningless concepts. Capitalism has proved itself unassailable, and sooner or later, all human life will be governed only by the random fluctuations of the market' (175). Finance rules indeed so that when economics student Veronica decides to found a theatre group, she first needs to look for sponsors: 'That's the way things are going these days: private enterprise' (122). She eventually accepts a lucrative job in financial services and suffers from 'Yuppie burn-out': 'You work your rocks off in the City for ten years, you make pots of money, and then one day you look at your life and can't remember what any of it was for' (214). This sense of void will lead Veronica to drive her car into a brick wall one night. In the short story 'The Dog Walker's Tale' (which will form part of Coe's new novel *Number 11*), Jane who has worked for years as a trader in the City for an investment bank, also gives up but ironically she manages to earn more money walking the dogs of wealthy people than she did in the City.

As in *The Rain Before it Falls*, the political dimension is however relatively secondary in *The House of Sleep* and the link with *What a Carve Up!* has more to do with similarities of structure, tone and content. Both novels have been conceived as dark comedies partly set in a gothic mansion: Winshaw Towers in *What a Carve Up!* owes its name to a 'mad conglomeration of gothic, neo-gothic, sub-gothic and pseudo-gothic towers' (186), and finds an echo in the later novel in Ashdown, the old house where students used to live in the mid-1980s and which has been transformed into a sleep clinic some 12 years later. Standing on the edge of a cliff by the ocean, it sports 'spires and tourelles', 'glacial rooms and mazy, echoing corridors' (3, 26), as well as a mysterious basement where gruesome experiments are being performed on rats, rabbits, dogs and even human beings, evoking the chilling atmosphere of horror films. As the narrator twice remarks, the house's 'bleak, element-defying beauty masked the fact that it was, essentially, unfit for human occupation' (4, 27). Such an eerie description is supplemented by yet another homage to crime writer Frank King as *The House of Sleep* takes its title from a spy novel of the same name (1934) by King, which comes to symbolize the link between Sarah, Veronica and Robert as they all read it and use it as a means to convey messages to each other (118, 122, 123, 126, 220, 226, 247). Sarah and Veronica are entranced by the thriller's 'dated 1930s jargon and the incredibly convoluted plot' which entails a 'baffling sequence of midnight kidnappings and grisly assassinations' (118), a description which partly recalls *What a Carve Up!* and confirms Coe's attachment to popular genre literature.

Like *What a Carve Up!*, *The House of Sleep* is structured around alternate chapters, two time-frames and various perspectives, as the narrator keeps moving from one narrative strand to another and one focalization to another, in a general disruption of linearity and continuity – 'I don't like continuous narratives', Terry asserts (146) – maybe mimetic of the merging of dreams in one's sleep. The odd-numbered chapters take place in 1983–84 and are centred on a group of students; the even-numbered chapters focus on the same characters in the last two weeks of June 1996. The novel is divided into six parts and four stages that mirror the different phases of sleep, and on occasion the last word at the end of one stage is repeated at the beginning of the next stage, thus providing a deceptive continuity between chapters while in fact the narrative has moved from one character's mind to another, and one time frame to another. As Suzanne Berne remarks, 'this deliberate conflation of time and identity neatly illustrates how fluid our perception of the world can be' (12). The time difference between chapters also enables the reader to observe the evolution of the protagonists 12 years apart while the back-and-forth movement requires a keen attention to details, coincidences, echoes and repeated phrases to reassemble the various pieces as with a jigsaw. It is thus only in 'Appendix 1' that the reader can finally make sense of the italicized phrases that have been disseminated throughout the book as they appear in Robert's poem to Sarah, 'Somniloquy' (333). In a similar way, the narrator skilfully retains some information (names, for instance) to maintain suspense and ensure the reader does not immediately identify some characters. For instance, when Dr. C. J. Madison meets a young woman on the beach, she forgets to ask for her name and does not reveal her own first name (26); if she had, she would have remembered Ruby Sharp, the little girl Sarah and Robert took to the beach back in 1984 and to whom Robert – now called Cleo Madison – confided his love for Sarah. The novel is thus ingeniously constructed, encouraging the reader to take an active role in the narration.

Recalling the polygenericity and discontinuity of *What a Carve Up!*, *The House of Sleep* incorporates various genres (romance, tragedy, farce, horror story) and offers comic pastiches of specialized discourses (film criticism, feminist theory, Lacanian psychoanalytical discourse, management course jargon). This led Malcolm Bradbury to qualify the novel as a '"postmodern" book' because it delights 'in language as much as sensibility, parodic surfaces and falsified references as much as shifting depths, plotted devices and borrowed gothic conventions' (46). According to José Ramón Prado Pérez, the mixture of genres and styles 'breaks the continuity of the narrative' and emphasizes 'the construct that all forms of discourse are' (970). One may further suggest that the pastiches turn the novel into an ironic version of postmodernism since Coe seems to be parodying postmodernism itself.

In *The House of Sleep*, Terry is plagued with a 'single-minded obsession with cinema' (82) and, just like Graham in *What a Carve*

Up!, has elitist and absolutist views about films. As a student, he writes his dissertation on a depressing neo-realist Italian film he has never seen, by fictitious director Salvatore Ortese (1913–75) and Coe interrupts the flow of the narrative to include an entry for Ortese, supposedly copied from the *Cambridge Companion to Film* (129–30) and imitating the style and mode of such biographical entries. A highbrow film buff, Terry is enthralled with such directors as Carol Reed, Orson Welles, Howard Hawks, Sergei Eisenstein, Kenji Mizoguchi or Wim Wenders, whom his ignorant friend Kingsley has never heard of, preferring such popular movies as *Ghostbusters*, *The Odd Couple* or *Dirty Harry* (197–99). Terry's ambition for his part is to 'write a screenplay that could be shot over a period of fifty years' (193), following a man from childhood to old age: 'a vertiginous, fast-forward chronicle of hope withering into despair' (128), a distant echo perhaps of B.S. Johnson's ten-minute film *Paradigm* (1968), which shows a man speaking in a fabricated language, transforming from young and verbose to old and inarticulate. In *The House of Sleep*, a film producer attributes the demise of the British film industry to snobbish people like Terry, intellectuals who 'go around proclaiming that film was an art form' (202). This echoes Terry's earlier pronouncement that film is 'fundamentally the expression of one artist's personal vision' and that the greatest director would be someone of 'uncompromising integrity' (128) – maybe someone as radical as B.S. Johnson.

Twelve years later, Terry has been fired from the prestigious film magazine *Frame* and ends up writing 'short, eye-catching résumés of the week's film' for a TV listings magazine: 'He was allowed an indiscriminate fifteen words per film, whether it was *Smokey and the Bandit* or *La Règle du jeu*' (274). He then becomes 'one of the leading spokesmen for a form of criticism which jettisoned all the concepts of value' he had held dear a few years earlier (275), and he cynically mocks the jargon of his colleagues. In one of his film reviews reproduced in italics – once again interrupting the narrative flow – Terry sneeringly recalls a discussion between two critics as to who might be the greatest film director. The member of the old school is praised for his '*antiquated coherence*' in choosing '*the veteran Portuguese director Manoel de Oliveira*', while the '*Young Turk*', carrying the banner for Quentin Tarantino, is derided for the '*crappiness of his argument – which was that by "revitalizing" B-movie clichés, Tarantino was actually achieving some sort of (and yes, he really did use this word) 'originality'. I think, God help him, he may even have mentioned postmodernism at some particularly desperate moment'* (73). The review ends as an ironic and clichéd praise for the type of popular American movies Terry used to despise. In 'Diary of an Obsession', Coe, who used to be a film reviewer, remarks: Terry's 'absurd critical outpourings are a kind of punishment for all the journalistic crimes I myself have committed over the years' (2005a, 52).

Besides film criticism, *The House of Sleep* pastiches the jargon of American management programmes through the course Gregory has signed up for, which is supposed to 'introduce leading members of the psychiatric profession to some basic business concepts' (251). The two course trainers speak in hollow slogans and write them on a flip-chart in foot-high capitals, such as 'EMBRACE THE CHANGE' or 'MOTIVATE YOU FOR CHANGE' (253). They ask the audience to take part in childish games, whose relation to change and management culture is never explained. For instance, participants are required to immerse jelly babies in water without touching the bucket the sweets are in and without stepping into the 12-foot circle that surrounds it (259). The triviality of the course is made blatant by the discrepancy between the ridiculous activities involved and Professor Cole's deep concern about a dangerous schizophrenic patient who might be released that very day because of a shortage of beds in his ward. While his colleagues are trying to drown the jelly babies, the doctor imagines a newspaper brief about the patient's knife aggression towards a man and his letter of condolences to the latter's parents, both transcribed in italics and interrupting the dialogue (261–2). Cole's imagined words will prove proleptic as the patient will be released and when Terry finds himself on Denmark Hill station platform, he will notice a man carrying a knife and resembling the doctor's description (322) – the reader may thus surmise that Terry may become his victim. The intermingling of the two discourses suggests what may happen when management culture is applied to the National Health Service, thus echoing passages in *What a Carve Up!* where Michael highlights the dreadful consequences of severe cuts in health budgets. The polyphony creates what Bakhtin would have called a dialogic mesh while simultaneously pointing to the constructedness and built-in stereotypes of each specialized discourse.

Lacanian psychoanalytical jargon is also subject to comic caricature in the novel. The sections set in 1996 include – without any preliminary introduction or contextualization – italicized snippets of conversations between an analyst and an analysand whom the reader soon enough identifies as Sarah, the woman who suffers from narcolepsy, whose symptoms are 'excessive daytime sleepiness; vivid pre-sleep dreaming; cataplexy brought on by laughter' (286). However, instead of diagnosing a case of narcolepsy, her psychotherapist, Russell Watts, offers a linguistic interpretation of her choice of words in his paper *The Case of Sarah T.: or an Eye for an 'I'* (283). The text is a witty pastiche of Lacanian psychoanalytical theory: Watts draws a parallel between the eroticization of Sarah's eyes during the sex act and a penetration of her 'I', a 'rape of her most intimate self' (292); he calls the phallus the masculine 'gender's magnificent, philoprogenitive signifier', and argues that Sarah's eyeballs, 'those twin desiring globes', had 'become, in her strange, private, opto-erotic sexual universe, nothing less than two vaginas which some freak of nature had placed on either side of her nose' (293). The pastiche produces comic effect and exposes the blindness of the psychotherapist who fails to see the obvious (Sarah's narcolepsy), so focused is he on making her case fit neatly into his preconceived theories and patterns. In her review of the novel, Anita Brookner writes that she heard 'echoes of Buñuel and Georges Bataille' in the narrative (37). The atmosphere of *The House of Sleep* is very different from that of Bataille's transgressive novella *The Story of the Eye* (1928), but one might perceive echoes of the sexual perversions of Bataille's exhibitionist teenagers who are fascinated with eyes, to the point that the male protagonist is shown inserting the enucleated eye of a dead priest within his girlfriend's vagina. One also recalls the infamous scene from Buñuel's surrealist film *An Andalusian Dog* (1929) – which uses dream logic or Freudian free association – when a man slits a woman's eye with a razor, as well as the Dali-inspired dream sequence in Hitchcock's *Spellbound* (1945), showing a room filled with curtains painted with over-sized eyes and a man walking around with a large pair of scissors cutting the drapes. While sight is often related to 'scenarios of knowing' in psychoanalytic writing (Brooks, 9), in *What a Carve Up!*, Thomas Winshaw is significantly punished for his peeping obsession by having his eyeballs pulled out of their sockets.

The House of Sleep does not spare feminist discourse either, as it is pastiched through the character of Veronica, whose nickname

(Ronnie) is interestingly and deliberately masculine. The reader first encounters her when she is engaged in conversation with friends, accumulating radical blunt statements. She states that 'objectivity ... is male subjectivity' (7) and argues that Harold Pinter's plays 'appeal to the misogyny deep within the male psyche' (6), concluding: 'All men hate women. ... All men have the potential to become rapists' (7). However Veronica's character will subsequently move away from such stereotypes and become more complex and nuanced. She is the one who introduces Sarah to Simone de Beauvoir's *The Second Sex*, Kate Millett's *Sexual Politics* and Angela Carter's *The Sadeian Woman* (48), and many years later, Sarah remembers: 'yes, we were reading our Julia Kristeva and our Andrea Dworkin and we never passed up an opportunity to complain about patriarchy' (217). In 1984, Veronica had argued that one could not have culture without gender: 'Gender's everywhere' (6). Twelve years later, Sarah sarcastically reflects on the 'intolerant' set of values her friends and other students used to believe in: 'We were so *obsessed* with politics all the time: gender politics, literary politics, film politics ... there was even that phrase, wasn't there, that awful phrase, "political lesbian"' (216). With the benefit of hindsight, Sarah is able to perceive the excesses of some radical theories which bring together issues of politics, identity and gender. The novel ends on a bitter-sweet note as Robert changes gender to appeal to Sarah but is told that Sarah's relationship with Veronica was probably just a phase, and that she is to be married to Anthony (309). To quote Carey Harrison, Coe 'makes us rethink the verities of gender' and puts forward such qualities as love, tenderness and affection. Reflecting on her past homosexuality, Sarah notes: 'I didn't know myself very well' (310). With these words, she points to the instability of her own identity and self-knowledge, which might explain why she was so interested in Weil's book, *Gravity and Grace*, and especially the chapter on 'The Self' (153). *The House of Sleep* thus keeps enforcing confusion and will not offer the reader the comfort of stability and firmly-set categories. For Prado Pérez, the novel depicts 'disjointed and chaotic characters at the point of dissolution' and challenges 'the moral certainties and monolithic representations of reality promoted by conservative ideological discourses' (971).

The House of Sleep not only probes questions of identity, but also of ontology. As in *What a Carve Up!*, the frontiers between fiction and reality, between dreams and the real world, are often blurred, so that characters sometimes wonder about the ontological status of the situations they find themselves in, or else they choose fantasy over real life, preferring to withdraw behind screens. Like Michael in *What a Carve Up!*, the older Terry finds refuge in the films he watches all night (70), a variation on the addictive dreams of his student days, 'which took on the quality of the most pristine and idealized childhood memories, which were beyond the most fertile, accomplished and assiduous fantasist' (81). Because these visions are far more rewarding than Terry's everyday life, he requires a minimum of fourteen hours' sleep to pursue them and gets disconnected from the real world. As for Robert, his unrequited love for Sarah makes him sink 'into a romantic coma from which there seemed to be no awakening …, his mind acting as a private cinema screen upon which ever more tantalizing scenes would be projected' (79). Here again, the imagined scripts are more satisfactory than real life and justify remaining in his room for days. Significantly enough, Robert's childhood dream about a woman pointing at a hospital (86), which he later interprets as the sign that he should change gender (268), corresponds to the only surviving photograph from Ortese's lost film (296, 316), about which Terry is obsessing. In both cases, the world of fantasy heavily determines the conduct of one's life.

In *What a Carve Up!*, the first epigraph (by Jean Cocteau), repeated twice within the book, advises sleepers to accept their dreams: 'Si vous dormez, si vous rêvez, acceptez vos rêves' (n.p., 167, 487). Like Michael Owen, Sarah in *The House of Sleep* is often 'liable to have a dream so real that she could not distinguish it from the events of her waking life' (46). Her 'hypnagogic hallucinations' (36) or impossibility to tell the difference between her vivid dreams and the events of her real life are repeatedly evoked in the novel, by Sarah herself but also by Gregory, Terry, her psychoanalyst and the narrator (18, 36, 38, 46, 48, 114, 264, 285), and they subsequently transform the lives of the characters. Gregory becomes a lunatic sleep scientist because of his fascination with Sarah's symptoms. Robert invents a twin sister to make Sarah's dream come true. One of Sarah's too vivid dreams leads her to put footnotes out of sequence in one of Terry's articles (270–4), so that 'each one accidentally makes a libellous or offensive remark' – this conceit a tribute to 'a sketch by David Renwick on The Two Ronnies TV show, where a contestant in the quiz show Mastermind is able only to answer the question before last' (Quantick). The effect is comic but, as a consequence, Terry loses his job and turns into an insomniac, alcoholic and cynical film reviewer. To quote Trev Broughton, all of these destinies 'stem from casual encounters with Sarah's unconscious' (19), and point to the fine boundary between two ontologically incompatible worlds, objective reality and subjective consciousness, sometimes leading to confusion as to what is a memory and what is fantasy. In *The Terrible Privacy of Maxwell Sim*, the narrator likewise sees images of his schoolfriend and his sister, but cannot 'tell if these images were from a dream or a memory' (83). Such uncertainty casts doubts as to the reliability of some episodes and points to the fallibility of memory, a recurrent theme in Coe's work. In *The House of Sleep*, when Gregory talks to Sarah about their evening with friends, she retorts: 'I have my own memory of what happened, and it's completely different' (44), a kind of 'alternative memory' (45). Whether they are dreams or memories, it is not always possible to scrape the surface of the palimpsest and recover lost events or feelings. When Sarah's analyst feels she is holding something back about a past event, she claims she simply does not remember much about it, but the analyst retorts: '*There's a fine line between forgetting an event, and suppressing the memory of it*' (227).

Coe described *The House of Sleep* as a 'novel about lost time, lost opportunities' (2005a, 52), concepts that are suggested by the ellipsis between 1984 and 1996, and by the routes some characters have failed to take, such as, for instance, when Robert declines to go to bed with Sarah after she invites him to (231). The theme of loss itself is related to death, absence and disappearance, for example when Robert paraphrases a passage from Weil's *Gravity and Grace*: 'when you lose somebody, when you miss them, you suffer because the departed person has become something imaginary; something unreal' (160). While Sarah interprets this as the sign that Robert misses his twin sister, Robert is actually already projecting into the future, anticipating his loss of Sarah and the void that loss will create. In his melancholy poem to her, he echoes Weil's book, addressing Sarah in the first lines – 'Your gravity, your grace have turned a tide / in me' – and then letting the house's ghosts warn him: '*Another lifetime is the least you'll need, to trace / The guarded secrets of her gravity, her grace*' (333).

While Robert might never pierce Sarah's essence in his lifetime, Terry might never find the film he has been looking for all his life. As suggested earlier, the narrator invents an apocryphal Italian director, Salvatore Ortese, who supposedly made a film called *Latrine Duty*, for which no print exists, but which Terry is obsessively trying to locate. For Terry, that lost film is the most tantalizing and he compares it to 'the most beautiful kind of dream of all ... the kind of dream that might just have been the best one you've ever had in your life, only it slips from your mind just as you're waking up' (127). Terry's unwritten book about Ortese was to be about 'the idea of loss' (70), and Coe argues that 'it is important for some things to remain lost'. He adds: 'A quality of evanescence is central to cinema' (2005a, 53). This evanescent quality (of a dream, a film, an emotion, a memory), this something that is beautiful because unattainable, is what the novel is trying to examine and what may be compared to 'the rain before it falls' that Thea likes so much, precisely because 'there's no such thing'. As she tells Rosamond in *The Rain Before it Falls*, 'something can still make you happy, can't it, even if it isn't real?' (162). As Paul Quinn argues, 'the phrase is itself an excursion away from strict realism, conjuring up an image of something that is paradoxical and whose truth-claim status is uncertain' (19). Many years later, when Gill hopes to decipher the design behind the lives of four generations of women, the promise of a revelation evaporates and vanishes: 'What she had been hoping for was a figment, a dream, an impossible thing: like the rain before it falls' (278).

The idea of loss and lost films in *The House of Sleep* was inspired by Coe's own obsession over Billy Wilder's film *The Private Life of Sherlock Holmes*. This 1970 film is briefly referred to in *The House of Sleep* and Billy Wilder is dismissed as 'a middlebrow talent' (127), but the narrative is also peppered with discreet allusions to Wilder's film: the name of the house, Ashdown, is the surname Holmes and Gabrielle Vallodon assume when they pretend to be a married couple to go to Scotland; Vallodon, the café where the students meet, is the name adopted by the German spy who pretends to be Emil Vallodon's wife (Coe 2005a, 52). In addition, the released version of *The Private Life of Sherlock Holmes* is only two-thirds of the completed film. Once Coe learned about the deleted scenes, he spent years looking for them, just as Terry did for Ortese's *Latrine Duty*, both resembling the readers of the short-lived magazine

Movie Collector, 'fanatics, fetishists, obsessives' who are fascinated with 'deleted footage, missing scenes, tiny shards of forgotten movies which have vanished into some kind of cinematic purgatory' (Coe, 2005a, 50). For Coe, Wilder's film became 'intimately bound up with ideas of loss: lost time, lost opportunities, the rapidity with which events recede into the past and can never be recaptured' (2005a, 50). However, when Coe was eventually given a copy of the missing scenes on DVD, he first decided not to watch them as he realized that part of him 'would *prefer* this material to remain lost, unseen. That is its very essence' (2005a, 51). In *The House of Sleep*, Terry also gives up on his quest as the lost film and the forgotten dream turn out to be more enticing than the retrieved one, the remembered one. In *The Rain Before it Falls*, Rosamond refers to the lost scenes of Michael Powell's film *Gone to Earth* (1950): 'the producer had loathed it, apparently, and given orders for it to be reshot, re-edited, retitled and generally hacked for its American release. In the years that followed, all traces of the original were believed to have disappeared' (98). Some thirty years later however, the film was restored to its former state, and Rosamond's memory could be refreshed and preserved.

Memory and the passage of time, but also the focus on female characters and the benign presence of Rosamond Lehmann's literary legacy, provide echoes between *The Accidental Woman*, *The House of Sleep* and *The Rain Before it Falls*. In Coe's first novel, when the narrator does not know if a year or more has passed, he admits: 'I get so confused about time' (99). This sense of disorientation is echoed in the epigraph to *The House of Sleep*, taken from Rosamond Lehmann's *The Echoing Grove* (1953): 'I do get confused about time. If one loses one's emotional focus … that's what happens. Aeons – split seconds – they interchange. One gets outside the usual way of counting' (n.p.). In his biography of B.S. Johnson, Coe quotes the same passage when referring to the last days before the writer's suicide, about which people had unclear memories and offered contradictory accounts, probably because 'when you are caught up in events of such emotional intensity … then chronology just goes into pieces' (377).

In *The Rain Before it Falls*, Rosamond's memory of a painful childhood event is also imprecise: 'How many weeks was it, I wonder …? Or was it only a matter of days? They say that split seconds and aeons become interchangeable when you experience intense emotion' (55). As Daniel Soar remarks, in her narrative, Rosamond 'collapses ages into instants, and her instants stand for ages' (33). The echo of Lehmann's quote in Coe's three novels is not a coincidence as ten years separate each of the three books (1987, 1997, 2007), and they each offer powerful portraits of female characters at various ages. The quotation is aptly chosen as the fallibility of memory and the loss of stable landmarks are common themes in Coe's novels, which exploit the capacity of time to collapse, expand or contract, as in dreams. One recalls W.S. Landor's epigraph to Lehmann's novel, *A Note in Music* (1930): 'The present, like a note in music, is nothing but as it appertains to what is past and what is to come'. In *The Terrible Privacy of Maxwell Sim*, the narrator also reflects on the relativity of time – 'Fifteen years ago. Is fifteen years a long time, or a short time?' (12) – before admitting later on: 'I lose track of time' (282), and eventually choosing a meaningful simile when phoning Clive: 'The phone rang for what seemed like aeons' (332). While *The House of Sleep* is divided into the various stages of sleep, Lehmann's *The Echoing Grove* comprises five parts entitled 'Afternoon', 'Morning', 'Nightfall', 'Midnight' and 'Early Hours', that testify to the novel's 'thorough collapse of conventional narrative time', to quote Coe's introduction to the novel (2013d). Coe also notes that Lehmann's novel is marked by a 'combination of passionate bleakness and extreme formal and narrative ingenuity', and 'a seductive blurring of memory and actuality' (2013d), characteristics that are shared by *The House of Sleep* with its alternate chapters, analepses and prolepses, as well as its confusion between dreams and reality. In that same novel, Veronica is collecting Lehmann's books in their first editions (153, 215) and Sarah takes one of her novels to the beach, reading aloud six words from that book – 'as still, as carved, as death' (151, 249) – which Robert will later include in his poem 'Somniloquy' (333) to describe the atmosphere of that afternoon. The narrator enigmatically never reveals the title of that novel – which is *Dusty Answer* (1927) – thus challenging the reader's curiosity.

These intertextual echoes in *The House of Sleep* already paved the way for a more extensive tribute to Lehmann in *The Rain Before it Falls*, in which the reader hears the confession of a woman named Rosamond, who, a few hours before committing suicide at the age of 73, narrates significant events of her life on a tape-recorder for the benefit of her cousin's granddaughter Imogen.

Each event is related to a photograph that is being described in detail, recalling *Rosamond Lehmann's Album* (1985), a retrospective survey of her life at 84, comprising some 140 snapshots of herself, her family and circle of friends accompanied by informal commentaries, which Lehmann considered as a 'simple, sketchy record of a life' as well as her 'farewell' to the reader a few years before her death (1985, 12). In Coe's novel, Rosamond's niece, Gill, is the one who is entrusted with her aunt's tapes and ends up listening to them with her daughters since Imogen is nowhere to be found. The novel thus comprises a framing narrative, written in the third person from Gill's perspective, and an embedded first-person narrative, made up of Rosamond's oral monologue. As Coe remarked, 'being able to write in the voice of the other gender is first base for a novelist' (in Laity). In her monologue, Rosamond often refers to her cousin or sister-in-blood Beatrix, who bears the same name as one of Lehmann's sisters, the actress Beatrix Lehmann, while the mother of the fictional Beatrix, Ivy, shares the name of another Virago writer, Ivy Compton-Burnett, who wrote about the dysfunctional families of the late-Victorian upper classes. In Coe's novel, the ambivalent relationship between Rosamond and Beatrix may recall the 'possible lesbian undercurrent in the friendship between Judith and Jennifer' (Coe, 2013d) in Lehmann's *Dusty Answer*. Coe claims that his favourite novel by Lehmann is *The Ballad and the Source* (1944), 'a story of the relationship between a mother, her daughter and her granddaughters, in which betrayal, manipulation and emotional histrionics are shown to have a cumulatively destructive effect across the generations' (2013d), a description that could partly apply to *The Rain Before it Falls* which offers a portrait of four generations of women (Ivy, Beatrix, Thea and Imogen) from the 1940s to 2007, leaving husbands, fathers and brothers in the shadows. Unlike Milan Kundera, reproved for 'his overwhelming androcentrism', Coe refuses to 'see the world from an exclusively male viewpoint' (Coe, 2015a). He argues that his novel is, 'in a veiled, oblique sort of way', about 'what "good parenting" is', 'a fable about what happens when a child is neglected, not wanted and not loved by her mother' (in Page, Benedicte, 20).

More specific echoes of Lehmann include the incident of the bird that took place in Auvergne in April 1992: Rosamond's niece, Gill, was driving in the countryside when she heard 'a loud, sudden thud on her windscreen' and saw a black shape bouncing off it. Looking out she saw 'a dark blot upon the asphalt – a dead bird, a young blackbird. And on the instant of seeing that lifeless shape another thud fell, leaden, upon her heart'. Gill 'picked up the small body gingerly ... and then placed it gently on a bed of moss under the branches of a lone shrub', thinking to herself: 'You know what it's supposed to mean: a death in the family' (22). In Lehmann's autobiographical work *The Swan in the Evening. Fragments of an Inner Life* (1967), which, in its new edition of 1982, she described as her 'last testament', Lehmann, like the fictional Rosamond, tells the story of her life not exhaustively but by 'fragments', focusing on significant episodes of her outer and inner life. The book is dedicated to Lehmann's granddaughter, Anna, and ends with a letter to Anna in which Lehmann addresses her in ways that are not dissimilar from Rosamond's own communication with Imogen. In the middle part of the book, Lehmann recalls hearing 'a loud, sudden thud' on one of the French windows in her house on the Isle of Wight in 1958 (82). Looking out, she saw on the paved terrace 'a dark blot upon the stone – a dead bird, a young blackbird'. She adds: 'on the instant of my seeing that lifeless shape a thud fell, leaden, upon my heart' because it seemed 'such an unpropitious omen' (83). Her companion 'picked up the small body and placed it gently on a bed of dead leaves under the shrubby branches' while Lehmann said: 'You know what it's supposed to mean: a death in the family' (83–4). A few hours later, Lehmann learned that her daughter Sally had just died in Java. In *The Rain Before it Falls*, it will take Gill fifteen years to understand the significance of the bird's death. On that very same day, 16 April 1992, Imogen, Rosamond's cousin's granddaughter, was hit and killed by a car in Toronto (275). The echoes between *The Rain Before it Falls* and *The Swan in the Evening*, to the extent of duplicating words and sentences, testify to Coe's great sense of indebtedness to Rosamond Lehmann for her style, tone and emotional commitment.

Like Lehmann, Gill is known to have had ominous experiences, 'clairvoyant episodes, intimations of the supernatural', such as a vision of her grandparents' ghosts, as recorded in the short story 'Ivy and her Nonsense' (2005a, 4) and *The Rain Before it Falls* (3). Having noticed that tragic patterns inevitably recur in her family, she postulates that there are no coincidences: 'Nothing was random, after all. There was a pattern' (276). One may refer to the case of the dog which inexplicably runs away from Beatrix in 1945 (77–8), echoed by another dog running away from Imogen some fifty years later (275). According to Charlotte Moore, the escaping dog is 'an emblem of the failure of fidelity and commitment which taints each succeeding generation' (58). Such patterning is common in Coe's novels: they are often built around what may only seem like coincidences and the meaningful repetition of phrases, sentences or events. In *The Rain Before it Falls*, the patterning is symbolized by a piece of music played by Gill's daughter, Catharine, half-way through the book, and inspired by Theo Travis's multi-tracked flute soundscapes on his album *Slow Life* (2003) as mentioned in the preliminary note. The concert interrupts Gill and her daughters' listening to Rosamond's tapes and thus provides a musical interlude. The location in a church in the West End of London recalls 'the church where Rosamond and Rebecca had attended their first concert together' more than half a century before (149), a 'coincidence' that makes Gill's 'skin tingle' (150). Catharine plays two single notes on her flute and then a phrase; the music is recorded instantaneously and then repeated back, while Catharine continues to play, thus creating 'loops of sounds … shifting in and out of phase with each other' (150). This sense of repetition with a difference, or incremental repetition, is a powerful musical allegory of the narrative construction of the book and of the hereditary patterns of love withheld or begrudged in the lives of four generations of women.

Coe's admiration for Lehmann extends more generally to her 'extraordinary gift for description, for evoking the tones and textures of the material world; an exceptionally sophisticated approach to structure …; and, above all, an astonishing, unembarrassed emotionality' (2013d). As Coe remarks, while 'there had been very little visual detail' in his previous novels which relied much more on dialogue (in Guignery, 2013, 32), in *The Rain Before it Falls* the story emerges from visual descriptions as Rosamond meticulously describes twenty photographs to a blind (and absent) woman, focusing on 'colours, shapes, buildings, landscapes, bodies, faces' (230). The novel is also marked by an emotional and nostalgic tone, as well as a sensitive portrayal of female characters, a quality shared by contemporary male novelists such as Ian McEwan in *On Chesil Beach* or Graham Swift in *Tomorrow*, both published in the same year as Coe's novel. Beyond Lehmann, *The Rain*

Before it Falls is an homage to the female novelists of the Virago Modern Classics imprint. Their books 'adumbrated the multiple confinements – psychological, political and economic – women experienced in the separate domestic sphere of (mainly) well-born British life' and *The Rain Before it Falls* follows in the steps of that great tradition (Lehmann, Chris, 26). Coe recalls in particular reading Dorothy Richardson's sequence *Pilgrimage* which had a profound influence on him: 'at a time when I was … struggling to find my own voice as a novelist, Dorothy Richardson flung open a door onto a new world of possibility' (2013d). He particularly values her 'deliberately elliptical narrative style', moving not 'in conventional linear chronology but rather sideways and by accretion' (in Lehmann, Chris, 26). In *The Rain Before it Falls,* although Rosamond's description of photographs follows a chronological order, she leaves ellipses of several years and regularly moves backwards and forwards to connect events and characters over the years and generations.

Another hint at the Virago novelists is to be found in the reference to the real-life shooting in Shropshire of the film *Gone to Earth* by Michael Powell, with Jennifer Jones and David Farrar, in which the fictional characters Rosamond and Beatrix played extras (in the second sequence of the actual film, two extras appear exactly as the invented cousins are described in the novel and go through the same motions, one piece of fiction thus drawing from another, as in *What a Carve Up!*). The film is adapted from a novel of the same title dating from 1917 by Mary Webb – 'the unofficial poet laureate of Western Shropshire' according to Coe (2013d) – three of whose novels had been reprinted by Virago. One may also suggest a comparison with May Sinclair's *The Life and Death of Harriett Frean* (1922), a short novel that encompasses the heroine's life from birth to death in 'pitiless economy', and 'looks unsparingly at the moral degeneration of one woman as her heart hardens into a protective bitterness' (Coe, 2013d). Coe notes that in Sinclair's novel 'the ageing process seems to become more and more remorseless and inevitable' (in Guignery, 2013, 31), a description that also applies to Coe's novel as the reader knows from the start that Rosamond is dead. A short novel that covers a long period of time – from 1941 to 2007 – *The Rain Before it Falls,* just like Sinclair's book, gives an 'incredible sense of time passing and time accelerating' (Coe in Guignery, 2013, 31). Through these numerous intertextual echoes, Coe has managed to bring together in his novel several members of a literary family he particularly values.

The novel finds its origin in an authentic encounter with a mysterious blind girl at a wedding near Birmingham in the late 1980s (in Guignery, 2013, 30), as well as in Coe's own nostalgia for the time he spent as a child with his grandparents in Shropshire. For the first part of the narrative, Coe drew on his parents' and grandparents' photograph albums, and particularly on the family farmhouse which becomes Warden Farm in the novel and which 'performs a similar symbolic function to [the fictional estate] Manderley in Daphne du Maurier's *Rebecca* [1938]' (Coe in Guignery, 2013, 32). In both books, the house becomes a character, an atmosphere, and is the conveyor and repository of diverse emotions across generations. It is certainly no coincidence that Coe should have chosen to refer to *Rebecca* which was republished by Virago, all the more as it is the name of Rosamond's lifelong companion in Coe's novel, of the narrator in Lehmann's *The Ballad and the Source*, and of Mortimer's wife in *What a Carve Up!*, in which the family mansion also holds a central place.

As a teenager, Coe was fascinated by Marcel Proust (whom he hadn't read yet), whose novels he imagined solving 'all the impossible riddles about loss, memory and the passing of time'; he too 'wanted to write a huge novel – a series of novels – which would follow a group of characters over time, exploring the complex relationships between their aspirations and reality, between real experience and the memories that subsequently moulded and falsified it' (Coe, 2015b). Several years later, he 'conceived of a series of interlinked stories and novellas and novels which might have the general title *An Easterly Wind*'. He 'imagined a novel which would begin with a family party, in the garden of a house on the outskirts of Birmingham, where the attention of the guest would be drawn to a young, fair-haired girl who would be blind, and whose relationship to the other family members would not at first be understood' (Website, *Rain*). The project, now called *Unrest*, was abandoned for a while until Coe wrote the short story 'Ivy and her Nonsense' in 1990, which focuses on a Christmas party in a Shropshire house and introduces the characters of Gill and her brother, but also Aunt Ivy and Uncle Owen, who reappear in *The Rain Before it Falls*, with Gill and David as Rosamond's niece and nephew. In 'Ivy and her Nonsense', David (who is also the narrator of the short story 'Pentatonic') finds a 'small wooden box filled with Kodak slides' and sees on the prints 'forgotten holidays, forgotten gardens, forgotten family cars, forgotten relatives' (2005a, 6), just as Rosamond will base her recollection on twenty photographs from the past. In 'Pentatonic', David's equivalent of Proust's madeleine is a pentatonic tune he composed at the age of ten – 'the only thing left of that time' (Coe, 2014a) – as well as a photograph of himself, his sister Gill, his daughter Amy, and Gill's daughters Catharine and Elizabeth, taken near his grandparents' old house, and which has gone missing, a sure sign that 'everything just … slips away' (Coe, 2014a).

Several precise details from 'Ivy and her Nonsense' reappear in Rosamond's description of the fifteenth photograph in *The Rain Before it Falls,* such as the fact that there were 11 of them at the kitchen table, that David's hat was too big for him and had slid down over his eyes, that David's grandmother (Rosamond's mother) seemed remote and preoccupied after completing a period of jury service (2005a, 7; 2007a, 195, 203). Both narrators (David and Rosamond) remember playing charades and going to church to attend midnight communion (2005a, 10, 14; 2007a, 203). Such connections point to Coe's subtle weaving together of threads, which the alert reader can identify. Coe explains in an interview that when he wrote *The Rain Before it Falls,* he 'created a big family dynasty' and had 'a big family tree planned out' (in Armitstead). From then on, *Unrest* developed, with David narrating 'Pentatonic', 'Rotary Park' focusing on Rosamond's cousin, Beatrix (who has renamed herself Annie), after she moved to Canada in 1967, and *Expo 58,* centring on Rosamond's brother-in-law, Thomas. As Coe remarks: 'I like the idea that these books coexist independently but they also have a relationship to each other' (in Armitstead). Both intertextuality (echoes of other books and authors) and intratextuality (echoes of one's own books) coexist in Coe's work, confirming that any text is an 'echo chamber' as Roland Barthes suggested (1975, 78).

In comparison with his previous long novels or 'epics', Coe called *The Rain Before it Falls* a 'micro novel' because it is 'about the relationships within one particular family, and it doesn't really take any account of historical forces at all' (in Tew, 2008, 46). It is certainly true that individual stories prevail over history in the novel, all the more as Rosamond admits that she is 'capable of, but not interested in, understanding the events that were unfolding around [her] in the wider world' (74). And yet, the first photograph enables Rosamond to reflect on a traumatic historical moment in Britain, 'the evacuation of children during the Second World War' (38). She recalls that at the very beginning of the war, more than a million children 'were taken away from their parents by train in the space of a few days' (38). Among them was Rosamond's friend Gracie, and the former can only imagine the evacuee's sense of abandonment at the separation from her parents and friends. When Gracie comes back home, one detail encapsulates the trauma of her evacuation: 'she spoke, by then, with a terrible stammer' (42). When Rosamond herself is evacuated, she is sent to her aunt and uncle's in the countryside and though they are not strangers, they treat her as 'the unwanted guest, the evacuee' (53) and Rosamond soon feels 'a sense of loneliness and homesickness … impossible to describe' (55). These painful reminiscences echo B.S. Johnson's own distressing memories of his evacuation in 1941, as recorded in *Trawl* (1966) and also in the accounts of others in the edited volume *The Evacuees* (1968) in which he wonders 'whether the number of lives saved was worth the psychological damage to several million schoolchildren' (20). In *The Terrible Privacy of Maxwell Sim,* Max notices the exit for 'High Wycombe' (144) on the motorway, the town where Johnson himself was evacuated during the war (Coe, 2004b, 47–8), as recorded in *Trawl* (54).

In *The Rain Before it Falls,* Rosamond briefly refers to the dispiriting news from abroad during the winter of 1944–45 (73–4) and then makes an allusion to London in the early 1950s: 'the signs of war damage, and subsequent attempts at reconstruction, were everywhere' (123). The psychological wounds and the emotional dislocation on which the novel focuses are less directly related to the consequences of the war than to the effects of mothers' indifference to or abuse of their daughters over several generations. And yet, by telling the lives of a woman and a family, Rosamond also gives an insight into those of a house (Warden Farm) and a county (Shropshire), if not a country. In *The Terrible Privacy of Maxwell Sim,* a character also points to the incredible repository of memories an elderly lady (in this case Miss Erith) can become: 'Imagine the changes she must have seen in her lifetime. Someone should fetch a tape recorder and keep her story for posterity. … stories like hers need to be remembered, don't you think? Otherwise, England has forgotten its own past' (192).

The preservation of England's national history and of one's personal story is a recurrent concern of contemporary British novels, but in *The Rain Before it Falls*, Rosamond's repeated use of the words 'story' and 'narrative' points to the affinities of her monologue with fiction. She tells Imogen she wants to give her 'a sense of [her] own history' (32), and for that purpose she will tell her 'the story of [her] own life' (33). Imogen's 'history', inscribed in the successive dramas of several generations of women, will thus emerge from Rosamond's 'story', a significant shift in vocabulary. A similar impulse makes Rosamond think that she should tell Thea the story of her own friendship with Thea's mother Beatrix – 'Perhaps if words – phrases – gestures – were not enough, then *narrative* was what Thea needed' (208, emphasis in the original) – but Thea is not interested in that story and will not let Rosamond indulge in her own storytelling. Frequently, Rosamond draws attention to her control of the narrative and her exclusion of irrelevant stories. When she is tempted to talk more about her relationship with Rebecca, her early love, she interrupts herself: 'I must stop thinking about Rebecca; it is the story of me and Beatrix I am meant to be telling' (173). When she refers to the 'fanciful and macabre legends' of the Stiperstones in south Shropshire, she uses the word 'story' again, as though putting these myths and her own story on the same level, but she soon discards those legends: 'now is perhaps not the time to elaborate upon those stories. I have my own story to tell' (95). Rosamond also takes on the attributes of the storyteller and uses the strategies of fiction writing when she imagines scenes she could not have attended, such as her friend's evacuation at the beginning of the war – 'I can only imagine' (41) – or the growing fondness between Beatrix and Jack: 'This is how I imagine it happened' (111).

In addition, Rosamond is skilful at creating suspense through elliptic prolepses, for instance when looking at a picture of Beatrix and herself – 'Both girls are smiling, broadly and happily, with no intimation of the disaster that is about to befall them' (71) – or when she refers to Thea in her pram, 'unaware of the turns her narrative is about to take' (96) – the term 'narrative' pointing towards fiction again. When Rosamond gets to the eighteenth picture, she is finally ready to tell Imogen 'the dreadful story that lies behind it' (228), the adjective preparing the reader for further drama – or melodrama. Like a seasoned story-teller, Rosamond teases and possibly frustrates the reader when introducing characters or topics without developing them any further for the time being: 'But I will come to the children later' (43); 'I shall explain what I mean by that shortly' (69); 'I have not yet told you who Rebecca was, and that, too, must wait its turn' (95); 'I will explain all of this in due course' (105). As a whole, Rosamond is very conscious and careful as to the construction of her story, and wants to impose a strict and reassuring frame through the choice of twenty photographs, arranged in a chronological order. Sometimes however, she cannot prevent her mind from digressing or getting ahead, thus disrupting the linearity of her narrative, and like the narrators of Fielding and Sterne she comments on the fragile construction of her tale: 'I am wandering from the point again …' (49); 'I have digressed from my task of describing this photograph' (69); 'Now I'm getting ahead of myself again' (219); 'How difficult it is to tell you all these things in the right order. … everything has gone higgledy-piggledy' (224). Although she ends up suspecting (as B.S. Johnson did) that 'perhaps chaos and randomness are the natural order of things' (224), Rosamond strives to limit digressions and maintain control over her narrative: 'I must get a grip on myself' (211). For that purpose she systematically reminds the reader of the number of the photograph she is describing, thus letting him/her know about the progression of her narrative. She even anticipates the potential exhaustion of Imogen and the reader/listener: 'Five more to go, then. Thank goodness! I am growing tired of this story, and you must be exhausted, listening to me chatter on for hours on end' (211). Through such comments, Rosamond constantly keeps her audience aware of her role as storyteller in charge of her narrative, however taxing it may be. In *The Terrible Privacy of Maxwell Sim*, Max will also adopt a spontaneous and easy tone, addressing the reader directly.

The tone of the embedded narrative in *The Rain Before it Falls* is thus deliberately oral as Rosamond regularly addresses Imogen as 'you', and sometimes hesitates, forgets things or repeats herself. The effect is one of spontaneity and immediacy, which does not however erase the sense of an impending doom as the reader knows Rosamond committed suicide, and the old lady keeps reminding us that she is nearing the end: 'It will be over now, all over, very soon. A relief all round, I am sure' (211), '[the bottle of whisky] will come in very handy, I am sure, in the short time that is left to me now' (238). The voice we 'hear' is thus that of a dead woman, a voice from beyond the grave which recalls the first (deceptive) sentence of another confessional novel, Graham Swift's *Ever After* (1992): 'These are, I should warn you, the words of a dead man' (1). Once Rosamond's tale is over, the reader witnesses her drink whisky and swallow pills, wondering 'how quickly they will work' (257). As in B.S. Johnson's *House Mother Normal* where blanks contaminate the page as the character of Rosetta Stone loses consciousness and eventually dies, Rosamond's discourse becomes disjointed, made up of shorter and shorter sentences or merely interjections, the blanks gaining ground: 'Not dark. Not here. Sunlight. Blue. Ceru ... The lake ...' (258). As she gradually slips into unconsciousness, her mind moves backwards to memories of Rebecca and Thea in the summer of 1955: 'A lake, first of all. Clear blue sky, absolutely cloudless. A rich cerulean blue' (155). The final blank on the page (259) is a mimetic representation of her final loss of consciousness and death.

Once Rosamond has died, a new voice takes over, in a short chapter written in italics: it is Thea's interior monologue as she comes back to Shropshire in 2007, six months after Rosamond died. Thea's internal voice in a stream-of-consciousness mode resembles Rosamond's in the last two pages of her monologue: nominal sentences predominate, thoughts are juxtaposed, and the short paragraphs are separated by blanks. In both cases, the voice is surreal. When the frame story in third-person narration takes control again, solid blocks of paragraphs reappear. But Thea's voice is to be heard a second time, though muted again, through the letter she sent Gill, which is reproduced. This written voice gathers all the threads of the narrative and provides a tragic closure with the revelation of Imogen's death some fifteen years before. Throughout the novel, the recorded voice of a dead woman, as 'English and undemonstrative' (24) as the Shropshire landscape, was therefore addressing a dead girl by describing still shots or recorded images, an exchange between spectres in which distance seems to be repeatedly doubled. The reader, as well as Gill and her daughters, are all made to realize they have been in effect eavesdropping on a spectral monologue, and the underlying implication is of a violation of the privacy of an intimate and painful confession.

Coe said that *The Rain Before it Falls* was his 'easiest book because it had no comedy at all' (in Charnock), and it is indeed a melancholy novel about loss – thus echoing *The House of Sleep* – as well as a book about trauma, which sometimes veers towards the melodramatic. Coe loves melodrama (in Guignery, 2013, 33), and says he has 'always seen life itself as being full of melodrama', so that it maybe only 'adds to [the book's] realism' (2013d). According to Paul Gilroy, the novel testifies to 'the need for and the difficulty of a systematic working through of the past' (201). To borrow a line from a poem in Coe's *Say Hi to the Rivers and the Mountains*, Rosamond is '*building on the past because this future cannot last for long*'. Trauma takes various forms in the novel (war evacuation, lack of love, abuse, separation, abandonment, psychological and physical violence, death …) and is made more poignant by the first-person narrative and the confessional mode. Nearing the end of her life, Rosamond is driven by both a desire and a reluctance to tell, what Beckett in *The Unnamable* (1958) called 'the inability to speak, the inability to be silent' (153). On the one hand, she needs to relieve herself of a burden by telling Imogen the story of the feckless women in her family, and thus explain how the girl came to be blind: 'The only important thing, at this stage, is that I do my duty: that I repay what is owed to you' (228). It almost sounds as if Rosamond were talking to a priest and looking for absolution, though one wonders what sin could drive her to that confession.

On the other hand, the elderly lady sometimes assumes the figure of the reluctant narrator, pointing to the limitations of language when it comes to recalling painful or emotional memories. When she nostalgically evokes her mother (one of the absent figures of the narrative), she writes: 'These things have resonance for me … but it's terribly hard to convey that, in words' (37). In the same way, Rosamond cannot 'put a name' to the 'shadowy, nebulous emotion' she felt – somewhere between regret and jealousy – on the day Beatrix got married. The photograph replaces words: 'the picture, the picture itself, is far more expressive than the words I can find to describe it' (86). Later on, when she is about to narrate the episode of Thea's violence against her daughter, she becomes hesitant – 'I find myself lost for words. … *words fail me*' (230) – and she also feels defeated when she tries to describe Thea's picture in the newspaper – 'Her expression …? Well, that is not easy to describe' (229) – or Thea in prison: 'Your mother looked … Well, once again, words are inadequate' (232). The emotion is sometimes so overwhelming that Rosamond needs to pause her recording, for instance after telling the story of how Beatrix drove a knife repeatedly into Thea's door – 'I think I need a few moments' rest, after telling you all that' (189) – or when she comes to the painful revelation of the origin of Imogen's blindness – 'I find myself having to tell you the most difficult thing of all, and I simply don't know where to begin. Let me turn this machine off for a moment, and allow myself a little while to reflect' (230) – or when she was refused the adoption of Imogen: 'Time to turn off the tape again. I'm sorry. I thought I had more self-control than this' (237). These pauses, marked by typographical blanks or dots, and her loss of adequate words are the equivalent of aposiopeses, rhetorical ways of suggesting a reluctance to tell or to confess. In *The Terrible Privacy of Maxwell Sim*, when Max is about to confess his shameful invention of a fake female identity in order to communicate with his ex-wife on the internet, he likewise becomes hesitant: 'I wasn't going to talk about it here but, well, I suppose the idea is that I tell you the whole story, warts and all, so I can't very well leave it out' (85); 'I'm digressing so much, I suppose, in order to put off telling you the really shameful thing' (87). Contrarily, when Clive makes a pause in his letter before telling the story of Donald Crowhurst – 'excuse me for a moment while I go and pour myself another cup of coffee' (46) – the interruption gives a comfortable feeling to the scene and arouses the reader's curiosity.

In *The Rain Before it Falls*, when Rosamond reveals 'It was your mother who blinded you' (230), the reader may wonder about the elderly lady's motives for disclosing this shocking information which Imogen had wiped from her memory: 'Do you remember that happening? They told me that you didn't, that you had blanked it out. That you remembered other things, things that happened to you before then; but that day, that morning, that … attack – no' (231). Why then would Rosamond want to bring the trauma back to the surface when Imogen had chosen to bury it deep? Rosamond asks herself that very question when she is about to divulge the loathsome content of Thea's letter – '(why on earth am I telling you this? It can do nothing but hurt you)' (247) – but the temporary self-doubt is only contained between brackets and Rosamond continues with her unpleasant revelation. One also wonders why she regularly implies that Imogen's foster family has not been giving her the proper love and attention, while Thea's letter in the last chapter contrarily suggests that

Imogen seemed happy with her new family in Canada. Rosamond conceives of herself as 'this secretive, self-effacing, benevolent agency, plotting behind the scenes in order to engineer climactic reunions and miraculous healing of wounds' (238), and may be a contemporary avatar of the *deus ex machina* of Victorian novels. However her insistent involvement may also be considered harmful to Imogen's recovery, as suggested by her new family and by Ruth herself, Rosamond's companion (252–3).

One may speculate that Rosamond's attachment to Imogen is a way to prolong her relationship with Beatrix and conjure up the unrequited love she used to feel for her cousin. When Beatrix accuses Rosamond of touching her daughter Thea while lying next to her in bed, the accusation seems outrageous, and yet Rosamond's last musings in that chapter are about 'the pressure of her body' (194), probably a reminder of 'the warmth of Beatrix's body' some twenty years earlier when they were both teenagers (61) and Rosamond 'pressed [her]self against her' (142). One therefore cannot help but wonder about the true motives behind Rosamond's confession (as her admission is probably as much about her unrequited love for Beatrix as about the other female characters), and even sometimes doubt her reliability as a narrator, all the more as she admits that she sometimes imagines scenes when her memory fails her. For instance, when she nostalgically recalls a particular morning as a teenager when she found Beatrix's bed empty next to hers, she confesses: 'Actually, I am allowing my imagination to run away with me again. Whether I looked across, on that first morning, and saw Bea's empty bed, I really cannot say' (51). When she writes about the sun setting on the countryside in Shropshire, she admits: 'But I think this is something I am now imagining, not a memory at all' (45–6). Coe himself said he had conceived Rosamond as 'a totally reliable narrator': according to him, the fact that she meditates on the reliability of her memory 'is an indication that she is being honest with the reader and that she is flagging up the fact that what she is about to say might not be the whole truth' (in Guignery, 2013, 35). However, she often appears as a manipulative and unreliable narrator, with motives of her own for telling the story.

In Coe's first novel, *The Accidental Woman*, the narrator remarked: 'We all have our memories, we hoard them up and shape them to our requirements. We do things simply so that one day, it may be the next, we shall have the pleasure of remembering them' (9). In *The Rain Before it Falls,* the journey into Rosamond's past (an impossible return to origins, as the title suggests) is an ideal opportunity for Coe to reflect on the vagaries of memory, the subjectivity of knowledge and the elusiveness of truth, a recurrent concern in novels by other contemporary British writers such as Julian Barnes, Kazuo Ishiguro or Graham Swift. Over time, Rosamond becomes aware of the multiplicity of truths, for example when the same roads seem to her 'utterly familiar' and at the same time, 'utterly strange and other-worldly'. She concludes: 'sometimes, it is possible – even necessary – to entertain contradictory ideas; to accept the truth of two things that flatly contradict each other' (201), a premise she will repeat later on: 'life only starts to make sense when you realize that sometimes – often – all the time – two completely contradictory ideas can be true' (249).

One's memory can obviously play tricks and affect truth, and Rosamond regularly points to its fragility: '"The mind has fuses," as somebody once said' (231). That 'someone' is the narrator of B.S. Johnson's *The Unfortunates,* when reflecting on the fallibility of memory: 'I fail to remember, the mind has fuses' ('Then they had moved', 5). He is echoed by Rolf in *The Closed Circle,* who says he cannot remember the episode of Paul saving him from drowning as a child – 'The mind has fuses, I suppose' (163) – but also by Max in *The Terrible Privacy of Maxwell Sim* when he refuses to recall the painful day his wife and daughter left him: 'human beings have mechanisms for dealing with that kind of thing – *the mind has fuses*' (207). Rosamond's earliest memories for her part are sensory ones: the play of colours on a small frosted window, 'like a kaleidoscope', 'the sweep of [her] mother's broom near by, behind [her], on the lino in the kitchen'. For her, the 'two things – the image and the sound – go together in [her] memory' (37). Remembering her aunt is also linked to senses: 'as soon as I think of her laugh, as if by some process of sensory association, I find myself remembering her smell. Strange how so few of our strongest memories are visual' (44). Later on, she remarks: 'The more I look at Ivy's face in this photograph, the more it serves to remind me, not of what she used to look like, but of her smell, and the sound of her voice' (46). It might be because Imogen is blind that Rosamond focuses so much on other senses, even though the foundation of her whole endeavour is visual since it is built around photographs.

Photographs feature regularly in Coe's fiction and are either deceptive or revelatory. In *The Dwarves of Death*, the album cover shows a woman flanked by two disquieting dwarves, who turn out to be that woman's young and innocent daughters (195). In *The House of Sleep*, Terry is obsessed with the movie-still of a woman pointing to a hospital (296, 316), which Robert will interpret as the sign that he should change gender. In *The Rotters' Club*, the picture of two lovers smiling strikes by its agelessness: 'There was nothing transitory, nothing evanescent about those smiles' (117), while another snapshot of the same two lovers with a third person half looking at them reveals a violation of their intimacy: 'It was an eloquent photograph. It told its unhappy story concisely, and without ambiguity' (117). In *The Terrible Privacy of Maxwell Sim*, the snapshot of two teenagers on a summer holiday in 1976 ('the folded photograph') reveals disquieting facts about Max's father. In *The Rain Before it Falls*, photographs become a full-blown narrative device. The description of clothes and haircuts help date the photographs; for instance in a 1945 snapshot: 'Most of the men are wearing flat caps – this is one of the things that dates the photograph – and that peculiar style of trouser that was so popular then' (73). But mostly, the photographs are considered valuable by Rosamond 'insofar as they corroborate [her] failing memory': 'They are the proof that the things I remember – some of the things I remember – really happened, and are not phantom memories or fantasies, imaginings' (39). As Roland Barthes argues in *Camera Lucida. Reflections on Photography* (1980), the essence or '*noeme*' of photography is 'That-has-been' (77), i.e. it certifies that '*the thing has been there*' (76); the photograph, as a 'certificate of presence' (87), is self-authenticating, attesting that the referent 'has indeed existed' (82): 'the *necessarily* real thing … has been placed before the lens' (76). Susan Sontag agrees that 'there is always a presumption that something exists, or did exist, which is like what's in the picture' (2001, 5). For Rosalind Krauss, drawing on C.S. Peirce's terminology, photography has a continuous, immediate, physical, concrete, and direct link with the referent, hence its value as index, whereas sketches and paintings, which one can draw from memory or imagination, are iconic in that they are only related to the referent through visual resemblance and imitation (77). This is the case of Imogen's portrait drawn by Ruth from snapshots of the little girl (which is therefore the representation and interpretation of other representations). Although Rosamond finds the painting truthful and faithful, Ruth argues that it is 'just a likeness' (245), probably because Ruth herself 'had a dislike of pure realism, in literature as well as art' (243).

If photographs authenticate one's memories, one may wonder like Rosamond: 'But what of the memories for which there are no pictures, no corroborations, no proof?' (39). Are these memories unreliable or less valuable than those which are mediated by photography? Rosamond seems to find them more expressive than snapshots: 'the images we remember, the ones we carry inside our heads, can be more vivid than anything a camera is able to preserve on film' (80). For indeed, the certificate of presence that photography offers is not synonymous with accuracy or transparency, concepts which, in any case, have become highly suspect in the postmodern era. As Susan Sontag argues, 'the photographic image ... cannot be simply a transparency of something that happened. It is always the image that someone chose; to photograph is to frame, and to frame is to exclude' (2003, 46). In addition, the photograph only offers a surface and never reveals the buried layers. For instance, when Elizabeth looks at a picture of her mother Gill, she wishes 'it could tell her what her mother might have been thinking, or feeling, at this momentous party, so soon after her marriage, so newly pregnant. Why did photographs – family photographs – make everyone appear so unreadable? What hopes, what secret anxieties lay behind that seemingly confident tilt of her mother's face, her mouth slipping into its characteristic, slightly crooked smile?' (14). The photographs not only fail to give access to the subject's inner thoughts, they are also deceptive in that they may only offer the illusion of happiness and hide true emotions behind performed smiles: 'everybody smiles for photographs – that's one of the reasons you should never trust them' (214). In *The Closed Circle,* Claire refers to a photograph of her mother and remarks: 'She was smiling the unknowable smile that people wear for the camera' (95). In *The Rain Before it Falls,* the subjects smile in the snapshot of Rebecca's graduation ceremony, even though Rosamond and Rebecca have just had a major quarrel. Rosamond remarks:

> Normally I don't like photographs of formal occasions. They are even more mendacious than usual. This next picture ... is a good

> example, because although it seems to record an occasion with perfect fidelity, it actually gives no indication of what was going through the minds of the people who were there. There is, if you like, the 'official' interpretation of the picture, and behind it, there is the unofficial, authentic version.
>
> (130)

Such formal photographs are deprived of what Barthes calls the '*punctum*' (27), a striking detail that captures the eye of the beholder and initiates a personal response. Instead, they are '*unary photographs*' (40) which transform reality 'without doubling it, without making it vacillate' (41), 'docile' pictures, 'invested by a simple *studium*' (49), a general field of cultural recognition marked by polite interest, 'unconcerned desire' and 'inconsequential taste' (27). In addition, these photographs are misleading because the subjects assume a pose and a role. As Barthes points out, 'once I feel myself observed by the lens, everything changes: I constitute myself in the process of "posing," I instantaneously make another body for myself, I transform myself in advance into an image' (10); and therefore, each time he is photographed, he 'invariably suffer[s] from a sensation of inauthenticity, sometimes of imposture' (14).

Rosamond becomes even more upset with a later picture of Beatrix, her children and herself at the beach, depicting an occasion when Beatrix was obnoxious and violent towards her daughter: 'The smiles on our faces nauseate me ... What a deceitful thing a photograph is. They say that memory plays tricks on one. Not nearly as much as a photograph does, in my view' (193). Rosamond has come to trust her memory more than the visual signs. Many of the photographs described in the novel give the illusion of a harmonious and cheerful family through several generations, but it is a fraudulent construction. According to Susan Sontag, 'through photographs, each family constructs a portrait-chronicle of itself – a portable kit of images that bears witness to its connectedness' (8). That connectedness is belied by Rosamond's narrative, which also points out that a photograph is 'a poor thing, really' because it 'can only capture one moment, out of millions of moments, in the life of a person, or the life of a house' (38–9). While Rosamond's tale provides duration, transitions and a sense of continuity over the years, photographs stop time and freeze movement, as, for instance, when people are ice-skating: 'They all look rather poignant like this, the way the photograph has reduced them to an unnatural stillness, just when they are doing something as dynamic and joyful as ice-skating' (73). Rosamond compares them to the 'figures embalmed in the molten lava at Pompeii' (73), and thus to dead subjects. According to Barthes, death is the '*eidos*' (92) of photography: immediately after the click of the shutter, the subject is lost forever, transformed into an object and the photograph testifies to its absolute pastness, its death as a subject (15). The twenty photographs described by Rosamond actually show people who are almost all dead by the end of the narrative, leaving the reader with a sense of loss similar to the one felt by Gill after she learns her daughter's boyfriend has left her – 'Catharine's sense of loss and abandonment was transmitting itself, stealing into her mother's heart' (277) – but which may also be similar to the 'atmosphere of loss and regret and something to do with the past that was somehow sinister and frightening', which is to be found in the poetry of Maxwell Sim's father (172).

While *The Rain Before it Falls* is a melancholy book concerned with the painful experiences of mothers and daughters, in which fathers and husbands are conspicuous by their absence, *The Terrible Privacy of Maxwell Sim* and *Expo 58* revert to a semi-comic mode and to Coe's favourite figure of the depressed and ordinary male character, as the next chapter will show.

7

EVERYMAN ON THE ROAD AND ABROAD: *THE TERRIBLE PRIVACY OF MAXWELL SIM* AND *EXPO 58*

While *The Rain Before it Falls* offered a retrospective of 60 years of a woman's life and *The House of Sleep* followed the destiny of a group of young people over two decades, Coe's most recent novels, *The Terrible Privacy of Maxwell Sim* (2010) and *Expo 58* (2013), focus on only one year – 2009 and 1958 respectively – and on the trajectory of ordinary men, on the road and abroad. Published in 2010, *The Terrible Privacy of Maxwell Sim*, had its origins twenty years earlier when Coe 'jotted down some ideas for a novel about a travelling salesman driving the length and breadth of Britain's motorway network' (Website, *Sim*). Coe describes his ninth novel as both a picaresque novel indebted to Fielding's *Joseph Andrews* and *Tom Jones* (Website, *Sim*) and a 'British "road movie", finding narrative interest in a journey along the M40, the A5192 and the A74(M)' (in Laity), a novel which was influenced by Lindsay Anderson's 1973 epic film *O Lucky Man!*. In an essay on Anderson, Coe compares the film to Jonathan Swift's *Gulliver's Travels* and describes it as 'a modern version of *Candide* or *The Pilgrim's Progress*, in which a naïve hero journeys through the cities and along the motorways of 70s Britain, looking for enlightenment and encountering a series of strange adventures' (2013d). Similarly, like the hero (or anti-hero) of an epic, Maxwell Sim 'undertakes a journey; faces diverse situations and characters; and, learning from his experiences, comes to some moral revelation by the end of the work' (Hoskin). At the end of the book Max himself sums up all his adventures of the last two months, and tries to understand their meaning. He moves from one cliché – 'if my recent experiences had taught me anything, they had taught me a lesson about the cruelty of the world' (326) – to another – 'maybe what I had really learned (or started to learn) was something about myself, about my own nature and my own problems' (326–7), and yet these stereotypes may well prove true. The book itself is divided into parts that chart Max's journey from Australia to England and Scotland, and back to Australia, a circular voyage that seems to belie any sense of teleology and progress. Lindsay Ashworth, the PR officer of Guest Toothbrushes, Max's employer, calls Max's trip a '*quest*', a 'journey', a 'voyage of discovery' (101), and conjures up grand images of the *Odyssey*, *Lord of the Rings*, and King Arthur and the Holy Grail. As for Max, he tells his GPS they are 'going on a sentimental journey' (153), seemingly unaware he is echoing Laurence Sterne.

The novel draws from the real-life experience of Donald Crowhurst, a British engineer who set out on an around-the-world voyage on 31 October 1968, but ended up faking his exploit, writing down a false account of the journey in his logbooks. The first embedded narrative, 'The Misfit', relates Crowhurst's intense isolation in the 'terrible privacy' of his tiny cabin (54, 59, 285), thereby announcing Max's own solitary journey. As the novel develops, Max, who has been given 'an old hardback copy of Ron Hall and Nicholas Tomalin's book, *The Strange Voyage of Donald Crowhurst*, and a DVD of *Deep Water*, the feature-length documentary that had recently been made about his journey' (115), identifies more and more with Crowhurst. Max's Toyota Prius, 'sleek, modern and radically innovative' (104), is described in the same terms as Crowhurst's boat (51), and when Max meets Alison, he explains to her 'all the parallels I had started to see between his situation and mine, and how strongly I was coming to identify with him' (236).

However, on reading Tomalin and Hall's book, differences appear between the two men: Crowhurst, both as a child and as an adult in the RAF and then as entrepreneur, is presented as 'ebullient, sharp with his tongue', 'brilliant with his hands' (23), 'always the wildest, bravest in any group, a compulsive risk-taker and defier of authority' (27), 'a real swashbuckler' (64), 'determined, confident' (81). Max, on the other hand, like Michael in *What a Carve Up!*, Benjamin in *The Rotters' Club* and *The Closed Circle*, and Thomas Foley in *Expo 58*, is an ordinary suburban man, 'perpetually nervous and uncertain' (119), a depressed Everyman whose ex-wife used to torment herself with 'the riddle of his unhappiness, his maladjustment, his sense of being forever ill at ease in the world' (131). Reflecting on his childhood, Max remarks that there 'was nothing much to shout about. Like everything else about me, I suppose. Unexceptional' (153). Echoing the comic epigraph from *The Fall and Rise of Reginald Perrin*, Max imagines what should be written on his gravestone: 'Here lies Maxwell Sim. He was a pretty ordinary bloke really' (154), later on turning it into the more gloomy: 'the most unnecessary person ever born' (286). Coe explains that in this novel, his ambition was 'to find a kind of mystery and romance and strangeness at the heart of the deeply ordinary' (Website, *Sim*). This ordinariness (which Coe maybe turns into a literary form in the way Georges Perec did in France) is particularly reflected in the description of places: when Max's father refers to the time he and his wife moved to Rubery, a southern suburb of Birmingham, he talks of 'an anonymous, pebble-dashed, three-bedroom house, in a characterless street of similar houses' (277); when going back to Watford, Max looks at 'the monochrome grimness of urban Hertfordshire' (72); when driving on the M40, Max is struck with boredom: 'There was absolutely nothing to see, nothing to look at'; 'There was countryside on both sides, but it was featureless'; 'These areas are wastelands' (146). While Max finds comfort in impersonal chain restaurants and motorway service stations, where he feels part of 'the business community' (147), an elderly woman laments the fact that 'everything that gives a community its own identity – the local shops, the local pubs' is being taken away and replaced by 'bland, soulless, corporate' businesses which 'play the same music and serve the same beer and the same food' (198) – the same coffee shops whose proliferation Claire deplores in *The Closed Circle* (6).

The novel reflects on the impact of modern technology on our private lives and interrogates such issues as loneliness and the difficulty of establishing ethical relationships with others. Early in the novel, while sitting on the toilet in a restaurant in Sydney, Max incongruously declares: 'that was when it really hit me. The loneliness' (14). The isolation of the noun makes the feeling of loneliness even more definitive, as does the repetition of the adjective in 'I was alone in the world, now, terribly alone' (14); 'I felt suddenly, terribly alone' (139). According to Coe, the 'terrible privacy' of the title refers to 'the two decades of isolated family life – barricaded by the institution of the nuclear family from any real contact with the outside world – which have turned [Max] into the dysfunctional person that he has become' (2013d) – possibly an echo of the defective mother-daughter relationships in *The Rain Before it Falls*. In her essay 'The Folded Photograph', Alison reflects on a family holiday in 1976 and on how Max's father seemed disconnected from his son (an only child) and probably never 'made a connection with him in the first place' (179). This contrasts with Clive (Poppy's uncle) who remembers his childhood in simple terms that suggest warmth and connections: 'Family life, ordinary life. A life surrounded by other people' (58). When Max is having dinner with his father in Sydney in 2009, he remarks: 'If the Chinese woman and her daughter were at one end of the scale of human intimacy, we were right at the other' (17). It is only at the very end of the novel that Max's father finally puts a hand on his son's shoulder: 'It was the first time I could remember him ever doing anything like that' (309).

The fragility of intimacy had already been a central topic in *The Rotters' Club* and *The Closed Circle*, but the recurring terms 'privacy' and 'intimacy' were always used in relation to a fake or failed connection rather than a genuine closeness. In *The Terrible Privacy of Maxwell Sim*, the chasm that used to separate father and son, the self and the other, is reproduced in the relationship between Max and his daughter Lucy. Lucy's mother notices 'the odd paradox of their closeness and separation' (124) during a family holiday. A few years later, when father and daughter, who had once 'lived together in conditions of absolute intimacy' (209), have dinner together, they spend their evening apart, texting absent friends. Max and his wife Carolyn are no better; the last years of their marriage are marked by an 'almost complete lack of communication': 'We seemed to have forgotten the art of talking to each other' (13). This disconnection contrasts with the 'settled, comfortable sort of intimacy' (40), that Max probably deludes himself into feeling, when sitting in 'companionable silence' (40–1) next to Poppy on a plane, or when she later on sleeps by his side, 'the most trusting and intimate thing you can do with another person' (66).

Mostly, however, relationships in the contemporary world are exposed as lacking any genuine human contact, bereft of any ethical relation to alterity, denied of what Emmanuel Levinas described as 'responsiveness to and responsibility for the other' (Gibson, 25). If, according to Derek Attridge, ethics is 'an encounter with alterity' (27–8), the postmodern world depicted in Coe's novel seems deprived of this ethical drive: 'We mill around every day, we rush here and there, we come within inches of touching each other but very little real contact goes on' (8), mankind having 'become very inventive about devising new ways for people to avoid talking to each other' (19). Michael Owen had already experienced that loss of sociability and engagement with other people in *What a Carve Up!* when he went for more than two years without talking to anybody. He told his neighbour: 'in the old days you'd have to have talked to someone: going into shops and things. But now you can do all your shopping in the supermarket, and you can do all your banking by machine' (54).

In the later novel, when Max stops for lunch at a motorway station, he notices: 'at this place, you didn't even have to talk to anyone to get your hamburger. You did it all on your debit card' (149). E. M. Forster's motto 'Only connect' – which Max's wife is fond of repeating and Max identifies as being 'from one of the fancy writers that she was always trying to get me to read' – has been replaced by a contemporary 'Only disconnect' (185). In 1973, B.S. Johnson quoted his friend Philip Pacey who was arguing that telling stories was 'an alternative to real communication … an escape from the challenge of coming to terms with real people' (1973b, 14). In his PhD thesis, Coe referred to D.W. Harding's definition of the novel as an 'ideal conversation' (which might echo Sterne's conversational style) and went on to refer to sociability as 'the recognition of our dependence on, and obligation to consult with, other people' (1986, 171). In the modern world however, new technologies tend to distance people. Coe remembers using his answering machine in the 1980s mainly to screen calls: 'like mobile phones (which put you in touch with people at a distance, but cut you off from the people around you) and VCRs (which turn TV- and film-watching into private rather than communal experiences), the answering machine is another 80s invention that puts up more barriers than it brings down' (2013d). Twenty years later, on his way to an interview, Coe describes himself turning off the CD player of his car, activating the central locking, setting his mobile phone to silent and checking his palmtop for any emails, 'the unthinking technological routines of middle-class British life in the summer of 2004' (2013d). In *The Terrible Privacy of Maxwell Sim*, emails, Facebook, blogs and GPS are tools of alienation and isolation rather than connection with others. Max, whose name evokes the anonymous digits of a SIM card, refers to the Internet as an 'invention which now allowed someone like Caroline to have her closest relationship with someone who was just a figment of my imagination' (90). He later comments on the simulacrum of connectedness it provides: 'the internet is something that puts up barriers between people as much as it connects them' (305). At the same time, these devices have the ability to track people and to deny them any sense of secrecy: 'There was no such thing as privacy any more. We were never really alone' (65). This echoes Jonathan Franzen's collection of essays *How to be Alone* (2002), in which the American writer laments the way mass culture and techno-consumerism impinge on the private sphere.

In Coe's novel, Max refers to his GPS (which he decides to call 'Emma') and declares: 'in Emma, I had found something like the perfect partner' (151); 'Sitting here in my Toyota Prius, with only Emma for company, I was cocooned from the rest of the world' (185). With Emma, Max may be trying to recreate the 'little cocoon of intimacy' (301) he had noticed between a Chinese woman and her daughter, playing cards at a restaurant in Sydney. Max, like his own creator (336), is fascinated by the 'wall of intimacy' and 'protective screen' around mother and daughter (8), 'the connection between them. The pleasure in each other's company. The love and closeness' (213): 'they had become, for me, a sort of totem, a symbol of everything that a real relationship between two human beings should be, at a time when people seemed to be losing the ability to connect with one another, even as technology created more and more ways in which it ought to be possible' (302). Mother-love, according to Levinas, is the most ethical form of affection as it gives priority to the other over one's self: 'In maternity what signifies is a responsibility for others' (75). Buoyed by such a hopeful image of ethical exchange, of communication and care for each other, Max suddenly feels an acute 'need for human contact': 'I wanted to talk. I was desperate to talk' (21), and his words rush out and flood in towards his travelling companion Charles on the plane: 'having said so much to Charlie, having unburdened myself so shamelessly of so many words, a tidal wave of words finally breaking through the floodgates, after months and months of withdrawal from the world, months made long by silence, by lack of human contact' (29). The sentence itself has a tidal potency, but the comic irony is that Max literally bores Charles to death with his flow of words, as his companion dies of a heart attack on the plane. Undeterred, Max continues on his desperate quest towards 'learning not to be scared of intimacy again, not being lonely any more' (283). Max's journey is therefore an emotional quest, which leads him to recognize and accept the alterity and singularity of the other, including his father's homosexuality and eventually his own.

One manifestation of Max's ethical opening towards the other takes the form of the four pieces embedded in the main text, where different voices, tones, genres and alternative stories emerge, in a way that recalls similar devices in *A Touch of Love* and *What a Carve Up!*. Clive's affectionate letter to his niece ('Water: The Misfit') narrates the real story of Donald Crowhurst's fake expedition around the world. Two other pieces in the first person – Alison's essay about privacy violation and her attraction to Max ('Fire: The Folded Photograph') and Harold's memoir about his failed relationship with Roger ('Air: The Rising Sun') – are written in the confessional mode. As for Caroline's autobiographical short story, 'Earth: The Nettle Pit', which was originally published as a separate short story in the *Earth* volume of *Ox-tales: Original Stories from Remarkable Writers* (2009), it is written in the third person, supposedly 'to give it a kind of "distance and objectivity"' (90, 118), but it relates a family holiday in Ireland and retains the real names of the characters, thus giving the reader a different perspective on Max.

The four stories correspond to the four elements, as indicated in the titles, and thus echo the organization of T.S. Eliot's *Four Quartets* – also 'themed around the four elements' (195) – the book Max's father is reading when he meets Roger for the first time (249), the one Max mistakenly remembers as '*String Quartets*' (284) and which Coe had already referred to in *A Touch of Love* (186–7) and *The Rotters' Club* (377). Eliot's insistence on the continuity between past, present and future, on the notion of circular time, memory and repetition is echoed in the novel which unearths traumatic experiences from the past and highlights their impact on the present. When Miss Erith asks Max if he has ever heard of Eliot, he gives a defensive and positive answer, before adding: 'He wrote the lyrics for *Cats*, didn't he?' (195). Max is of course correct: the musical *Cats* is based on Eliot's *Old Possum's Book of Practical Cats* (1939) and was composed by Andrew Lloyd Webber – a composer William despises in *The Dwarves of Death* for his 'facile and unmemorable' music, 'harmonically primitive and melodically derivative' (26). Such a network of references, combining music and literature, but also high and popular culture, is emblematic of Coe's fondness for intermediality and serves to lighten the potentially melodramatic mode.

However, like Terry's friend Kingsley in *The House of Sleep*, Max is regularly mocked for his lack of literary credentials. He admits from the start: 'I hardly ever read novels, never mind trying to write one' (11) – an ironical comment when we surmise that Max is probably writing the very book we are reading – and he repeats the same claim at the end: 'I don't read much fiction' (335). He did however read Jane Austen's *Emma*, which led him to call his GPS by that name for its 'classiness and sophistication', even if he admits he 'hated the book' (150). When his wife suggests he might broaden his horizons by reading contemporary American fiction such as 'one of the Rabbit books' (John Updike's series about a middle-class Everyman called Harry 'Rabbit' Angstrom), Max mistakenly buys Richard Adams's *Watership Down* (1972) – '(Bloody good book, actually, if you ask me.)' (87) – a book that features a group of anthropomorphized rabbits and which nine-year-old Paul Trotter is 'precociously' reading at the beginning of *The Rotters' Club* (9).

The most overwhelming (although sometimes shadowy) intertextual presence in the book is that of B.S. Johnson. In his biography of the British writer, Coe laments the lack of information on Johnson in the mid-1950s: 'So much of this period is lost, lost beyond retrieval. If I were to write a novel about B.S. Johnson … this is the period I would home in on: so little is known, which leaves so much scope for the imagination' (2004b, 64). And indeed, the fourth embedded story in *The Terrible Privacy of Maxwell Sim*, 'The Rising Sun', is a memoir by Max's father, Harold, who remembers his unusual friendship, at the end of the 1950s, with Roger Anstruther – an ironic homonym of the protagonist in Elizabeth von Arnim's *Fraulein Schmidt and Mr Anstruther* (1907), a romantic epistolary novel involving a '*Fraulein*' and a '*Mr*'. The relationship between Harold and Roger is heavily indebted to that between Graham and Samuel (later renamed Albert) in a deleted passage from Johnson's *Albert Angelo*, reproduced in the coda of Coe's biography (437–45) – a friendship which could itself be based on the ambiguous relationship between Johnson and Michael Bannard in the 1950s. Johnson's purpose in his novels was to explore the depths of his own self, to convey the truth of his experiences and emotions through first-person narrations that revealed the extent of his painful involvement with his own past. The guiding principle of his work is pronounced in the last part of *Albert Angelo*: 'telling stories is telling lies and I want to tell the truth about me about my experience about my truth about my truth to reality' (167). This led Coe to surmise (in his biography) that the deleted episode from *Albert Angelo* might offer autobiographical information about an obscure dimension of Johnson's life. In *The Terrible Privacy of Maxwell Sim*, Coe's fictional alter ego (the assumed author of the book who meets his character at the end) expresses his position as regards truth in a last chapter which is said to come after the story is over: 'you're absolutely correct that the kind of thing I write, from a literal point of view, is not objectively "true". But what I like to think is that there's another kind of truth – a more universal …' (339). It is therefore probably not surprising that the family name 'Anstruther' should contain the word 'truth'.

Coe's ethics of truth might apply to the way he honestly but also creatively wrote his own version of the deleted passage from *Albert Angelo* in *The Terrible Privacy of Maxwell Sim*. A comparison between Johnson's text and Coe's 'The Rising Sun' reveals a series of similarities between Harold-Samuel-Johnson and Roger-Graham-Bannard. Both Harold (in 'The Rising Sun') and Samuel (in *Albert Angelo*) are interested in the 'revolution in architecture' in the City of London (2010a, 246) and share a passion for music, going to concerts at the Royal Festival Hall and other places 'almost every night' (2010a, 250), or '4 or 5 times a week' (2004b, 439). In real life, a friend of Johnson's recalls going to a 1950s performance of *The Rite of Spring* with Michael Bannard: 'the whole performance was done in modern dress and dancers wore dungarees: Bannard stormed out halfway through, declaring that it was a travesty' (Coe, 2004b, 428). In 'The Rising Sun', fictional Harold recalls a similar episode during a performance of *Titus Andronicus* in modern dress, which Roger disapproved of: 'Twenty minutes into the performance he stood up, and declared at the top of his voice: "I see that we are being bamboozled ..."' (253). Harold remarks: 'On this occasion he was wearing – as was often his way – a black, silk-lined cape, which he swirled around himself' (253), a cape that evokes one worn by Michael Bannard at a V&A concert. At the end of the performance, Bannard 'shouted criticism at the performers' and then 'came floating down the staircase, swirling his cape around him' (Coe, 2004b, 428).

Bannard's 'bombastic exterior' (2004b, 68) may however have concealed a more complex inner self, suggested in particular by his ambivalent relation with Johnson, of which the clearest evidence might be the deleted passage from *Albert Angelo*. In that fictional text, the narrator notes from the start: 'There was an electric unspeakable inexplicable knowing between them' (in Coe, 2004b, 437), which finds an equivalent in the 'electric thrill' felt by Harold in the presence of Roger in Coe's novel (2010a, 249). Harold admits: 'our first instance of real physical contact ... sent a pulse of exhilaration through my body' (255), while in Johnson's text, when Samuel and Graham sit back to back, 'the points of contact seemed to burn together', and when they touch hands, they feel 'an intense feeling ..., at once exhilarating and terrifying' (in Coe, 2004b, 441). And yet, the narrator insists that 'Graham was not homosexual, just neuter' (in Coe, 2004b, 441). In 'The Rising Sun', fictional Roger tells Harold about a mysterious Goddess and warns him: 'she absolutely disapproves of homosexuality, and has terrible punishments in store for those who practise it. Bad news for the likes of us' (2010a, 262) – sending a shiver of protest through Harold who does not consider himself a homosexual. The Goddess mentioned here is Robert Graves's 'White Goddess', a figure who so obsessed Johnson he believed he had a supernatural encounter with her in 1955 (Coe, 2004b, 71). In a 1961 diary entry, Johnson wrote: 'M wanted to go too deep and I was too scared to follow him', adding: 'homosexuality would be such an affront to the Goddess that I am tempted' (in Coe, 2004b, 70). In 'The Rising Sun', Harold confesses to being 'in thrall to Roger' – 'However cruel he was to me, I could not escape him' (255) – and yet, he tries to set himself free from his unhealthy domination: 'Why have I let you treat me this way for months, doing everything at your behest, running around at your beck and call as if I were your mistress?' (269). This question recalls that of Johnson's friend Frank Lissauer in a letter of 2 October 1961 about Michael Bannard: 'Who's he, after all, to order you around like a mistress?' (in Coe, 2004b, 433).

These numerous echoes between two fictional texts and (auto) biographical material point to the porous frontier that separates truth from imagination, reality from artefact, and testify to Coe's fascination for this obscure episode in Johnson's life. The resonances confirm Coe's indebtedness to Johnson's work, which also resurfaces through more random allusions. For instance, when Harold refers to the first time he made love to Barbara (Max's mother), he takes issue with the common saying 'You always remember the first time' (276), the title of an anthology edited by Johnson, in which writers were invited to recall the first time they had had sex (published posthumously in 1975). Max also wonders what led Crowhurst to commit suicide and asks a series of questions that could have been put either to Johnson (who took his life at the age of 40), or indeed to Max who was just about to kill himself: 'Was that what tipped you over the edge, finally – the loneliness? The terrible privacy, as Clive called it? I'm not surprised. Nobody could be expected to handle solitude like that, and why should you be any different? You're human like the rest of them' (285). The last sentence is the title of Johnson's 1964 verse play and 1967 film, in which a schoolteacher after going to hospital becomes painfully aware of his own mortality, and later tells his pupils that from the moment of birth we all start to decay and die. While the message of Johnson's play is very bleak and Crowhurst's last notes before he dies are desperate, Coe's novel is written in a comic, albeit sometimes melancholy, mode.

The anti-bookish narrator-protagonist of *The Terrible Privacy of Maxwell Sim* addresses the reader in a way familiar to readers of both Johnson and Coe. He lays bare the artefact of fiction when he describes a woman and adds: '(Sorry, I am just not very good at describing people.'), or remarks: '(I am not very good at describing clothes either – are you looking forward to the next 300 pages?)' (7). He may be echoing Lois's frustration in her diary in *The Rotters' Club* when she writes: '*The sky is blue, I am no good at describing things*' (327), or Benjamin's when he is at pains to convey the details of Cicely's suede jacket: 'how on earth am I ever going to be a writer if I can't describe clothes properly' (374). In *The Terrible Privacy of Maxwell Sim*, Max refers to the beautiful voice of his GPS and notes: 'Don't ask me to describe it. You'll have realized by now that I'm not great at this sort of thing' (149). Such interventions suggest that Max might actually be writing the book that is being read and he is indeed regularly reminding the reader of his control over the narrative. For instance, when he declares: 'So I flew to Sydney and saw my father, and everything else you know. Or at least, everything that I've chosen to tell you' (107), he is emphasizing his power of selection as a storyteller. Later on, aiming to describe his father's apartment, he muses on the inadequacy of language: 'Just then I tapped out a couple of sentences but I decided to delete them again because they didn't seem to do justice to the atmosphere in there: I used words like cold, sparsely furnished and eerie, but somehow that's not enough' (193). Ironically a sense of the deletions is included in his account of their inadequacy. He even tries to fool the reader by inventing a rather clumsy erotic conclusion to his evening with Alison (240–1), only to confess in the next chapter that none of it was true, but still taking pride in his imaginative skills: 'I think I'm finally beginning to get the hang of this writing business' (242). He eventually embeds and synthesizes his own story when telling it to the Chinese woman, thus providing the reader with a brief summary of the book and a list of all the characters he has met (326–7). However, Max also confesses that his inept narrative lacks connections and transitions, and that he has not yet mastered the art of storytelling: 'what I found myself telling her didn't feel much like a proper story at all, any more, just a series of random, unconnected episodes' (327).

He fails possibly because he turns out not to be the author of his own story. At the end of the novel, what sounds like a new voice intervenes to address the reader with a series of warnings – '(Stop me if you've had enough of this by now.)' (333), '(You don't have to read any more if you don't want to. The story is over.)' (333) – but also thanks and compliments: '(It's been a long haul, I know. Thanks to all the people who have stayed with me. Really, I appreciate it. And I admire your stamina, I must say. Most impressive.)' (333). After a blank on the page, Max relates how a middle-aged man, very much resembling Jonathan Coe, introduced himself to Max as the author of the very book Max thought he was writing, a book which until then had been 'a perfectly conventional, realist novel' (Coe, 2013d). The author, who had made a cameo appearance at Heathrow airport earlier (71), cheekily asks Max: 'So how does it feel ... to be part of someone else's story?' (336). This shattering of illusion recalls the conclusion of Johnson's *Christie Malry's Own Double-Entry* when the author meets Christie on his hospital bed and tells him: 'it does not seem possible to take this novel much further. I'm sorry' (165).

In Coe's novel, Max protests when the author tells him the story is over and even tries to go away: 'It can't be finished, ... I still don't know how it ends' (339). After a 'brief and fond but high-handed conversation with [his] creation' (Coe, 2011), the 'Author-God', as Roland Barthes called him (146), consigns Max to oblivion with a click of his fingers. This literary device may correspond to the first type of intrusion Coe described in his PhD thesis on Fielding: 'a coming-clean about the fact that the author exists, that she/he is responsible for the words on the page and that, if there were no author, there would be no story' (1986, 4). While many readers felt betrayed in their willing suspension of disbelief by this brutal intervention of the author as a *deus ex machina,* one of them aptly expressed what the writer had in mind with the coda: 'Maxwell creates artificial relationships and ignores opportunities to develop real ones. At the same time the reader (and author) is creating a relationship with an imagined character – Maxwell himself'. By exposing Max as an artefact, Coe sends an ethical message to the reader: 'away with artificiality, find a human being with whom you can connect' (Coe, 2013d). The urge to connect and to assume ethical responsibility for the other prevails in a novel which describes the loneliness of a long-distance driver (Max) and a long-distance sailor (Crowhurst), and may anticipate the loneliness of an Everyman abroad in Coe's *Expo 58*.

Thomas Foley in *Expo 58* could have been Maxwell Sim's father, but the mild-mannered and unprepossessing civil servant working for the Central Office of Information first made a cameo appearance in the short story 'Ivy and her Nonsense' and in *The Rain Before It Falls* as the father of Gill (Rosamond's niece) and David. In the earlier novel, Rosamond talks about Thomas in an agreeable way and tells Imogen: 'You should get him to tell you about his life one day, if you ever meet him. He was a dark horse, Thomas. There was more to him than met the eye' (250). Even though Imogen died before getting a chance to meet Thomas,

Expo 58 is the story of an important period in his early life. Gill is still a baby and David has not been born yet, though his parents have already agreed their son would be called thus (236). Thomas's wife Sylvia is heard talking to her mother about cousin Beatrix – 'a compulsive romantic adventuress rarely held back by the fact that she had an infant daughter to look after' (18–19) – and especially about her car accident, an episode reported in *The Rain Before it Falls* (168). In *Expo 58*, Thomas's marriage to Sylvia is wobbly as he leaves his wife and daughter and his humdrum life behind while he goes to Brussels for six months during the eleventh World Fair (which had already been the setting for an obscure pulp noir novel by F. Furnes, *Meurtres à l'Expo 58*, published in 1958). Thomas will reappear in the short story 'Pentatonic' in which his son David shares memories of his father travelling, buying a portable cassette recorder in the late 1960s and collecting records of classical pieces. David recalls that his parents' 'marriage was always a bit rocky', that 'there was always an edginess – some feeling of instability' between them (2014a), probably the lasting consequence of what happened in Brussels in 1958.

Expo 58 shares with *The Rain Before It Falls* not only the time frame but also a vein of melancholy, although it returns to comedy. As the title suggests, the novel is set during the Brussels World Fair in 1958, a time that represents a new era of modernity – or postmodernity – in Europe, as epitomized by the Atomium, a 300-feet futurist structure made of nine stainless steel spheres connected to each other, meant to resemble the unit cell of an iron crystal and to symbolize the connectedness between nations. Held on the Heysel plateau north of Brussels, the Fair was organized to show off each country's best achievements, innovations and designs in arts, science and technology, and to celebrate the peaceful relations between nations after the end of the Second World War. As evidenced by the British industries pavilion, the Fair was also a 'marketplace. It was there to sell, to drum up business' (Coe in Arter), which could lead some to consider it as 'a sordid marketplace powered not by idealism at all, but by the forces of capitalism' (Coe, 2013a, 36).

The idea was indeed 'to sell' or, as one of the characters of the novel puts it, 'to *project* – an image of the British character' (6). Coe wrote *Expo 58*, which he defined as 'a very British book about a very English Englishman' (in Snoekx), while Danny Boyle aimed to convey a sense of Britishness with the opening ceremony of the Olympic Games in July 2012. The novel examines the definition of 'that maddening, elusive topic of "Britishness"' (Coe, 2013a, 3) and how it can be presented to the rest of the world:

> What did it mean to be British, in 1958? Nobody seemed to know. Britain was steeped in tradition, everybody agreed upon that: its traditions, its pageantry, its ceremony were admired and envied all over the world. At the same time, it was mired in the past: scared of innovations, riddled with archaic class distinctions, in thrall to a secretive and untouchable Establishment. Which way were you supposed to look, when defining Britishness? Forwards, or backwards?
>
> (3)

Such crucial interrogations about Britishness are shared by several contemporary writers, such as Kazuo Ishiguro in *The Remains of the Day* (1989), Peter Ackroyd in *English Music* (1992), Julian Barnes in *England, England* (1998), or Ian McEwan in *Atonement* (2001). In *Expo 58*, the British are shown entering the Fair 'a bit grudgingly and a bit sceptically', with a touch of 'snobby amusement' – which was 'characteristic of Britain's attitude to Europe at that time' – as well as an 'arrogant, aristocratic indifference to the whole notion of the modern' (Coe in Armitstead). This explains why a senior officer fails to find the word 'future' to round up his speech: 'We're trying to look back, of course, on our rich and varied history. But we're also trying to look forward. Looking forward to the … to the …' (Coe, 2013a, 6–7). In 1958, Britain's resistance to modernity is symptomatic of its misgivings about the construction of a European identity during the Cold War, an attitude which finds resonances in the contemporary world and in recent literature. Coe summed up the underlying political theme of the book with two questions: 'how does Britain think of itself in relationship to Europe? Has the way that we thought of our position in Europe changed much since 1958?' (in Armitstead). In 1958, Britain was still mired in the past, diminished by the ongoing loss of its Empire and reluctant to engage with Europe and with the modern. This is symbolized by the construction of a full-scale model of a pub, the Britannia, as the centrepiece to the British pavilion and a symbol of the national character. The pub was indeed constructed for the World Fair in Brussels and later copied in Dover.

In Barnes's *England, England*, where a theme park of England in miniature is built on the Isle of Wight (called 'England, England'), pubs appear in fifth position on the list of 'Fifty Quintessences of Englishness' according to market research into clichés of Englishness (83). Both the World Fair and Barnes's England, England present a world of make-believe, a 'mirage', a 'chimera' (Coe, 2013a, 212), all the more as the pub in *Expo 58*, instead of sporting the traditional thatched roof, horse brasses and pewter tankards, is designed like a modern yacht club, decorated with lifebuoys and models of ships. As the overseer of 'a fake pub, projecting a fake vision of England, transported into a fake setting where every other country was projecting fake visions of their national identity', 32-year-old Foley realizes that he is 'living in a world constructed entirely out of simulacra' (179), thus anticipating Jean Baudrillard's own development of the concept in *Simulacra and Simulations* (1981). Baudrillard points to four successive phases in the simulation of an image, at the end of which the 'simulacrum' no longer bears any resemblance to the original and occupies what the sociologist calls 'hyperreality', 'a real without origin or reality', best exemplified by the fake world of Disneyland (1). In *Expo 58*, Thomas is looking after 'a replica pub' (73), which houses the replica of an anchor from HMS *Victory* (78) and a 'scale model of the Britannia aeroplane' (212); his friend Tony is looking after a replica ZETA machine (73); and Emily is performing '*faux*-domestic activities at the American pavilion' (212). The Fair sports a fake Bavarian beerhouse with lederhosen-clad orchestra, a replica of a Congolese village with traditional huts and a section called 'Gay Belgium' (30, 97), a name with quite a different connotation in the new millennium. All the contributing countries thus offer revealing (though fake) symbols of their national identities.

This world is all the more deceptive as it is populated by spies, hiding their true identities and purposes. As a Cold War comedy of manners with the ingredients of a thriller, *Expo 58* bears some similarities with Ian McEwan's *Sweet Tooth* (2012), though Coe replaces the intellectual background with slapstick comedy. Coe described his own novel as a 'John le Carré meets Evelyn Waugh' comic novel, which mixes espionage, politics, romance and comedy. It recalls Graham Greene's *Our Man in Havana* (1958), a comic novel set in Cuba during the Cold War, in which a vacuum cleaner retailer becomes a spy for the British secret service but fakes the reports he sends to London. *Expo 58* also pays homage to Ian Fleming's James Bond series of spy novels which Coe enjoyed so much as a child that at the age of 11, he wrote a story that was an 'imitation of a James Bond' (in Tew, 2008, 35). In *Expo 58*, secret agents Wayne and Radford dismiss Fleming's novels as implausible: '"Pure fiction, of course. Gadding around the world …" "Bumping people off without so much as a by your leave …" "Sleeping with a different woman every night …"' (140). In *The Closed Circle*, Paul Trotter, from the time he has given Malvina a key to his flat, has 'been half-expecting to encounter what he liked to call a "James Bond moment"' – when Fleming's hero 'returns to his hotel room late at night in an exotic foreign location' and finds a 'naked *femme fatale*' on the bed (63) – but Paul's own bedroom remains 'Malvina-less' (64). In *What a Carve Up!*, Michael refers to *Goldfinger*, in which Shirley Eaton 'gets covered in gold paint and suffocates' (152), which inspired the title of her autobiography, *Golden Girl* (1999); the corrupt art dealer Roddy suffers the same fate in Coe's novel (479).

In *Expo 58*, Thomas, like most of Coe's male characters, is a naive and dithery middle-class man from Tooting, playing the role of the innocent abroad, and is thus very much an anti-James Bond, even if he is seen reading *From Russia with Love* (150), published the previous year – in *The Rotters' Club*, the PE master is known as 'Rosa', 'on account of his passing resemblance to the mannish villainess in *From Russia with Love*' (64). Thomas is reluctant to discard the novel as 'pure fantasy', as Fleming appears 'to be writing with great authority' (150). When unable to know what to do next, he wonders: 'How would James Bond have acted in this situation ?' (153), and he hopes the Belgian hostess Anneke might respond like the young Soviet spy Tatiana Romanova in Fleming's novel, but eventually he has to admit that 'the differences between himself and Fleming's hero were probably too great for any meaningful comparison (153–4). Far from excelling in espionage, Thomas does not realize that most of the people he meets are spies and proves unable to prevent the Russians from stealing nuclear secrets from the British and the Americans. As such, the book is thus a parody of spy novels and very different from the contemporary versions of James Bond novels such as Sebastian Faulks's *Devil May Care* (2008), and William Boyd's *Solo* (2013). And yet, Coe's German publisher decided to highlight the James Bond flavour by calling the book *From Brussels with Love*.

Comparing it to his previous work, Coe insists on the lighter and subtler pace of this book: 'I love the classic light comedy films of the 1930s and 40s and wanted to do something delicate like that, something that floats, rather than hammering things home as I did in *What a Carve Up!*' (in Higgins). *Expo 58* confirms Coe's attachment to popular culture as the book evokes the tone and atmosphere of the Ealing Comedies (1947–57) and the *Carry On* comedy series (1958–92), but also the films starring Dirk Bogarde, with whom Thomas shares a striking resemblance (2, 21, 148) according to some, while others think he has a hint of the American actor Gary Cooper. Coe argues that the novel is 'quite a postmodern … allusive book' because of its frequent references to British comedy and literature. For instance, Thomas's colleagues at work, Tracepurcel and Stanley Windrush (17, 235), are named after characters in the Boulting brothers' comedy film *I'm All Right Jack* (1959), featuring Peter Sellers, while another colleague, Carlton-Browne (13, 235), takes his name from *Carlton-Browne of the F.O.*, another 1959 comedy by the Boulting Brothers. Two characters are called Carter (41) and Wilkins (125) after the teachers in the Jennings series, humorous children's novels by Anthony Buckeridge about a schoolboy in a preparatory school in England between the Second World War and the 1960s. The pub's landlord is Mr Rossiter (50), an homage to Leonard Rossiter who played the title role of Reginald Perrin in the TV series.

As for the two British secret service agents Mr Radford and Mr Wayne, wearing 'long beige raincoats and trilby hats' (Coe 2013a, 33), they are said to behave 'like something out of a cheap novel' (158), but as the first epigraph points out, they are named after the actors Basil Radford and Naunton Wayne who played the buttoned-up cricket enthusiasts Caldicott and Charters in Alfred Hitchcock's 1938 comic thriller *The Lady Vanishes* (in Coe's novel, it is the British gentleman in charge of the ZETA machine, Tony Buttress, who has suddenly 'vanished' [127]). In an essay, Coe remarks that Caldicott and Charters are 'two of the finest creations in British cinema' and provide 'a blissful satire on stiff-upper-lip Englishness': the film is his favourite of Hitchcock's production because it is 'a comedy as much as a thriller' (2012a), a combination Coe aimed to emulate in *Expo 58*. Some reviewers suggested that the two bumbling spies recalled the Thomson and Thompson of the *Tintin* books by Belgian cartoonist Hergé, but Coe admitted he was 'not a huge Tintin reader' and therefore did not have this reference in mind (in Armitstead). On the other hand, Coe says the two agents have a little 'of the two sinister interrogators from Harold Pinter's first play, *The Birthday Party*, and from two characters in *Diamonds Are Forever*', the seventh film in the James Bond series (1971), which Coe saw when he was about ten years old. Coe also remarks that Radford and Wayne are meant 'to be archetypes of a political presence that we don't really understand or control, but which is at all times directing our actions', and he mischievously suggests that they may have 'a little bit of David Cameron and George Osborne about them as well' (in Snoekx) – respectively Britain's Conservative Prime Minister and the Chancellor of the Exchequer since 2010.

Some details about the two agents may also recall comic scenes from Jacques Tati's films, for instance when the two overweight agents and Thomas squeeze into a Volkswagen Beetle and Thomas attempts to take his coat off (133–4), while the novel's humour is reminiscent of P.G. Wodehouse, Kingsley Amis's early novels and Evelyn Waugh's *Scoop* (1938). Humour comes in the form of puns – the barmaid at the pub is called 'Shirley Knott', pronounced 'Surely not' – as well as running jokes, such as one about the health-giving properties of cigarettes which pregnant women are advised to smoke because they counter stress. The reader can also delight in the reproduction of 1950s lingo, with such expressions as 'jolly', 'tickety-boo', 'top-notch', 'shindig', 'ballyhoo', 'malarkey' and 'old chap', as well as in linguistic playfulness, for instance when one of the spies is said to have had 'the sachet and the packet in the pocket of his jacket' (244).

Though comedy prevails in the book, melancholy and sadness exude from the letters exchanged by Thomas and his wife, Sylvia. They are a model of understatement as husband and wife never truly communicate what they feel but hide behind mundane anecdotes. The growing gaps between the letters suggest their progressive estrangement and alienation from each other. In terms of narrative technique, plot and characterization, this is probably Coe's most conventional novel, which also represents a change in writing method – 'It's the first time I've written sequentially', Coe says (in Charnock). However, the book ends with a fast-forward to 2009 when an elderly Foley returns to Brussels. Like Rosamond in *The Rain Before it Falls*, he reminisces about the past with nostalgia, and thus contradicts his earlier belief (upon visiting the site of his grandfather's farm in 1958) that 'it was pointless trying to recapture the past, returning to scenes of long-lost happiness in search of relics, consoling souvenirs' (204).

Expo 58 marks an interesting evolution in Coe's literary production. After a series of early novels that were fairly experimental and partly indebted to Fielding and B.S. Johnson, he moved on to postmodernist playfulness as well as satirical portraits of contemporary British society and intimate reflections on solitary lives. With *Expo 58,* Coe proceeded further in the direction of the conventional realist novel, moving back to the 1950s and a tradition of comic and popular literature and culture. The next novel, *Number 11,* will shift the cursor forward again as it is set in contemporary Britain and marks the reappearance of some of the characters from *What a Carve Up!,* whom the author had magnanimously kept alive.

Part III

CRITICISM AND CONTEXTS

8

AUTHOR INTERVIEW

Would you agree with a description of your first three novels as 'Funny, Brutalist, and Short' (to quote B.S. Johnson's Christie Malry*)?*

I don't know if I would agree with that description now, but it was certainly on my mind at the time. My introduction to B.S. Johnson was the King Penguin reissue of *Christie Malry* which came out in 1984, and I believe I started writing *The Accidental Woman* a few months later. (Incidentally the title of the novel was always simply *Maria,* until I came up with a new one at the insistence of Colin Haycraft at Duckworth when he published it in 1987. '*Maria*' appealed to me as a title because it was an homage to all the Beckett protagonists whose names began with M – Murphy, Molloy, Malone etc.) The phrase 'funny, brutalist and short' – which I don't think I recognized at the time as an echo of Samuel Johnson – certainly appealed to me and indeed I quoted it in some of the many letters which I sent out to publishers with my manuscript. *Christie Malry*, which I had read so recently, is clearly a huge influence on *The Accidental Woman*, mainly because of the idea of the narrator being in a close and dialogic relationship with his hero, or in this case heroine. But then this was the very aspect of Henry Fielding's technique that I was exploring in my PhD thesis, so Fielding is probably the older and more fundamental influence.

I suppose the description could apply to the other two novels as well. *A Touch of Love* (another change of title – it was originally called *The Separatist*) is not especially funny, although it does contain one of my favourite jokes in all my books (the suicidal family who leave a note saying 'Goodbye Cruel World – From All at 49'). *The Dwarves of Death* is simply not a book that I look back upon or think about very much.

A recurrent device in your novels is the insertion of embedded stories. At the same time, you say you're not tempted by the short story format. Aren't your embedded stories a way of testing the genre of the short story within a novel?

The 'embedded short story' is my answer to the personal problem I have with writing short stories. I've written eight of them – four in *A Touch of Love*, four in *The Terrible Privacy of Maxwell Sim* – which is more than my total output of 'real' short stories collected in *Loggerheads and Other Stories*. They are a way of writing short self-contained stories which also involve connections, either in theme or use of recurring characters, with longer narratives. In a way my current novel-in-progress, *Number 11*, is a continuation of the process as it could be read simply as five separate short stories or novellas.

The technique has always started from practical reasons. When I was writing *A Touch of Love* I had very little money and had never had anything published. I wanted to write a novel but I also had the idea of writing something that could be 'asset-stripped' and sold in separate parts. I thought that if no one wanted to publish the whole book I could at least try placing the short stories in different magazines. The final section was even written as a radio play, at first, in the hope of selling it to the BBC. Nothing came of these plans, however. Of all my novels I think *A Touch of Love* went through the biggest changes and somewhere in my archive I have a draft in which the whole of the first section is narrated in the first person by Ted.

With *The Terrible Privacy of Maxwell Sim* I was asked to write a short story on the theme of one of the four elements in aid of Oxfam. I wanted to do it but was busy working on my novel and didn't want to get distracted. So I had the idea of writing a short story which could also be part of the novel again. And once I'd written it, I thought it would be formally pleasing to have three other stories which told you something about Maxwell and his life, each one based on one of the elements in order to tie in with the references to Eliot's *Four Quartets* which were starting to appear in the book. But I don't think I would have thought of any of this if Oxfam hadn't approached me. Contingency plays a large part in the writing process, for me.

In The Rotters' Club, *the narrator refers to a 'curious, lengthy digression' in* Tom Jones, *'which seems to have nothing to do with the main narrative but is in fact its cornerstone' (127). Just before, you included the story of the Jews Inger and Emil – a digression. Why is that episode so important in the novel?*

At first I included it purely because I had my eye on the sequel, *The Closed Circle*, and wanted to set up a situation in which Paul Trotter would be owed a huge debt of gratitude by another character for having saved his life. But the story of Inger and Emil got bigger and more complicated as soon as I started to think about it – it began to seem like a big story of its own, having very little to do with *The Rotters' Club*. So I included that comparison with Fielding's 'Man of the Hill' episode in *Tom Jones* almost as a way of apologising for it, by saying 'Look, there are other writers, much greater writers than me, who've gone off on a big tangent like this in the middle of books'.

Two other things about the Inger and Emil story: it is placed immediately after the detonation of the Birmingham pub bomb which wreaks such havoc on Lois and the rest of the Trotter family. I thought that, in the aftermath of a brutal tragedy like that, one of the things the characters might feel would be a sense of total disorientation and confusion, so I wanted to make the reader feel rather the same way. A few pages into the story I wanted the reader to be thinking 'Hold on, I'm confused now – what does this have to do with anything?' But of course, the important thing is that the Jewish story does tie in with the whole racism theme of *The Rotters' Club* and *The Closed Circle,* where the entire plot, on one level, is driven along by the consequences of hostility and discrimination against minorities.

Could you talk about your literary project Unrest *which traces the history of a family over several decades? Could it be related to such sequences of books as Marcel Proust's* In Search of Lost Time, *Anthony Powell's* A Dance to the Music of Time *or Dorothy Richardson's* Pilgrimage?

This is difficult to discuss because it's work-in-progress and most of it is still just inside my head, in a very abstract form. Of course I love all the *romans fleuves* that you've mentioned (particularly the Dorothy Richardson) but what I envisage is something looser in form, and which would not proceed chronologically. There would be 15 narratives, arranged as five volumes – three to a volume. So far all I've written is *Expo 58* (which is Part 2 of the 15) and *The Rain Before It Falls* (which is Part 1), although some of the stories in *Loggerheads* are meant to crop up in Parts 10–12. But who knows if I'll get any further with it!

You said you considered your children's book The Broken Mirror *as your 'most serious and politically engaged book' and* The Rain Before It Falls *as 'perhaps the most purely political of all [your] novels'. In which ways is that so and what do you mean by 'political'?*

Both of these descriptions, I suspect, were reactions on my part to being asked by journalists 'Why don't you write political novels any more?' (This is a very common question from journalists who like *What a Carve Up!* the best of all my books and want me to write another one just like it.) I was trying to expand the definition of 'political' beyond the way it is often used in literary discussions, where it becomes a synonym for 'polemical' or 'satirical'. In the case of *The Rain Before it Falls,* I've been acutely conscious – ever since becoming a father myself – that the family unit is also a political unit, and within the confines of this unit (which is an intensely private space) there is scope for terrible abuse of power. (I suppose what *I* mean by a 'political novel' is a novel in which power is one the central themes: it can equally be the power of a government over its people, or the power of a mother over her daughter.) *The Rain Before It Falls*, therefore, is – within this expanded definition – a political novel in the sense that it examines a systematic abuse of power over several generations.

The case of *The Broken Mirror* is slightly different. I first wrote a children's story about a fragment of mirror which reflects not a real but an imagined world back in 1983, when I was 22 years old. Almost 30 years later I had the idea of salvaging what I could from it. It became a parable about a child's developing consciousness, about how perception of the world's injustices and imperfections creeps up on the adolescent mind. In the final chapter the central character, Claire, realizes that she is not the only person to possess a 'broken mirror', that in fact many people feel about society the way she does, and by joining together they can construct a collective vision of how the world might be a better place. It is a call for collective thinking in an atomized and fragmented world (the logical extension, in a way, of *Maxwell Sim*, the book that came before it) and in fact this explicitly polemical aspect of the book was inspired by Stéphane Hessel's bestselling pamphlet *Indignez-vous!* Sadly, although my European editors embraced this idea of a political message wrapped up in a kind of fairy tale, British editors found the story too didactic and it remains the only one of my books not to be published in the UK or indeed in the English language.

Your new novel, Number 11, *takes up a few characters from* What a Carve Up! *and alludes to the legacy of the Winshaws. Why did you decide to 'exhume' the Winshaws some 20 years later?*

One of the most frequent questions I've been asked over the last few years is 'Why don't you write a sequel to *What a Carve Up!?*', or 'What would the Winshaw family be doing today?' You try to turn a deaf ear to such things but eventually they worm their way into your consciousness and start setting off thought processes. In the case of *What a Carve Up!* I always thought there was no point in writing a sequel as the political message of the book had not really changed. As I'm always saying to people, the novel was never about Mrs Thatcher (whom it barely mentions) but about Thatcherism; and Thatcherism has never gone away in the 24 years since Mrs Thatcher herself left office. John Major, Tony Blair, Gordon

Brown and David Cameron have all presided over Thatcherite governments.

After a while, however, I realised that this was an argument *in favour* of writing a sequel, rather than argument against it. If I wanted to write a novel set in Cameron's Britain, and if the Winshaws were my metaphor for the Thatcherite establishment, then I felt they should very much be present in the novel, as they were in 1994. This presented a difficulty, of course, because almost all of the Winshaw family are killed off at the end of *What a Carve Up!*. I toyed with the idea of bringing them back as ghosts, or even implying that the whole massacre at the end of the original novel was just a dream taking place in Michael Owen's feverish head. But I couldn't make either of these ideas work. Eventually I realised that there were only three potentially significant characters left standing at the end of *What a Carve Up!* – Phoebe, the nurse, Josephine Winshaw (Hilary's daughter) and Helke Winshaw (Mark's widow). Not much to go on, in a way, but I decided that this in itself might be liberating: instead of tying me down to a whole cast of existing characters, I could merely have these people make a fleeting appearance, and concentrate on creating new characters, which is a much more interesting process for me anyway.

On the day after the general election in Britain in May 2015, which saw the re-election of the Conservatives, you tweeted: 'My new book satirises greed, inequality, non-doms, cuts, Katie Hopkins types'. Does this mean Number 11 *marks a return to satire after* Expo 58 *which tended more towards comedy?*

Well, you shouldn't read too much into a tweet. Usually the main purpose – as with this one – is simply to exploit current events to generate a bit of publicity for your new book! The OED definition of satire is 'the use of humour, irony, exaggeration or ridicule to expose and criticize people's stupidity or vices'. When it's put like that, maybe there isn't so much difference between the two books. You could read *Expo 58* as being a satire on indecisiveness and marital weakness. *Number 11* is a satire on greed, inequality, social media, reality TV and so on. So really there are only two differences: in tone (the satire in *Number 11* is more severe) and subject (the objects of satire in *Number 11* are social and political issues rather than personal qualities). To put it more simply: *Expo 58* is a gentle satire on human frailty; *Number 11* is a fierce satire on social injustice. But I would say that both are satires according to the dictionary definition.

You are currently writing a play The Magnificent Death of Henry Fielding, *inspired by Fielding's posthumously published* Journal of a Voyage to Lisbon. *What attracted you to this project?*

The Magnificent Death of Henry Fielding is another work-in-progress: as soon as I've finished my current novel I intend to go back to it and attempt another draft. Of course I read all of Fielding's works when I was writing my thesis back in the 1980s, but the *Journal of a Voyage to Lisbon* had never stayed in my mind particularly. However a few years ago I was invited to Lisbon by my Portuguese publishers and I took Fielding's book with me as appropriate reading for the journey. (Rather ironic, in retrospect, because as I realized after re-reading it, there are almost no references to Lisbon in it at all: only in the final sentence.) As soon as I began to read it again, however, I was seized by the idea that it could be adapted for the stage. The first image in particular – the bloated and decrepit Fielding being winched on board the *Queen of Portugal* in a harness, to the jeers and catcalls of the mob gathered on shore – struck me as a wonderful opening scene. I was slightly worried because I hadn't written for the stage since I was a student (I had a little satirical play called *Victims of the Recession* performed when I was at Warwick), so I've really been learning the technique as I go along. Also, in the first couple of drafts I stuck too closely to the source material, rather than finding a new dramatic shape for my homage to Fielding – which is what the play really is, of course, as far as I'm concerned.

How do you feel about the film adaptations of your novels?

Only three of my novels have been adapted for the screen. The most recent is *The Terrible Privacy of Maxwell Sim*, which has been filmed in France as *La vie très privée de Mr Sim*, with Jean-Pierre Bacri. At the time of writing the shooting is still in progress, so it's too early to say what the end result will be like, although I have to say I'm extremely impressed by the screenplay, written by the director, Michel Leclerc, with his partner Baya Kasmi. It manages to retain nearly all the major episodes from a very complex and digressive novel, while also giving the narrative the sort of clean linear shape that a feature film requires.

The first of my novels to be filmed was *The Dwarves of Death* (as *Five Seconds to Spare*). It was neither a commercial nor an artistic success, mainly because – for financial reasons which I never really understood – the film had to be rushed into production before the script was ready. I'd agreed to write the screenplay myself which was itself a bad decision: my feelings about the original novel were too ambivalent and I tried to deviate too much from the source material, in ways which were not helpful. The film's director then came on board and wrote his own draft which didn't meld very convincingly with mine. It had a handful of good scenes but the tone and the storytelling of the film were so unclear that the few audiences who saw it were so confused that they couldn't enjoy even the few moments that worked.

In between was the BBC's television adaptation of *The Rotters' Club*, which was a much happier experience. The most important thing was that it was adapted by two experienced and brilliant TV writers, Dick Clement and Ian La Frenais, whose work (especially the rhythms of their dialogue) had itself been a huge influence on me ever since the 1970s. And then there was the fact that they had the relative luxury of a three 50-minute episodes rather than a 120-minute feature film. Even so, the last episode was rushed and the adaptation would have benefited from being 200 minutes long. Enough usable material was certainly shot.

Incidentally I've just taken my daughter to see the final part of Peter Jackson's adaptation of *The Hobbit*. Jackson has been widely criticized for taking a relatively short children's book and filming it in three parts, totalling more than eight hours' running time. I have many problems with the tone of his adaptation but I have no problem at all with the length of the films. Eight hours is a perfectly reasonable amount of screen time to devote even to a relatively simple novel. When ITV filmed *Brideshead Revisited* in the 1980s they spent more than 13 hours on it, and as a result it was one of the few genuinely faithful and successful screen adaptations of a work of literature. Hitchcock was once asked if he would ever consider making a screen adaptation of a great novel such as *Crime and Punishment*, and answered: 'Well, I shall never do that, precisely because *Crime and Punishment* is somebody else's achievement. And even if I did, it probably wouldn't be any good.' 'Why not?' his interviewer (François Truffaut) asked. 'Well, in Dostoevsky's novel there are many, many words and all of them have a function.' 'You mean that theoretically,' Truffaut prompted, 'a masterpiece is something that has already found its perfection of form, its definitive form.' 'Exactly,' Hitchcock answered, 'and to really convey that in cinematic terms, substituting the language of the camera for the written word, one would have to make a six to ten-hour film. Otherwise, it won't be any good.'

Here we have the truth about screen adaptations stated very simply. The reason great novels never translate successfully to the screen is quite obvious: film companies and distributors are in thrall to the tyranny of the 120-minute movie (in order to maximize the number of screenings per day). But you can almost never condense even the simplest of full-length novels into two hours. It's an incredibly difficult thing to ask of any screenwriter.

9

OTHER WRITINGS

Although Jonathan Coe is mainly known as a novelist, he is also a biographer, an essayist, a short story writer, an as yet unpublished playwright, a film and book reviewer, as well as a music composer. Coe's most recent experiments in fiction include the writing of two children's books: *The Broken Mirror* (2012) and *The Story of Gulliver* (2013), both first published in Italy. While the latter confirms Coe's attachment to Jonathan Swift, the former (which has not yet been published in Britain) is a fable which expounds the necessity to believe in dreams and, above all, to dream collectively. The story had an earlier version, entitled *Fragment of a Glass*, which Coe wrote some 30 years earlier when he was a student. He retained the central metaphor of the broken mirror which reflects a better world than the one we live in and attempted in both versions to 'capture something about what it was like to grow up, leaving your childhood and your youthful fantasies ruefully behind' (Website, *Broken*). In *The Broken Mirror*, the lonely and melancholy eight-year-old Claire plays in a rubbish dump where she finds a fragment of mirror which reflects 'not the ordinary, over-familiar things of which her everyday world consisted, but the things she might dream about'. As Claire grows up, the reflections in the mirror change: the 'vibrant, colourful fantasy world' of childhood is lost and replaced by familiar surroundings, but always 'transformed, made more welcoming and beautiful'. As a teenager, her parents separate and Claire is now old enough to listen to the story of 'George the Homeless Man' who fell 'through the cracks' after being swamped with debts and losing his wife and children, and to lament the closing down of the library, replaced by a shopping mall, and the hospital, turned into luxury flats. Claire eventually learns that other children have been carrying a fragment of mirror for years and they all gather one night to put them together and see if they can 'make their town a better place to live'.

The symbol of the fragmented mirror may recall Jacques Lacan's concept of the 'mirror stage' in the formation of identity, when the baby sees in the mirror the reflection of an imaginary whole, which compensates for the experience of his/her fragmentary real. In Coe's fable, the fragmented mirror gives access to the magical world of imagination until the children grow up and the pieces are assembled to form a whole and attempt to change the real. As such, *The Broken Mirror* is a plea for collectivity and a sense of communion to counter individualism and the atomization of society. While the book is gently optimistic and idealist in its conclusion and exploits the conventional codes of the fable (through the use of fantasy and magic, the presence of evil characters and obstacles to the heroine's development), it also tackles contemporary issues such as social inequalities, injustice, and consumerism, which find echoes in the novels for adults.

Coe defines himself first and foremost as a writer tempted by expansiveness, which explains why his favourite genre is the novel: 'I have trouble keeping things out of books, which is why I don't write short stories because they turn into novels' (in Taylor, Charles). To date, Coe has published six short stories, composed between 1990 and 2012, and included in *Loggerheads and Other Stories* (2014). The shortest story, 'Loggerheads', is the subtle and melancholy interior monologue of a retired woman who reflects on her marriage but also on the memory of an image from childhood that suddenly springs back to her mind. Three stories – '9th & 13th', 'V.O.' and 'Ivy and Her Nonsense' – had originally appeared in his first collection *9th & 13th* (2005), published in honour of Penguin's 70th anniversary.

The stories reveal the extent to which Coe's interest in music and film permeates his shorter fiction. In '9th & 13th', the narrator David, a pianist in New York, explains how to play these chords: while the 9th is 'slightly rootless', bringing out 'an audible sense of indecision', the 13th is open, 'brimming with potential' (2005a, 20–1), and the two of them form 'the sound of endless, infinite, unresolved possibilities' (28), just as the question asked by a female customer in the bar (who is looking for a place to stay for the night) raises 'infinite possibilities' and leads the pianist to let his imagination run wild and dream of a fantasized future with that stranger, a would-be writer (22). The short story uses the musical theme to reflect in a pensive mode on 'what would have happened' (22), on paths not taken and missed opportunities, a recurrent topic in Coe's longer prose in which indecisive male protagonists often take refuge in imagined lives and narratives rather than assume control over their destiny.

In 'Pentatonic', subtitled 'A Story of Music' – a story also available as a digital download accompanied by the piece of music by Danny Manners which originally inspired the story – David (Thomas Foley's son) listens to the tape of his first piano composition, made when he was ten years old and based on the pentatonic scale (which contains five notes per octave instead of seven). The tune symbolizes his lost childhood and triggers off a feeling of nostalgia for the past that has slipped away. When listening to his 12-year-old daughter sing during a school reunion, he deeply feels that this is the end of her childhood, which means his own painful loss of her. His wife Jennifer's reaction to the singing of the hymn about sacrifice, 'I Vow To Thee My Country', differs greatly as it reminds her of her father fighting in the Second World War and how this trauma later provoked nightmares and panic attacks that shattered her own childhood. Instead of bringing them together, music thus sends husband and wife along different tracks and memories, and eventually drives them apart. In 'Rotary Park' on the other hand, music bonds the father and children together and helps them cope with the mother's erratic behaviour and instability. On Christmas Day 1969, Joseph is impatient to get his 12-string Hofner guitar while his father is proud to display an '8-track cartridge. The recorded music medium of the future', which they try in the car (2014a). In both cases, music, listened to or performed in the comforting seclusion of a garage or a bedroom, is a refuge from painful emotions. These few examples from Coe's short stories point to the central role music plays in his literary work. Coe defines himself as 'a (professional) producer of words and an (amateur) composer of music' (in Okereke), and an important part of his production includes his musical compositions and collaborations with musicians. He has argued that 'all art aspires to the condition of music' (2013d) and points out: 'If my life had worked out the way I would have wanted it to, I would be a composer' (in Guignery, 2013, 36). In May 2015, Coe released his first album, *Unnecessary Music*, which includes compositions from the mid-1980s to the present.

The short story 'V.O.' revisits the hero of Coe's third novel *The Dwarves of Death*, William, who has become a well-known composer of film music and is taking part in a Festival of Horror and Fantasy Cinema in France, probably inspired by the several festivals in which Coe has himself participated as member of the jury or president. As in *What a Carve Up!* where the ontological boundaries between Pat Jackson's film and Michael's life become so blurred that the character seems to inhabit the film, in 'V.O.', William gets confused when he simultaneously reads the French subtitles of the film *The Haunted Heart* (directed by Gertrud who left her husband for William), and hears the original German soundtrack and the English translation by the interpreter Pascale, who sits next to him and has fallen in love with him. As the film he watches deals with a love triangle, he can 'no longer be sure whether it was Gertrud or Pascale that was speaking to him' (2005a, 42). Voices, music and images thus intertwine, just as the threads of fiction and reality interweave.

Coe's fascination for the cinema has led him to write biographies of American actors Humphrey Bogart and James Stewart as well as film reviews and longer pieces on film adaptations (2013d), Alfred Hitchcock (2012a), Billy Wilder (2005a, 44–55) and the actress Shirley Eaton (1999). These non-fictional pieces help identify Coe's filmic interests and obsessions; they illuminate some of the film references in his novels and can encourage one to perceive subtle echoes from Coe's fictional creation. For instance, in his biography of Bogart, Coe points to a quality in the actor's most popular performances (including Rick in *Casablanca*), which consists in 'combining toughness with an appealing vulnerability: the harder the shell, according to this theory, the more precious and fragile are the feelings it seeks to protect' (8). This epitome of masculinity in American cinema may be said to contrast with the ineffective and hapless male characters of Coe's novels, but vulnerability is also a quality Coe is interested in exploring.

Coe has seen various television, film and radio adaptations of his novels. They include the 1999 film adaptation of *The Dwarves of Death – Five Seconds to Spare* – for which he drafted the early versions of the screenplay. In 1997 Coe had published in the *New Statesman* an extract from a never-completed film script, *The Decoy*, which gives insight into the adulterous relationship between a Labour MP and a young journalist – perhaps the inspiration for the interaction between Paul and Malvina in *The Closed Circle*. In 2004, BBC Radio 4 broadcast an eight-part adaptation of *What a Carve Up!*, with a script by David Nobbs, the creator of *The Fall and Rise of Reginald Perrin*, while *The Rotters' Club* was adapted for BBC Radio in 2003 and for BBC television in 2005, as three hour-long episodes. The script was written by Dick Clement and Ian La Frenais, famous in Britain for their successful television series *The Likely Lads* (1964–66) and *What Happened to the Likely Lads* (1973–74), featuring two working class men, Bob and Terry, which are also the names of two characters in Coe's *The House of Sleep*. *The Rotters' Club* TV 'mini series' is very successful both as an adaptation of Coe's novel and as a visual and musical representation of the 1970s. In 2014, *The Terrible Privacy of Maxwell Sim* was adapted in France by Michel Leclerc and Baya Kasmi, with Jean-Pierre Bacri and Mathieu Amalric in the main roles, and with the road trip being transposed to France and Italy. Coe's experimentation with various literary genres has recently extended to playwriting with his play in eight scenes, yet to be performed, *The Magnificent Death of Henry Fielding* (2014).

Coe's non-fictional work includes introductions to novels by his much admired predecessors or contemporaries such as Henry Fielding, Rosamond Lehmann, B.S. Johnson, David Nobbs and the Spanish novelist Javier Marías. Some of these are reproduced in Coe's anthology of journalism and essays, *Marginal Notes, Doubtful Statements. Non-Fiction, 1990–2012 (2013)*, which confirms Coe's interest in music, cinema, satire, comedy and politics. In the final essay, he refers to his 'persistent *doubts* about the value of fiction', which has led him to question the conventions of the form he is working in, and he contrasts these doubts with the certainties of B.S. Johnson who 'had a strong and well-developed hatred' of fiction (2013d). Coe's full-fledged admiration for B.S. Johnson has already been mentioned and is evidenced by the essays he wrote on the latter's novels and poems, and also by his coediting with Philip Tew and Julia Jordan of *Well Done, God!* (2013) – a selection of Johnson's uncollected or unavailable plays, reviews, essays and short stories – as well as by his outstanding biography, *Like a Fiery*

Elephant. The Story of B.S. Johnson (2004). The biography presents 'the apparent paradox of a novelist who loves (traditional) novels writing the biography of a novelist who seemed to hate them' (Coe, 2004b, 7) and combines the two essential aspects of Johnson's novel writing in its very form: on the one hand, Coe implements the principle of truth-telling which is expected from a biography and is advocated by Johnson for the novel; on the other hand, he challenges the established genre of the biography and proposes formal innovations that deconstruct certain biographical conventions and echo some of the devices used by Johnson in his novels. In so doing, Coe's book engages a dialogue both with the traditional codes of the biography and with Johnson's own guidelines for the novel.

The book is divided into three parts: 'A life in seven novels' briefly presents Johnson's books; 'A life in 160 fragments' constitutes the core of the work and includes extracts from letters, manuscripts and reviews that constantly interrupt the main text, thus denying any sense of genuine continuity; 'A life in 44 voices' is composed of extracts from interviews with people whom Johnson knew and Coe interviewed, moving back and forth between various voices in a polyphonic mode, without any direct intervention from the biographer. Coe announces from the start that the book will be 'at times more of a dossier than a conventional literary biography', compiled with 'plenty of selectivity' and containing 'its fair share of guesswork' (8). Echoing Johnson's wish to reflect the chaos and fragmentation of reality in his novels, Coe says his biography is 'fragmentary, unpolished' (9). For instance, although the middle section generally follows a chronological order, fragment 46 is held back until the end of the biography because it is almost the last thing Coe found in Johnson's archive. In a footnote, the biographer addresses the reader: '(No flicking forward, by the way: this is a bound object, a work of "enforced consecutiveness", not some box full of loose sections to be shuffled and read in any order that you choose!)' (128) – a playful reference to the unbound format of *The Unfortunates*. Such cases of direct address are frequent in the book as Coe often comments on the progression of his work and the difficulties he encounters. As he comes to the point when he needs to relate Johnson's death 'in a few pages', he wonders: 'How can this be done? How can these pages be written?' (375). He also shares his frustration with the reader when a piece of information is missing, forcing him to leave gaps in his narrative (422, 423, 431), the equivalent of the cut-out rectangle on pages 149–52 of Johnson's *Albert Angelo*.

In addition, Coe advocates the need for selectivity and adds to it a creative and narrative dimension: 'no pretence of inclusiveness, no aspirations towards objectivity. The biography as creative enterprise, artwork: the chaos of reality rigorously sifted through, selected and moulded into appealing narrative shapes' (35). The biography is presented as *The Story of B.S. Johnson*, and although Coe is aiming to tell the truth, he often bluntly admits to hypothesising, imagining or speculating (203–4). In *Like a Fiery Elephant*, Coe has thus managed to combine the biographer's need to transmit the facts of a life – 'something of granite-like solidity' –, with the necessity to reveal the inner truth of his subject – 'something of rainbow-like intangibility' (Woolf, 229). It is above all the novelist's sense of gripping narrative which enables him to transcend the genre of the biography.

10

CRITICAL RECEPTION

The criticism devoted to Coe's work may be broadly divided into two categories: while some critics mainly draw attention to the political dimension of the books, seeing them as a satirical portrait of contemporary British society, others are more interested in formal aspects relating to genre, narration, self-reflexivity and intermediality. If Coe's novels have been extensively reviewed over the years and he himself frequently interviewed, academic criticism of his work has only recently begun to emerge. Serge Chauvin published the first analysis of *What a Carve Up!* in 1998 (in French), examining the contemporary forms of the detective novel in the book – a generic approach further developed by Vanessa Guignery in 2002 – but it is really only since 2006 (starting with Pamela Thurschwell's insightful essay on *What a Carve Up!*) that academics have started taking Coe's work into serious consideration. His fiction thus features in recent surveys of contemporary British fiction, most notably Dominic Head's *Cambridge Introduction to Modern British Fiction* (2002), Nick Rennison's *Contemporary British Novelists* (2005), Philip Tew's *The Contemporary British Novel* (2007) and Richard Bradford's *The Novel Now – Contemporary British Fiction* (2007). To this date, only one academic paper (by Lidia Vianu in 2008) has been devoted to Coe's first novel *The Accidental Woman*, while most analyses centre on *What a Carve Up!*, *The Rotters' Club* and *The Closed Circle*.

Coe's keen interest in the contemporary has led a majority of critics to place him within the broad category of realist and political writing. Richard Bradford posits that *The Rotters' Club* and *The*

Closed Circle are set 'firmly within the traditional, realist camp' (45) while *What a Carve Up!* is 'generally traditional and realist in form with a slight nod towards postmodernism' (40). Laurence Driscoll notes that Coe is generally considered as 'the political realist novelist par excellence' because of his accurate presentation of strikes, IRA bombings and NHS cuts, as well as '"the" political writer of the current generation', a description the critic himself will qualify (157). In 'The State and the Novel' (2002), Dominic Head argues that *What a Carve Up!* is the 'most significant novel about the effects of Thatcherism' (35) and it is indeed through that prism that Ryan Trimm analyses Coe's work in his excellent 'Carving up Value: The Tragicomic Thatcher Years in Jonathan Coe' (2010). Trimm examines the Thatcher legacy that manifests itself at all levels of society and compares *What a Carve Up!* with other contemporary British novels engaged with Thatcherism such as Margaret Drabble's Headleand Trilogy (1987–91), Ian McEwan's *The Child in Time* (1987) and Alan Hollinghurst's *The Line of Beauty* (2004). Trimm argues that the most striking difference is that in these latter books, 'Thatcherism operates largely as period backdrop to other thematics' while Coe's novel keeps 'characters and plot at a remove' and concentrates on 'the political and social impact of Thatcherism' (174). In 'Beauty and the Beastly Prime Minister', John Su also examines *What a Carve Up!* as a literary response to Thatcherite policies of deregulation and privatization: drawing from Colin Hutchinson's analysis (50), Su shows how, in contrast to the 'beastliness' of the 1980s' neoliberalist forces and moral bankruptcy, the novel 'projects an alternative, more communitarian set of values onto the realm of the beautiful – the English countryside' (1088). The farm associated with Michael's childhood and the place in Eastbourne by the seaside where he goes with Fiona are thus cast as melancholy 'fragments of a lost past' (1089).

In his insightful review of *What a Carve Up!*, Terry Eagleton writes that the novel is 'one of the few pieces of genuinely political Post-Modern fiction around' (12), two adjectives that are viewed by some theoreticians (such as Ihab Hassan or Jean-François Lyotard) as incompatible, since postmodernism is often presented as separate from politics and economics, as a cultural phenomenon related to notions of randomness, contingency, arbitrariness, chaos, playfulness, an incredulity towards metanarratives and the dissipation of truth in a multiplicity of micro-narratives. Eagleton and Fredric Jameson on the other hand consider postmodernism as the manifestation of specific political and historical circumstances, and that Coe's novels propose a thorough picture of the condition of contemporary British society. Coe is indeed not inclined to create fantasy worlds as his gift is 'criticising existing institutions, not imagining new ones' (Coe, 2013d). His work is thus often discussed as borrowing from the tradition of the social realistic novel and the state-of-the-nation novel satirising the corrupt ruling classes (Bradford, 40; Guignery, 2015; Head, 2002, 36; Thurschwell, 28; Tew, 2004, 187).

Among 'state-of-the-nation' topics examined by critics in Coe's fiction is the ascendant political authority of the money economy in Britain, as analysed by Nicky Marsh in *Money, Speculation and Finance in Contemporary British Fiction* (2007), in which he calls *What a Carve Up!* an 'acerbically critical account of the shifts in political power in the 1980s' when political authority was devolved to the market (86). Hywel Dix, in his study of 'The Retrospective Novel' (2010), explores for his part the way Coe integrates 'personal drama and public activism' (34) in *The Rotters' Club*, and hints at the interconnections between 'labour unrest, racial tension, Irish paramilitarism and class conflict', and 'the tensions thrown up by a capitalist society' (33) in Britain. In 'The Closed Circle of Britain's Postcolonial Melancholia' (2011), Paul Gilroy addresses the issue of Britain's xenophobic nationalism and takes as a literary example the 'loud and unusual anti-racist advocacy' of *The Rotters' Club* (200), focusing on the digressive story of the Danish Jews trying to escape Nazi persecution, seen as 'an allegory and an argument ... about the primary significance of racism' (201).

A crucial aspect discussed by critics in relation to Coe's work is that of class. If reviewers and academics praise Coe's work for his depiction of contemporary Britain, the major dissonant note comes from Lawrence Driscoll who, in a chapter entitled 'We're All Bourgeois Now: Realism and Class in Alan Hollinghurst, Graham Swift, and Jonathan Coe' (2009), objects to Coe's lack of 'meaningful political link to working-class culture' (227). Writing about *What a Carve Up!*, Driscoll contends that Coe's 'desire to attack Thatcherism for its greed, callousness, and its inhuman distaste for all things decent, leads [him] directly toward a satire of his [*sic*] social and economic moment, as opposed to any radical desire to overturn capitalism' (158). The purpose of a literary work is probably not to 'overturn' an economic regime, but Driscoll insists on pointing to the persistence of class ambiguities in contemporary literature. For him, Coe belongs to a 'tradition of épater le bourgeois ... in which the middle-class author, struck between the upper and lower classes turns his anger toward the upper classes and their excesses (as well as those of his own class) while never really having any real economic connection to the working classes' (158). Driscoll argues that such writers as Zadie Smith, Graham Swift, Will Self or Alan Hollinghurst, who are all part of the British literary establishment, occupy a similar position, that of the 'middle class, decent, honorable center' (158), and as such, their novels leave 'class formations unaltered' (159). Colin Hutchinson, in *Reaganism, Thatcherism and the Social Novel* (2008), had already argued that the fantasies of communitarian values in *What a Carve Up!* conceal the more difficult aspects of class antagonism, and that the narrator fails to 'channel his anger into effective political action' (50). John Su concurs that the novel does not suggest 'a development of class consciousness or a move towards political activism' (1091). Philip Tew argues on the other hand that all social classes are represented in Coe's novels, which allows for a 'plurality of sorts' (2004, 80), but he also adds: 'If there is any priority in Coe, it is to the instinct of the working classes and those of the lower middle class when uninfluenced by its love affair with aesthetic intellectualism' (2004, 84).

Rather than adhere to one specific mode of writing, Coe's work is characterized by an aesthetic of compromise. On the one hand, he maintains 'a solid commitment to realism' (Bradford, 47); on the other, he is attached to the pleasures of storytelling and of a willing suspension of disbelief, as he states in the conclusion of an essay on B.S. Johnson's quest for an 'authentic naturalism':

> ... in the end – for all my inescapable Britishness, my horror of the abstract, my love of the rooted and the specific – even I have to reject naturalism. Yes, I want my novels to be plausible, I want them to be believable. But I also know, as a reader, that it is when I allow myself to be seduced by the enchanting untruthfulness of fiction that I feel myself to be most alive.
>
> (2003)

In addition, Coe is not averse to postmodernist playfulness and *What a Carve Up!* – but also *The House of Sleep* to a lesser extent – has been hailed as a postmodernist exemplar because of its mixture of genres, embedded narratives, ontological uncertainties, histrionic play with coincidences and patterns, shifting perspectives and blurring of the narrative voice.

A second group of critics is precisely interested in examining the formal and generic complexity of Coe's production (interconnecting aesthetics, politics and ethics), more specifically the intricate narrative constructions with embedded stories, the intertwining of farce and tragedy, the parodies of the Gothic novel, the horror movie and detective fiction, and the use of intermediality. This is especially the case of the earliest extensive analysis of Coe's condition-of-England novels, by Pamela Thurschwell (2006), who analyses the mixture of genres and literary traditions in *What a Carve Up!* and wonders if one may combine laughter and empathy, Greek tragedy and gritty social realism. Several articles analyse Coe's insertion of film and music into his books, as well as his combination of genres from high, popular and vernacular culture. Gerry Smyth (2008) and William May (2014) both explore the multifarious musical scene conjured up in *The Rotters' Club*. While Smyth points to the 'uses of nostalgia' through music in Coe's book as well as in Hanif Kureishi's *The Buddha of Suburbia*, Claus-Ulrich Viol (2005) explores the nostalgic turn of British historical fiction towards the reconstruction of the 1970s as exemplified in Coe's novel and Kureishi's *Gabriel's Gift*, both published in 2001.

In his 1994 essay quoted in the Introduction, Coe reproached academic critics for praising the contemporary 'middlebrow and deeply, irredeemably unpopular' novel that resides at 'the very margins of cultural life in England' (1994d, 10), and being indifferent or even hostile to popular culture. According to José Ramón Prado Pérez (2006), 'the popular must be reinserted into the canon of literature, or at least into certain literary forms, as a challenge to the homogeneization, appropriation and nostalgia of conservative ideologies and postmodernist trends' (966). Prado Pérez argues that this is what Coe proceeds to do in *What a Carve Up!* and *The House of Sleep*, combining the parody of several literary discourses and popular forms with a disruption of realism and of monolithic representations of reality.

The simultaneous use and abuse of the popular genre of detective fiction in *What a Carve Up!*, has been analysed by

Véronique Alexandre (2009) and by Vanessa Guignery (2011), while Laurent Mellet, in a forthcoming article, analyses the figures of excess and the traces of absence in Coe's novel. On the one hand, Coe relies on 'absence as a narrative motif', withholding information, postponing comprehension, delaying the 'bridging of narrative gaps for the reader' in a postmodernist fashion. On the other hand, he accumulates motifs and themes that offer a 'comprehensive picture of 1990s Britain' and portrays characters with disproportionate obsessions. According to Mellet, these structures of absence and excess lead to the predominance of exclusion, that of characters, bodies (hidden behind screens), narrative links and, ultimately, readers who 'cannot interact with the blanks to make them meaningful'. Alexandre argues for her part that all the secrets of the realist, political and historical frame are revealed (225) while the enigmas relating to love, identity and lineage remain unsolved (236).

Besides academic criticism, interviews often provide valuable insight into Coe's work. In addition to many that were published in the press, three have been reprinted in Coe's *Marginal Notes, Doubtful Statements*. Philip Tew's 2006 interview (published in *Writers' Talk*, and followed by an overview of his work) provides helpful information about Coe's formative years, his literary heroes and writing methods, and addresses the issue of recording contemporary historical events in *What a Carve Up!*, *The Rotters' Club* and *The Closed Circle* (2008, 44–5). François Gallix and Vanessa Guignery's 2008 interview (published in Guignery's *Novelists in the New Millennium* in 2013) focuses more specifically on *The Rain Before it Falls* and on the importance of music and film in Coe's life and work. Roberto Bertinetti's 2011 interview dwells on Coe's literary influences (Johnson, Orwell, Sterne, O'Brien) and addresses the theme of loneliness in *The Terrible Privacy of Maxwell Sim*.

While no book in English has yet been published on Coe's work, Laurent Mellet wrote a monograph in French, *Jonathan Coe. Les politiques de l'intime* (2015), in which he explores ethical issues related to forms of vulnerability and intimacy, and the representation of affects; he analyses as well the relations between politics and aesthetics in Coe's work, drawing on the reflections of philosopher Jacques Rancière. Merritt Moseley (one of the rare American academics who have taken an interest in Coe's work) wrote an early entry on Coe in the *Dictionary of Literary Biography* (2000) and will publish *Understanding Jonathan Coe* in 2016 in a series of the University of California Press that offers helpful introductions to writers' major works and themes.

This profuse critical activity around Coe's fictional work in recent years and months suggests that Coe has now joined the literary canon, for novels that are 'challenging, erudite, politically charged, humane, and always supremely entertaining and accessible', a description of Alasdair Gray's books by Coe (2013d), that fits his own production equally well.

BIBLIOGRAPHY

SELECTED WORKS BY JONATHAN COE

NOVELS AND SHORT STORIES
The Accidental Woman. 1987. London: Penguin, 2008.
A Touch of Love. 1989a. London: Penguin, 2008.
The Dwarves of Death. 1990. London: Penguin, 2008.
What a Carve Up! 1994a. London: Penguin, 2008.
The House of Sleep. 1997a. London: Penguin, 2008.
The Rotters' Club. 2001a. London: Penguin, 2008.
The Closed Circle. 2004a. London: Penguin, 2008.
9th & 13th. London: Penguin, 2005a.
The Rain Before it Falls. 2007a. London: Penguin, 2008.
The Terrible Privacy of Maxwell Sim. London: Penguin, 2010a.
Expo 58. London: Penguin, 2013a.
Loggerheads and Other Stories. London: Penguin ebook, 2014a.
'La promeneuse de chiens', *Le Point*. 20 November 2014: 84–97.

BIOGRAPHIES
Humphrey Bogart: Take it and Like it. New York: Grove Weidenfeld, 1991.
James Stewart: Leading Man. London: Bloomsbury, 1994b.
Like a Fiery Elephant – The Story of B.S. Johnson. London: Picador, 2004b.

EDITION
Well Done God! Selected Prose and Drama of B.S. Johnson. Edited with Philip Tew and Julia Jordan. London: Picador, 2013b.

CHILDREN'S BOOKS
Lo Specchio dei Desideri [The Broken Mirror]. Milano: Feltrinelli, 2012b.
The Story of Gulliver. London: Pushkin Children's Books, 2013c.

ESSAYS, JOURNALISM AND OTHER WRITING
Website (including blog and message board): http://jonathancoewriter.com; accessed 19 January 2015.
'Satire and Sympathy: Some Consequences of Intrusive Narration in *Tom Jones* and Other Comic Novels', PhD Dissertation. Warwick University. September 1986.

'The Heights of Lowdown', *The Guardian*, 12 October 1989b: n.p. http://www.theguardian.com/books/1989/oct/12/fiction.jonathancoe; accessed 19 January 2015.

'About Men, About Women', *The Observer* 14 March 1994c: n.p. http://books.guardian.co.uk/departments/generalfiction/story/0,6000,102093,00.html; accessed 19 January 2015.

'Low Culture Rises above its Critics: the Culture Essay', *Sunday Times* 20 November 1994d: Section 10, 8–11.

'London: The Dislocated City', in Malcolm Bradbury, ed. *The Atlas of Literature*. London: De Agostini Editions, 1996a. 320–3.

'Close-Up on Hitchcock. Jonathan Coe – *Sabotage*', BB2 10 May 1997b. http://the.hitchcock.zone/wiki/Close-Up_on_Hitchcock_%28BBC2,_1997%29; accessed 19 January 2015.

'Introduction', *Golden Girl*, by Shirley Eaton. London: Batsford Ltd, 1999. 6–7.

'*9th & 13th*', Louis Philippe's Website. January 2001b. http://www.louisphilippe.co.uk/cd_9th.html; accessed 19 January 2015.

'Death by Naturalism', *Prospect Magazine* 83 (February 2003).

'A Fan's Notes', Hatfield and the North. *Hatwise Choice*. 2005b. CD.

'A Book that Changed my Life', *Time Out 1000 Books to Change your Life*. London: Random, 2007b. 55.

'I am Less Convinced that Satire is Good for Democracy', *The Financial Times* 11 September 2010b: n.p. http://www.ft.com/intl/cms/s/2/5784ac84-bc50-11df-8c02-00144feab49a.html#axzz2c9Y2fZFw; accessed 19 January 2015.

'*What a Carve Up!* by Jonathan Coe', *The Guardian* 16 April 2011: n.p. http://www.guardian.co.uk/books/2011/apr/16/jonathan-coe-carve-book-club; accessed 19 January 2015.

'My Favourite Hitchcock Film: *The Lady Vanishes*', *The Observer* 16 June 2012a: n.p. http://www.theguardian.com/film/2012/jun/17/favourite-hitchcock-film-lady-vanishes-jonathan-coe; accessed 19 January 2015.

Marginal Notes, Doubtful Statements. London: Penguin ebook, 2013d.

'Tenevo un diario in forma de note', *El Corriere della Sera* 6 July 2014b: n.p. http://lettura.corriere.it/tenevo-un-diario-in-forma-di-note; accessed 19 January 2015.

'Introduction', *Different Every Time: The Authorised Biography of Robert Wyatt*, by Marcus O'Dair. London: Serpent's Tail, 2014c. 9–12.

'How Important is Milan Kundera Today?', *The Guardian* 22 May 2015a: n.p. http://www.theguardian.com/books/2015/may/22/milan-kundera-immortality-jonathan-coe-novels-women; accessed 22 May 2015.

'Préface' ['Preface to *The Rotters' Club* and *The Closed Circle*'], *Les enfants de Longbridge*, by Jonathan Coe. Paris: Gallimard, 2015b.

OTHER WORKS CITED

Adams, Tim. 'The Way We Write Now', *The Observer* 10 November 2001: n.p. http://www.theguardian.com/books/2001/nov/11/fiction.comment; accessed 19 January 2015.

Alexandre, Véronique. 'Le Statut des énigmes dans *What a Carve Up!* de Jonathan Coe', in Michel Briand, Colette Camelin et Liliane Louvel, eds. *Les Écritures secrètes*. Rennes: Presses Universitaires de Rennes, 2009. 225–37.

Armitstead, Claire. 'Tash Aw, Jonathan Coe and the Best Autumn Fiction – Books Podcast', *The Guardian* 6 September 2013: n.p. http://audio.theguardian.tv/audio/kip/books/series/books/1378469436149/7896/gdn.book.130906.tm.Jonathan-Coe-Booker-Tash-Aw.mp3; accessed 19 January 2015.

Arter, Danny. 'Return to Satire: Jonathan Coe', *We Love This Book* 4 September 2013: n.p. http://www.welovethisbook.com/features/return-satire-jonathan-coe; accessed 19 January 2015.

Attridge, Derek. *The Singularity of Literature*. London & New York: Routledge, 2004.

Bakhtin, Mikhail. *Speech Genres and Other Late Essays*. 1986. Austin, TX: University of Texas Press, 2004.

Barnes, Julian. *England, England*. London: Jonathan Cape, 1998.

Barthes, Roland. *Roland Barthes par Roland Barthes*. Paris: Seuil, 1975.

———. *Camera Lucida. Reflections on Photography*. Trans. Richard Howard. 1980. London: Vintage Classics, 2000.

———. 'The Death of the Author', *Image – Music – Text*. Ed. and trans. Stephen Heath. New York: Hill and Wang, 1977. 142–8.

Baudrillard, Jean. *Simulacra and Simulation*. 1981. Ann Arbor: University of Michigan Press, 1994.

Beck, Stefan. 'The Information', *The New Criterion* 29.9 (May 2011): 32–7.

Beckett, Samuel. *The Unnamable*. New York: Grove Press, 1958.

Berne, Suzanne. 'Snooze Alarm', *New York Times* 29 March 1998: n.p. http://www.nytimes.com/1998/03/29/books/snooze-alarm.html; accessed 19 January 2015.

Booth, Wayne C. *The Rhetoric of Fiction*. Chicago: The University of Chicago Press, 1961.

Bradbury, Malcolm. '*The House of Sleep*', *New Statesman* 27 June 1997: 46.

Bradford, Richard. 'The Effects of Thatcherism', *The Novel Now – Contemporary British Fiction*. Malden: Blackwell, 2007. 39–45.

Brookner, Anita. 'The Sleeve Stays Unravelled', *The Spectator* 24 May 1997: 37.

Brooks, Peter. *Body Work – Objects of Desire in Modern Narrative.* Cambridge, MA: Harvard University Press, 1993.

Broughton, Trev. 'Crashing Out', *Times Literary Supplement* 23 May 1997: 19.

Charnock, Anne. 'Hay Festival #4: 7 Fiction Writers on Writing', 7 June 2013: n.p. http://annecharnock.com/tag/jonathan-coe; accessed 19 January 2015.

Chauvin, Serge. 'Le mystère du vase fêlé. Jonathan Coe, Martin Amis: retours sur un lieu clos', *La Licorne* 44, 'Formes policières du roman contemporain' (1998): 143–8.

Cowley, Jason. 'After Orwell', *The Financial Times* 19 April 2013: n.p. http://www.ft.com/intl/cms/s/2/bc93773c-a74d-11e2-bfcd-00144feabdc0.html#axzz2c9Y2fZFw; accessed 19 January 2015.

Dickens, Charles. *Great Expectations.* 1861. London: Penguin, 1985.

Diderot, Denis. *Rameau's Nephew and Other Works.* Trans. Jacques Barzun and Ralph H. Bowen. Indianapolis, IN: Hackett, 1956.

Dix, Hywel. 'The Retrospective Novel', *Postmodern Fiction and the Break-Up of Britain.* London and New York: Continuum, 2010. 31–6.

Driscoll, Lawrence. 'We're All Bourgeois Now: Realism and Class in Alan Hollinghurst, Graham Swift, and Jonathan Coe', *Evading Class in Contemporary British Literature.* Basingstoke: Palgrave Macmillan, 2009. 133–67.

Eagleton, Terry. 'Theydunnit', *London Review of Books* 16.8 (28 April 1994): 12.

Forster, E. M. *Commonplace Book.* 1987. Ed. Philip Gardner. Aldershot: Wildwood House, 1988.

Frye, Northrop. *Anatomy of Criticism: Four Essays.* 1971. Princeton, NJ: Princeton University Press, 1990.

Gasiorek, Andrzej, David James. 'Introduction: Fiction since 2000: Postmillennial Commitments', *Contemporary Literature* 53.4 (2012): 609–27.

Gibson, Andrew. *Postmodernity, Ethics and the Novel. From Leavis to Levinas.* London: Routledge, 1999.

Gilroy, Paul. 'The Closed Circle of Britain's Postcolonial Melancholia', in Martin Middeke and Christina Wald, eds. *The Literature of Melancholia: Early Modern to Postmodern.* Basingstoke: Palgrave Macmillan, 2011. 187–204.

Guignery, Vanessa. 'Transfiguration des genres littéraires dans la littérature britannique contemporaine', in Monique Chassagnol and Guy Laprevotte, eds. *Les Littératures de genre.* Nanterre: Université Paris X – Nanterre, 2002. 35–66.

———. '"Colonel Mustard, in the billiard room, with the revolver": Jonathan Coe's *What a Carve Up!* as a Postmodern Whodunit', *Études Anglaises* 64.4 (October–December 2011): 427–38.

———. 'Jonathan Coe', *Novelists in the New Millennium. Conversations with Writers*. Basingstoke: Palgrave Macmillan, 2013. 27–43.
———. 'The Way We Live Now: Jonathan Coe's Re-evaluation of Political Satire', *Études Anglaises* 68.2 (April–June 2015): 156–69.
Harrison, Carey. 'He'll Even Change His Sex for the Woman of His Dreams', *San Francisco Chronicle* 26 April 1998: n.p. http://www.sfgate.com/books/article/He-ll-Even-Change-His-Sex-for-the-Woman-of-His-3008317.php; accessed 19 January 2015.
Head, Dominic. 'The State and the Novel', *The Cambridge Introduction to Modern British Fiction, 1950–2000*. Cambridge: Cambridge University Press, 2002. 13–48.
———. 'The Demise of Class Fiction', in James F. English, ed. *A Concise Companion to Contemporary British Fiction*. Malden: Blackwell, 2006. 229–47.
Higgins, Charlotte. 'Edinburgh Book Festival Diary', *The Guardian* 16 August 2013: n.p. http://www.theguardian.com/culture/2013/aug/16/edinburgh-festival-diary-jonathan-coe; accessed 19 January 2015.
Hoskin, Peter. '*O Lucky Man!*: a Hopeless Kind of Optimism', *DVDBeaver*: n.p. http://www.dvdbeaver.com/film/articles/o_lucky_man.htm#3; accessed 19 January 2015.
Hutcheon, Linda. *A Poetics of Postmodernism. History, Theory, Fiction*. New York and London: Routledge, 1988.
Hutchinson, Colin. *Reaganism, Thatcherism and the Social Novel*. Basingstoke: Palgrave Macmillan, 2008.
Johnson, B.S. *Albert Angelo*. 1964. In *B.S. Johnson Omnibus*. London: Picador, 2004.
———. *The Unfortunates*. 1969. London, Picador, 1999.
———. *House Mother Normal. A Geriatric Comedy*. 1971. In *B.S. Johnson Omnibus*. London: Picador, 2004.
———. *Christie Malry's Own Double-Entry*. 1973a. London: Picador, 2001.
———. *Aren't You Rather Young to be Writing Your Memoirs?* London: Hutchinson, 1973b.
———. *Everyone Knows Somebody Who's Dead*. London: Covent Garden Press, 1973c.
———. *Fat Man on a Beach*, in Giles Gordon, ed. *Beyond the Words, Eleven Writers in Search of a New Fiction*. London: Hutchinson, 1975. 149–81.
Johnson, B.S., ed. *The Evacuees*. London: Victor Gollancz LTD, 1968.
Kellaway, Kate. 'Jonathan Coe: "Britain has sleepwalked into a crisis"', *The Observer* 1 September 2013: n.p. http://www.theguardian.com/theobserver/2013/sep/01/jonathan-coe-expo-58-interview; accessed 19 January 2015.
Krauss, Rosalind. *Le Photographique. Pour une théorie des écarts*. Trans. Jean Kempf and Marc Bloch. Paris: Macula, 1990.

Laity, Paul. 'A Life in Writing: Jonathan Coe', *The Guardian* 29 May 2010: n.p. http://www.theguardian.com/books/2010/may/29/life-writing-jonathan-coe; accessed 19 January 2015.
Lakin, Rich. 'Porridge and Perrin – Jonathan Coe at Birmingham Lit Fest', 11 October 2013. http://richlakin.wordpress.com/2013/10/11/porridge-and-perrin-jonathan-coe-at-birmingham-lit-fest; accessed on 19 January 2015.
Lappin, Tom. 'Waiting for Tony', *Scotland on Sunday* 17 August 1997: 11.
Lawson, Nigella. 'The Unreality Device', *Times Literary Supplement* 15 May 1987: 515.
Lehmann, Chris. 'The Counter-Family', *The Nation* 26 May 2008: 25–7.
Lehmann, Rosamond. *A Note in Music*. 1930. London: Virago, 2001.
———. *The Swan in the Evening. Fragments of an Inner Life*. New York: Harcourt, Brace & World, 1967.
———. *Rosamond Lehmann's Album*. London: Chatto and Windus, 1985.
Levinas, Emmanuel. *Otherwise than Being: or, Beyond Essence*. 1974. The Hague: Martinus Nijhoff, 1981.
Magarian, Baret. 'What Happens if the Wrong Sort of Dreams Come True?', *The Independent* 24 August 1998: 13.
Marsh, Nicky. 'Revision and Retrospect: Representations of the City in Jonathan Coe's *What a Carve Up!* and Alan Hollinghurst's *The Line of Beauty*', *Money, Speculation and Finance in Contemporary British Fiction*. London and New York: Continuum, 2007. 80–96.
May, William. 'Unrest and Silence: The Faithless Music of the Contemporary British Novel', in Erich Hertz and Jeffrey Roessner, eds. *Write in Tune: Contemporary Music in Fiction*. London: Bloomsbury, 2014. 227–39.
———. 'Closing the Circle: An Interview with Jonathan Coe', *in* Sally Bayley and William May, eds. *From Self to Shelf: The Artist under Construction*. Newcastle upon Tyne: Cambridge Scholars Publishing, 2007. 66–73.
McHale, Brian. *Postmodernist Fiction*. New York and London: Methuen, 1987.
Mellet, Laurent. *Jonathan Coe. Les politiques de l'intime*. Paris: PUPS, 2015.
———. 'From a Missing Brother to Reconstructive Fiction: Retention and Excessive Compensation in Jonathan Coe's *What a Carve up!*' *In-Between* (India), forthcoming.
Moore, Charlotte. 'A Life in Pictures', *Spectator* 22 September 2007: 58.
Moseley, Merritt. 'Jonathan Coe', in Merritt Moseley, ed. *Dictionary of Literary Biography, Volume 231: British Novelists Since 1960*, Fourth Series. Detroit: The Gale Group, 2000. 67–73.
———. *Understanding Jonathan Coe*. Columbia, South Carolina: University of South Carolina Press, forthcoming in 2016.

Murphy, Jessica. 'Fast Times at King William's High', *The Atlantic* 27 March 2002. http://www.theatlantic.com/magazine/archive/2002/03/fast-times-at-king-williams-high/303066; accessed 19 March 2015.

Noiville, Florence. 'The Contemporary British Novel. A French Perspective', *European Journal of English Studies* 10.3 (December 2006): 297–300.

Okereke, Kele. 'Author Q&A with Jonathan Coe', *Litro* 7 July 2014. http://www.litro.co.uk/?s=jonathan+coe; accessed 19 January 2015.

Page, Benedicte. 'No Kidding', *The Bookseller* 29 June 2007: 20.

Prado Pérez, José Ramón. 'Popular Culture, Formal Experiment and Social Critique in Jonathan Coe's Postmodern Fictions', in Manuel Cousillas Rodríguez et al., eds. *Literatura y Cultura Popular en el Nuevo Milenio*. Coruña: SELICUP y Universidade da Coruña, 2006. 963–76.

Quantick, David. 'Jonathan Coe is Funny', unpublished paper, *The Life & Work of Jonathan Coe Symposium*, Senate House, London, 28 April 2015.

Quinn, Paul. 'Curious Circles of Experience', *Times Literary Supplement* 21 September 2007: 19.

Rennison, Nick. 'Jonathan Coe', *Contemporary British Novelists*. London: Routledge, 2004. 34–6.

Rushdie, Salman. 'Outside the Whale' (1984), *Imaginary Homelands. Essays and Criticism 1981–1991*. London: Granta Books, 1991. 87–101.

Simons, John. 'Beyond Human Communities: Self-identity, Animal Rights and Vegetarianism', *Critical Survey* 8.1 (1996): 49–57.

Smyth, Gerry. 'The Uses of Nostalgia: Hanif Kureishi, *The Buddha of Suburbia* (1990); Jonathan Coe, *The Rotters' Club* (2004) [*sic*]; Bill Broady, *Eternity is Temporary* (2007)', *Music in Contemporary British Fiction. Listening to the Novel*. Houndmills, Basingstoke: Palgrave Macmillan, 2008. 184–7.

Snoekx, Kurt. 'Jonathan Coe: Stirred, not Shaken', *agendamagazine.blog* 10 October 2013. http://www.agendamagazine.be/en/blog/jonathan-coe-stirred-not-shaken; accessed 19 January 2015.

Soar, Daniel. 'Beatrix and Rosamond', *London Review of Books* 29.20 (18 October 2007): 32–33.

Sontag, Susan. *On Photography*. 1977. London: Picador, 2001.

———. *Regarding the Pain of Others*. New York: Picador, Farrar, Straus and Giroux, 2003.

Su, John. 'Beauty and the Beastly Prime Minister', *ELH* 81.3 (Fall 2014): 1083–110.

Taylor, Charles. 'A Conversation with Jonathan Coe', *Salon* 12 March 2002. http://www.salon.com/people/conv/2002/03/12/jonathan_coe; accessed 19 January 2015.

Taylor, D. J. 'Battered by Unappeasable Contingency', *Spectator* 15 September 1990: 40–1.

Tew, Philip. *The Contemporary British Novel*. London and New York: Continuum, 2004.

Tew, Philip. 'Jonathan Coe', in Tew, Philip, Fiona Tolan and Leigh Wilson, eds. 'Jonathan Coe', *Writers Talk. Conversations with Contemporary British Novelists*. London and New York: Continuum, 2008. 35–55.

Thurschwell, Pamela. 'Genre, Repetition and History in Jonathan Coe', in Philip Tew and Rod Mengham, eds. *British Fiction Today*. London and New York: Continuum, 2006. 28–39.

Tomalin, Nicholas and Ron Hall. *The Strange Last Voyage of Donald Crowhurst*. New York: Stein and Day, 1970.

Trimm, Ryan. 'Carving up Value: The Tragicomic Thatcher Years in Jonathan Coe', in Louisa Hadley and Elizabeth Ho, eds. *Thatcher and After – Margaret Thatcher and her Afterlife in Contemporary Culture*. Basingstoke and New York: Palgrave Macmillan, 2010. 158–79.

Vianu, Lidia. 'The Accidental Theme: Jonathan Coe, *The Accidental Woman*', *Philologica Jassyensia* 4.1 (2008): 147–65.

Vincent, Sally. 'A Bit of a Rotter', *The Guardian* 24 February 2001: n.p. http://www.guardian.co.uk/books/2001/feb/24/fiction.jonathancoe1; accessed 19 January 2015.

Viol, Claus-Ulrich. 'Golden Years or Dark Ages? Cultural Memories of the 1970s in Recent British Fiction', *Anglistik und Englischunterricht* 66 (2005): 149–69.

Woolf, Virginia. 'The New Biography', in Leonard Woolf, ed. *Collected Essays*. Vol. IV. London: The Hogarth Press, 1966–1967. 229–35.

INDEX